"Marybeth Mayhew Whalen's character-driven suspense propelled me through the pages with a relentless need to absorb every word. Unputdownable!"

—Robyn Carr, *New York Times* bestselling author

"A missing bride, a handful of unrequited loves, and unsolved mysteries threaten to bring a small southern town to its knees. Each character Whalen has created is a grace note of longing, pain, or strength, and in the search for the missing woman, each is pushed to face the darkest truths he or she has attempted to hide. The characters felt like real people to me, the plot, a singular, haunting melody holding them together. A gorgeous book."

—Emily Carpenter, author of *Every Single Secret*

"A seductive and emotional page-turner, *Only Ever Her* is a moving exploration of love, loss, and regret. Told in multiple points of view, where every character has something to hide, this mysterious tale asks the question: How well do you really know the ones you love? You won't be able to put it down, but you won't want it to end either."

—Karen Katchur, bestselling author of *River Bodies*

"A brilliant portrayal of the dark undercurrents of a small town and the complex shadings of relationships between flawed but lovable people, all of whom are keeping secrets. The plot, deftly interwoven through the voices of four characters, builds into suspense that keeps the pages turning all the way to the end. A book club must read!"

—Kerry Anne King, bestselling author of *Whisper Me This*

"The long-buried secrets of a small southern town take center stage in Marybeth Mayhew Whalen's *Only Ever Her*, an intricately woven tale about the pitfalls of self-deception and the damage that can ensue when tragedy sends carefully crafted 'truths' toppling. Whalen creates a cast of compelling and wonderfully fleshed-out characters, then slowly teases back their layers, exposing their dark places in delicious and sometimes heartbreaking fashion. Engaging, honest, and deeply compassionate, *Only Ever Her* is one of those wonderful books that teaches us about ourselves and reminds us that in order to live fully and honestly, we must first embrace our truth."

—Barbara Davis, bestselling author of *When Never Comes*

ONLY

EVER

HER

OTHER TITLES BY
MARYBETH MAYHEW WHALEN

When We Were Worthy
The Things We Wish Were True

ONLY EVER HER

MARYBETH MAYHEW WHALEN

LAKE UNION
PUBLISHING

Text copyright © 2019 by Marybeth Mayhew Whalen
All rights reserved.

Published by Lake Union Publishing, Seattle

www.apub.com

Amazon, the Amazon logo, and Lake Union Publishing are trademarks of Amazon.com, Inc., or its affiliates.

ISBN-13: 9781503903890
ISBN-10: 1503903893

Cover design by Faceout Studio, Tim Green

Printed in the United States of America

For Ashleigh Whalen Fraley, who didn't go missing.

I said, "O that I had the wings of a dove! I would fly away and be at rest. I would flee far away and stay in the desert; I would hurry to my place of shelter, far from the tempest and storm."

Psalm 55:6–8

Prologue: Wedding Day

June 1

He tugs at his collar and takes a swig of tepid coffee. He doesn't care for coffee, but he will accept any liquid at this point, especially liquid that contains caffeine. He hasn't slept in so long, he's too tired to count up how many hours it's been.

The sheriff presses his big, meaty palms on the table and leans in. "Well, Mr. Spacey," he says. "You ready to give your statement?"

"Yes, sir," he says. "I'm ready." The last time he was sitting across from Hal York like this, he was just a kid, brought in for shoplifting. No one believed him then, either.

"You going to tell the truth now?"

He holds up his right hand, pretends to lay his left one on an imaginary Bible. "And nothing but. So help me God." He hopes his voice sounds sincere.

"Well," the sheriff says, "let's hear your story."

MAY 15–16

Two Weeks until the Wedding

Annie

Though she has made it as far as parking outside the lawyer's office, she finds herself unable to go in. She has her fingers around the door handle, ready to tug it open at any moment. The car is new, so the door won't creak loudly when she opens it like her old car did. (Ah, the Jetta, may she rest in peace.) This SUV, a pristine, mature vehicle choice, will not give her any problems. Like her fiancé, Scott, who selected and bought her the Honda CR-V as an early wedding gift, this car is new and reliable and suitable for starting her new life in a few weeks as Mrs. Annie Hanson.

She lets go of the door handle and glances down at the letter on her lap, sees her name in the salutation just above the fold, her name as it is now: *Ms. Annie Taft.* She is not Annie Hanson yet. She has things she must do before that can happen. And showing up for a meeting at this attorney's office is one of those things.

She looks at the building just in front of her, a two-story red-brick colonial-style office that could house any sort of business at all—an insurance agency or dental practice or accounting firm. She scans the numerous windows as if someone might be watching her out of one of them. But there are no faces framed in the window-panes, no pairs of eyes peeking through the blinds. No one is even aware she is here.

She didn't call to make an appointment, even though the letter had suggested she do so. She wanted no guarantee the attorney would have time for her. All the better if he told her to come back and then she just never did. She's going to be very busy in the coming days, after all. She will scarcely have time for anything besides preparing for her wedding. Then she can tell herself—and anyone else—that she tried. She can say she did the right thing. Annie cares very much about doing the right thing; it is a part of who she is.

But what is the right thing? That is the question.

In her head, her aunt Faye starts to speak, reiterating what she, Faye, thinks is the right thing. (Which is not what Annie is now doing, for the record.) Some people hear their mother's voices in their heads, but Annie hears her aunt's, the closest thing she has to a mother. Annie quiets Aunt Faye's disapproving voice by distracting herself. She checks her makeup in the visor mirror, smiling to make sure there isn't any lipstick on her teeth. There's nothing on her teeth, but she sees that she could use a touch-up. She's chewed at her bottom lip so much that the lipstick she applied this morning is mostly gone.

She gets out her cosmetic bag from her purse and plunks it right on top of the letter, hiding it from sight. She pulls out her favorite lipstick and reapplies a swath of berry stain across her bow of a mouth. (She has her mother's smile, everyone says. Based on the photos she's seen, this is true.) Then, just for good measure, she touches up her nose with fresh powder. The early-summer heat is making her shiny, and sitting in this car isn't helping.

She should just get out and go inside. Pull the trigger, rip off the Band-Aid, as they say. But then she notices her eyebrows—the bright sunlight reveals some stray hairs that need to be plucked. She pulls tweezers from the cosmetic bag and removes the offensive hairs. It's always good to look your best when meeting anyone new, she reasons, and this attorney is someone new. He is a total stranger who has barged into her life uninvited through this letter he sent to her, presuming more about her than she is capable of.

Dear Ms. Annie Taft,

I am writing to deliver some news about my client, Mr. Cordell Lewis, a man I believe was unfairly sentenced to life in prison without the possibility of parole after being wrongfully convicted of the death of your mother, Lydia Taft. As a witness—and a key part of the prosecution's case against him—Ms. Taft, I understand that for you this story is a part of your past, but it is far from that for Mr. Lewis. It's very much in the present, and to any hope he has for a future.

I would appreciate it if you could come in to my office for a short meeting to allow me to inform you face-to-face of some new developments in the case as well as ask for one small favor. I look forward to meeting with you at your earliest convenience, as time is of the essence. Please know that, as the information I will be passing along to you is sensitive in nature, this meeting will need to be strictly confidential. Again, I will look forward to hearing from you and to sharing with you the exciting things that are happening.

Thank you for your time,
Tyson Barnes

It is a short letter—not a lot to it, really—but long enough to levy the right amount of guilt to get her here for this meeting, to talk about doing "a small favor" for the man she's grown up believing murdered her mother. *But what if he didn't?* Her stupid conscience keeps asking this one unending question. One she has to entertain before she can start a life of her own, a life away from here. That is part of her plan with Scott: get married, move somewhere else, start fresh. At the time they devised it, it sounded like a good plan. But the closer she gets to leaving, the more she wonders if she can.

She inspects her face one final time before flipping the visor back into place and stowing her cosmetic bag in her purse. Her stomach rumbles, and she thinks about her lunch appointment—another thing she doesn't want to do but feels obligated to show up for. If she isn't careful, she's going to be late for that. If the attorney is in and does want to talk, she might miss it altogether. She can't decide which would be worse: talking to the attorney who is trying to get Cordell Lewis, the man currently in prison for her mother's murder, released or showing up for an interview with a reporter from the town paper to talk about her wedding.

Annie is certain the reporter will find a way to also ask about Cordell Lewis's upcoming hearing. She suspects that this is what the reporter really wants to talk about, that this interview is just subterfuge. She and Laurel, the reporter, went to high school together. Laurel was always the aggressive type, and Annie doubts she's changed much in the eight years since graduation. If anything, her years away from Ludlow working for larger papers has probably made her more relentless. Lewis's release is a bigger story than Annie's wedding, after all. Annie wouldn't put it past Laurel to pull something like that. She will be on her guard.

She makes her decision and turns off the car, deciding that she will do what she came here to do, selecting the lesser of the two evils. She will go in and talk to—she looks down at the letter again to double-check the name of the man she has come here to see. She reads the signature line, imagines telling the receptionist that she is there to see Tyson Barnes. The receptionist will either say, "Oh yes, he's been expecting you. Right this way!" Or she will say, "I'm so sorry, but he's in court. Would you like me to let him know you stopped by?"

Whatever the outcome, Annie must go through with this. She must go and hear what this attorney has to say about Cordell Lewis, who has spent the last twenty-three years in prison for killing her mother. According to his letter, Tyson Barnes thinks that Cordell Lewis is innocent. He thinks he was wrongly convicted all those years ago and that

Annie was part of the witch hunt that made the wrongful conviction stick. He wants to talk about what she can do now, as a twenty-six-year-old woman, to make up for what she did as a three-year-old child. He thinks she can help set things right.

Annie knows one thing: nothing can set things right. No matter what she does or does not do, her mother will not be there when she walks down the aisle in a matter of days. Her mother will not wear a mother-of-the-bride dress that is slightly dowdy but appropriate for the occasion. She will not give Annie a family heirloom to be her "something blue." She will not offer marriage advice based on her own years of wisdom. Because Annie's mother did not have years to grow wise. Lydia Taft died when she was twenty-three years old. She didn't even get to live as long as Annie herself has.

"Okay, Tyson Barnes," Annie says aloud in the car. "You've got fifteen minutes. And that's all you get." Then she opens the car door and steps out.

Laurel

She has sorted the sugar packets by color, then in alphabetical order—the Splenda should be before the Sweet'N Low—and then created a repeating pattern of white, then pink, then yellow, then blue, a rainbow of packets. Done with that, she scans the restaurant, huffing her frustration as she, again, comes up empty. She checks her watch. Annie Taft is twenty-two minutes late and, though Laurel really has nowhere else to be other than this restaurant in the middle of the lunch rush, she is unhappy at being kept waiting this long. Five minutes, okay. But twenty-two? It's disrespectful.

She dumps the sugar packets out on the table, uses her hand to make them into a jumbled array, pondering the many options there are now for making life sweet, many of them noncaloric—all of the sweetness, none of the guilt, she thinks. Isn't that what we all want? She opens the notebook in front of her, jots down her thoughts. This might make a good essay. She could sell it to a magazine, she thinks. One like *Good Housekeeping* or *Woman's Day*. She adds these two magazine names down beside her idea, then draws stars around it, if for no other reason than to look busy—and less alone than she does right now sitting at this table waiting for someone who has most likely stood her up.

The server comes over and points at Laurel's empty water glass, the ice cubes sinking into each other as they collapse. "Would you like some more water?" the girl asks. She is probably twenty years old, with a high ponytail that pulls the corners of her eyelids upward, making her look perennially surprised.

"No, thank you," Laurel replies in her kindest, most patient voice. Thankfully, the girl scurries away without asking more questions. Like the most obvious one: "Do you think the person you're waiting for is going to show up?"

Laurel picks up her phone and stares at it, debating whether to just text Annie and ask where she is already. But that looks desperate and might make her seem like a nuisance. As put off as she is, she's also proceeding with caution. Though she is ostensibly at this restaurant to interview Annie Taft about her upcoming wedding ("The wedding of the year!" as Laurel's mother keeps saying) for the local paper, she is also here for her own reasons.

She thinks about her book idea—the one with Annie's murdered mother at the center of it, the one that could allow her to finally make her mark as a writer. Seeing as how nothing else she's tried has worked out. Annie Taft granting her access could make all the difference. So she will take things as they come; she will not push too hard. She's been known to push too hard when she wants something really badly. Just ask her family or her last boyfriend.

She puts down her phone and picks up her pen again, using it to cross through the sugar essay idea. If she's going to be a great writer, she needs to spend her time on truly worthy efforts. An essay on sugar is just a silly distraction. She's got to do better, govern herself better. She's got to be more intentional and not flit around from idea to idea. She'd be better served to do more research on the man they're supposedly letting out of prison. Yes, that would be a better use of her time. Perhaps she could track down his attorney, ask him some questions. She thinks of Professor Sharp, who taught her that "the enemy of great writing is distraction."

She wonders what Professor Sharp would think of her now, his prized pupil who has slunk back to her hometown after having been let go from yet another paper, writing instead for her tiny town paper, which is no better than a high school newspaper when you get down to it. Hell, she'd guess the *Ludlow Ledger* is actually beneath some high school papers. She thinks of her "boss," Damon, and cringes. She is far, far away from the dreams that lit her from within when she was a writing student a mere matter of years ago.

She gathers her things and puts them in her new tote bag, a colorful designer thing her mother bought her as a "welcome home" present, complete with her monogram in huge curlicue woven letters smack-dab in the center. Glynnis, her mother, thinks her homecoming is something to be celebrated, not something to be mourned. She bought her the tote to take to the country club so she can sit by the pool and "get some color."

"You look so pale from all that city living," Glynnis had said.

Laurel signals the server that she is ready to go by waving the credit card Damon so graciously allowed her to take to this lunch, his way of making it less awful that she's been reduced to covering Annie Taft's wedding, the closest thing Ludlow has to a society event. But now she hasn't even managed that.

"You're leaving?" the server asks, and her surprised look is real this time.

"Yes," Laurel says. She gestures to the empty chair across from her. "My guest appears to be a no-show."

"Oh," the girl says, then rests her hand on Laurel's shoulder. She pats her three times. Now it's Laurel's turn to look surprised. "First date?" the server asks in a low, sympathetic voice. "I've heard it's better to do lunch than dinner. Less . . . commitment."

"N-no, this was a business lunch. Uh, an interview."

"Oh." The server shakes her head gravely. "I bet they hired someone else and forgot to tell you." She nods, agreeing with herself. "That happened to me once."

"No, no, it wasn't a job interview," Laurel says, not knowing why she feels the need to explain to this server. But she does anyway. "I was interviewing someone for a story."

"Oh!" the girl says, the surprised look back in place. "You're, like, a reporter?"

"Yes," Laurel says, stifling a sigh. "I'm, *like*, a reporter."

The girl raises her eyebrows and nods her approval. "Cool," she says.

Laurel hands her the credit card, even though the girl seems to have forgotten her role in this exchange. "I'd like to pay for what I ordered. I need to get going."

The girl hands her back the card with a laugh. "You don't need to pay for a water," she says. She pats her on the shoulder again, and Laurel vaguely wonders how long it has been since she has been touched by a person she is not related to. "Good luck with your story." She points to the empty chair. "Hope you find what you need."

Laurel also looks at the chair that was supposed to hold Annie and wonders how she will get the wedding—or the murder—story out of her now. This hasn't gone anything like she'd hoped, much less dreamed of. (In her fantasy, she and Annie forgot all about the fact that they never really liked each other in high school. Annie had poured her heart out about the wedding, the murder, and her secret insecurities, then admitted that she was short a bridesmaid and asked Laurel to be part of the festivities.)

Laurel throws an absentminded "thank you" over her shoulder as she leaves the server, the restaurant, and her humiliation behind, refocusing her thoughts on what to do next, on how to salvage what should not already be lost.

Kenny

He watches the woman leave the restaurant, her feet moving so fast they barely touch the ground, her chin set in that familiar jut he remembers from high school. Laurel Haines was one of his regular tormentors back then. She'd been so certain about things: that she was above everyone in this town and would rise even higher after high school.

"See how far the mighty have fallen," he says to himself as he wipes away the sweat from his glass of iced tea. It is May, and spring has been swiftly toppled by a South Carolina summer, just like every year for as long as he can remember.

"Did you say something, sir?" the young waitress asks. He'd been so distracted watching Laurel leave that he hadn't seen her sidle up to his table, quick and agile. Seconds ago, she'd been at Laurel's table, patting her shoulder and acting chummy. He's glad the girl didn't hear what he said. No sense airing his personal grievances to strangers.

"Oh no," he says, and waves his hand in the direction of the path Laurel beat out of the restaurant. "I was just watching that woman over there leave. I think I might've gone to high school with her." He works to keep his voice vague and noncommittal.

"She's a reporter," the girl tells him, her voice weighted with perceived importance. Laurel would like people to think she's important. But from what he's heard, her grand plans of being a globe-trotting reporter have come crashing down, and she's run home to Mama. Now all the trotting she's doing is over to the *Ludlow Ledger* to cover such big news as the Garden Club home tour or the winner of the Little League fund-raiser.

"Be nice," he hears Annie's voice in his head say. But Annie is not here. She's not here for Laurel Haines, and she's not here for him. She's stood them both up. He hears something else in his head: Annie again, this time from earlier today, when she'd called and begged him to show up at this restaurant. "You can't just leave me in there with her," she'd whined. "You have to be there to rescue me." She'd taken a well-timed dramatic pause. Annie is the queen of the dramatic pause. "You know how snotty she is."

And of course, that had been what hit home, that memory of Laurel Haines looking down her pug nose at him, her friends flanking her as she leveled him with one of her zingers. How was it she always knew what to say to him that would hurt the most? And who'd always stood up for him? Annie. That was who. Without Annie by his side all those years, he would've had no social cred at all; his adolescence would've been even more miserable.

And so he is here today, in this restaurant, to protect his oldest friend, even though she didn't show up to need protecting. He grabs his phone and texts her a second time. The first text was measured and patient. Hey, I'm here, but I don't see you. She's here, though. Are you running late? Please tell me you didn't forget.

There'd been no reply.

This text is less patient and devoid of measure. Well, she just left and now I'm leaving, too. You better have a good explanation for not showing up. Sometimes he gets tough with her just to prove that he's not her whipping boy. He can't always be there for her. Especially not now that she's getting married. To someone else. Someone who didn't get tormented in high school. Someone who isn't even from Ludlow.

He sighs and shoves his phone in his pocket as he counts out cash to leave for the server, who is, thankfully, engaged in conversation with another customer. With any luck, he can slip out, and away, before he has to talk to anyone else. He's used to working from home, with little human interaction during his day. Some weeks, when his girlfriend goes out of town, he can go a whole day without talking to anyone. He likes those days. They're peaceful.

Safely outside the restaurant, he scans the parking lot for Annie's new car, the one Scott bought her as a wedding present. She loves the new-car smell, always asking him to inhale it reverently when he gets in. He acquiesces, never admitting he's one of an apparently small minority who doesn't prefer the smell of a new car. He liked the smell of her old car, the way it reminded him of a unique mixture of the half-drunk coffee cups always sitting in the cupholders, drive-through french fry splurges, and her soap. The way her car smelled like her. Her new car smells like nothing.

But her new car is not there. She is not sitting in it screwing up the courage to go inside, as she is prone to do whenever she's nervous about something. She has simply not shown up. She has pulled one of her disappearing acts, something she does from time to time. Something most people wouldn't guess, based on her reputation as the town darling. To everyone else, Annie is hearts and sunshine. But to those who know her best, she's got a dark side, usually brought on by stress or anything that has to do with her mother.

Considering they're talking about letting the guy convicted of murdering her mother out of prison, he should've seen this coming. He regrets the text he sent, pulls his phone out of his pocket to text her again. Then he thinks better of it. He can guess where she's gone. He will do better than a text. He will find her, and he will forgive her for disappearing, just like he always does.

Clary

The dove is really and truly gone. The one she calls Mica—her favorite, if she's being honest—has not returned. He wasn't just later getting back than the others, as she told herself when she arrived home from the release to find the other three doves there and him missing. Sometimes it happens—she knows this. A bird who didn't make it home is how she got into raising these birds, after all. She'd found one, years ago, on a day she'd needed to be needed. And that bird had needed her. So she knows it can happen; she knows it does happen. It's just never happened to her.

She needs to pee, and badly, but she ignores the urgent sensation, choosing instead to count again, as if she has merely miscounted. As if, in counting, she will make the dove appear, like a magician with a hat. One-two-three kazam! But the counting yields nothing, and the spot on the perch where Mica should be remains empty. She pictures him there, studying her the way he always does, his head cocked as if he's analyzing her, as if he can see right through to her soul. He is her most interesting dove, easily spotted among the others, with the iridescent silver feathers on the tips of his wings, the ones that remind her of those rocks she and Annie used to collect, thinking they'd found something valuable, that the silver veins within them were the real thing.

At Willie McGuirt's funeral today, Mica was the bird she chose to represent the spirit of the departed for the release. The other three birds symbolized the Father, the Son, and the Holy Spirit, there to show Willie's spirit the way to heaven. The whole thing was perhaps a little over-the-top, but it never failed to comfort the grieving. She herself still got a lump in her throat every time she witnessed it. But today had been especially moving—shocking, even. She gets one of those full-body shivers as she thinks about it, especially considering Mica has not returned with the others.

She'd let Willie's widow, Myra, hold Mica for a moment before letting him go with the other three birds. Myra had kissed the top of his little head, then released him. The birds had taken flight, just like always, but as they ascended, they must've spotted some sort of predator, because they quickly retreated back inside the funeral tent at the graveside. But to the dearly beloved who had gathered there, it had probably seemed like the birds had chosen to return to the tent of their own volition. The other three doves had chosen the floral spray atop Willie's casket as their perch. And Mica had chosen the empty chair beside Myra as his.

The gathered mourners had all inhaled in one collective breath as they watched Mica study Myra for a few moments. The other three birds watched Mica watch Myra, and it was as if Willie—who'd been married to Myra for fifty-four years—was saying one last goodbye as the Trinity looked on in approval. No one spoke. Clary doubts anyone breathed. And then, without warning and in unison, the four of them took off again. Silently, the mourners had all stood up, walked outside the tent, and watched until the doves disappeared into the clouds.

But Mica has not returned from that flight, and Clary wonders, and worries, that it all meant something she had missed. Clary hollers his name in desperation. "Mica!" she calls, her chin pointed toward the sky.

The loud noise startles the other birds—she has fifteen in all—and they flap their wings in response. The power in their wings creates a roaring sound and stirs up a wind that blows through the loft. Two of them swoop over her head, barely brushing the top of her spiky hair as they come just close enough before returning to their perch. The sound dies down, and the loft is still again except for her heart pounding. They study her with those intense eyes of theirs, knowing eyes. She wishes she could ask them where Mica is. She wishes they could tell her or show her. But she will have to look for him herself. It is up to her to find what she has lost.

Annie

"I should go," she says, but makes no move beyond the movement of her lips, saying the words. Kenny ignores the words, pulls her closer, and kisses the top of her head in a brotherly way. Sometimes she wishes Kenny were her brother or a cousin—someone related. Though some parts of their relationship pushed the boundaries of brotherly behavior. They'd never crossed a line, though, not since that one time back in high school. If Kenny were a family member, she wouldn't have to give him up in a few weeks. Take a new name, lose a best friend. She sighs.

"Stay," he says. "Let 'em wonder."

"Oh, they're wondering all right. You're not the only person I stood up today. I bet my phone has fifty-seven missed calls and texts." She holds up her fingers and ticks off the people who are likely looking for her. "Barbara Todd from the country club, Aunt Faye, Tracy, Laurel Haines—"

"She was pissed," Kenny says, and laughs. "You should've seen the way she tore out of that restaurant."

"Yeah, well she can take a number. I bet she's only after me for a story about my mom. Like she really cares about me getting married."

"It is the wedding of the year in this town," Kenny says. He thinks about it. "Maybe even the decade."

"And to think you're going to miss it." Annie shakes her head and tuts. "Shame." She feels him stiffen and elbows him. "Don't get all sensitive," she says. "I'm kidding."

He looks at her. Through the thick lenses of his glasses, his green eyes seem larger than they are. He looks like Clark Kent with those glasses on. He's even got the little swoop of dark hair across his forehead. But if you take off Kenny's glasses, he doesn't become Superman. He just becomes a better-looking version of himself. Kenny cannot leap tall buildings or fly through the air. But he is pretty good at knowing when she needs rescuing. She will miss him when he's out of her life. She starts to tell him so, but he speaks before she can.

"Maybe you *should* get going," he says, and moves away from her slightly. "Don't want to keep you from all the people who need you."

She is not in the mood to bicker with him, to beg him to relent. And she does need to get going. So she just says, "Okay." Then she adds, "Thanks for coming to find me today."

"It's not like where you were was a big mystery," he says.

She makes a face. "It is to some people."

"Well, you know what I think about that. The fact that you haven't told your fiancé where you like to go when you're upset but you did tell me speaks volumes."

"You know me . . . differently . . . than he does." She offers the same old argument she always does. "You've known me longer. That's all. There's never been a reason to tell him."

"You've never found a reason because you don't want him to know," Kenny says. "You want him to think you're the pretty little princess you've led him to believe you are—all sunshine and roses and that winning smile. You've let him fall under the same impression that the rest of the town has," he says.

She shoves him lightly. "I have not."

"Oh yes, you have; you've convinced him—like you have everyone else—that you're all sweetness and light with no darkness in you. Hell, you're even marrying him because of it. If you were honest with him—if you were honest with yourself—you wouldn't go through with it."

"Oh, and I guess you think I'd marry you."

A look passes across his face that is every bit as hurt as if she'd slapped him. They look at each other without speaking for a few seconds. She can see him decide not to go any further.

"You wouldn't be entering this business deal you're calling a love story," he says. "You wouldn't be selling yourself short." He rolls his eyes and moves farther away, increasing the distance between them by another fraction, signaling that the conversation is over. He has his pride.

If she wanted to, she could close the distance between them; she could smooth things over. But she holds her ground. They have to let each other go, give each other the space to do it. She needs to be kind to him now. Even though he thinks she's being cruel. She does not know how to end this, and she does not want to, but she has made a promise to someone else; she has made her choice. To let him think she will do anything else is unfair and unkind. And yet . . . She leans over and kisses him, a chaste peck, friendly, the kind Europeans give each other all the time.

He remains stony, impassive.

"I guess I'll go now," she says, willing him to speak up, to stop her. She doesn't have to leave just yet. She could stay a few more minutes. They could keep talking.

But Kenny stays silent, averts his eyes as she stands up and smooths her rumpled clothes. She brushes off the pine needles and bits of dead leaves that are stuck to her shorts, her gaze falling on the place where her mother died, the spot she likes to come to when her life gets overwhelming and confusing, which is often these days. Kenny is the only one she's ever told about this place. She's never felt comfortable telling anyone else.

She knows that counts for something, Kenny's right about that. She's cruel to pretend otherwise. But to do so is to open a door she's trying desperately to close. So she can do the right thing, so she can marry the right guy. Kenny is not the right guy. Scott is. Kenny, of course, does not understand this. He's not aware of the protocol. But she knows—as she always has—what's expected of her, what her role is in this town. She cannot marry the odd duck, her quirky friend. She has to marry the guy who is her perfect match, the one people expect to see waiting for her at the end of the aisle in a few weeks. She has to make the town happy, like she always has. It is her act of service, her offering on behalf of the greater good. When you're the only survivor of the town's darkest moment, you do whatever you can to bring light.

When she walks away, Kenny doesn't call after her, doesn't try to stop her. He just lets her go.

Faye

"I can't believe she's not here," Faye says, glancing at the oversize clock she keeps on the wall so that everyone—both customers and stylists—will know what time it is and hopefully stay on track. *You can't say you didn't know what time it is when there's a big-ass clock hanging in plain sight,* she always says. She tried this at home with the girls when they were teenagers, but they were harder to convince than her customers and employees. Annie and Clary run on their own time and by their own rules.

Which is why she's both surprised and not surprised that Annie isn't here for the practice run for the bridesmaids' hairstyle. She'd reminded Annie several times, but she had the distinct feeling each time that Annie wasn't listening. Annie has been so distracted lately, with all this talk of Cordell Lewis being released. It's put a real damper on the wedding plans. Which is why she cooked up this practice-run idea in the first place, to get Annie's mind where it should be—on her upcoming wedding—and not on this man who has dominated their lives far too much and for far too long.

In the chair in front of her, Tracy Douglas sits with a barely perceptible pout on her face. She's trying to be okay with being stood up by Annie, but she's not quite there yet. Faye feels the same way. Some days Annie requires more grace than others. Today is one of those days. She'd sensed it would be when she saw Annie reading something at the breakfast table this morning, something she quickly folded up and tucked into the pages of a bridal magazine she then pretended to be interested in when Faye walked in with her morning coffee in hand.

"Whatcha reading?" Faye had asked, giving Annie the chance to tell her the truth.

Annie tapped the magazine page and lied. "An article about seating arrangements for the wedding." She'd looked up at Faye, feigning innocence. "We really should go over that soon."

"Sure." Faye had decided not to push the issue. Let Annie have her secrets. The girl was entitled, seeing as how she was no longer a girl at all. In a few weeks, she would be a married woman. A married woman moving out and leaving town. Faye tries not to think about that. "Maybe after we finish at the salon today?" Faye had asked.

"Mm-hmm," Annie had replied, her nose buried in the magazine. Faye had known she wasn't paying a bit of attention to her. Now she wishes she'd pushed harder, made sure Annie acknowledged that she would in fact be at the salon immediately after her lunch with the reporter. Ugh. The reporter. Laurel Haines, back in town and hungry for a story. Faye fears Annie's wedding isn't the only story she's after. She's keeping her eye on Laurel Haines. She has spent her life protecting Annie, and that compulsion won't go away anytime soon.

When Annie got up to shower, Faye had flipped through the magazine to find whatever Annie had tucked inside. But whatever it was, it was gone. It had looked like some sort of official letter. Faye has an idea who it was from. She'd like to string up that attorney by his thumbs. This case of his—this Innocence Inquiry Commission—isn't any concern of Annie's. Whether or not Cordell Lewis belongs in jail is not for Annie to help determine. Let the girl get on with her life, for crying out loud!

"Do you think we should call her?" Tracy asks, interrupting Faye's fingers as they craft the braided part of the updo Annie had shown her a photo of, from that same magazine she'd been pretending to read that morning. Faye is doing the style from memory, and she can tell that Tracy doesn't quite believe that she's doing it right without the photo to prove it. But Annie has the magazine, and Annie isn't here.

"I tried," says Faye. "But she didn't answer. And she hasn't called back."

"I could text her," Tracy says, trying to be helpful. She has that eager look on her face that says she will do most anything she's asked. She was always such a pleaser in high school. Annie's best friend, for better or worse. But sometimes Faye suspects that Annie can take or leave Tracy, that the two will quickly lose touch once Annie moves away. *Annie is moving away.* The thought catches her up short, as it always does. Faye bemoans the fact that Annie couldn't find a nice hometown boy. She likes Scott Hanson well enough. But she does hold it against him that he's taking Annie away from them. She never thought Annie would be the one to leave Ludlow while she would stay behind.

Faye shakes her head. "I've already tried. A bunch of times." She rolls her eyes, a skill she learned from Annie and Clary. "She's probably off making goo-goo eyes at Scott," she says, just to say something.

"Or maybe more than that," Louise Hendrix suggests from a nearby chair, then cackles loudly, willing everyone to join her. A few customers politely do.

"Well, that's a visual I don't need in my head, thank you very much," Faye teasingly scolds Louise.

Louise laughs again but with less exuberance, then sits back, realizing she'd best not say more. Faye is not a prude, but she doesn't exactly want to think about her niece's sex life, either.

"You know what you should do? You should get a facial," she says to Tracy. "I can give you a free one. For your trouble."

"I want a free facial," Louise grumbles to herself, but just loud enough that someone could hear if they wanted. But no one pays her any mind. Louise is one of the richest women in town but not one of the smartest. She was once quite the beauty, but that ship has sailed. She spends most of her time standing on the dock waving a hankie, begging it to come back to her. Which means she spends a lot of time in Faye's salon. She's as much a fixture here as that big-ass clock on the wall.

"It's okay," Tracy says. "I don't really need one." Tracy leans toward the mirror in front of her as if to confirm that she is correct.

Faye pats Tracy's shoulder. "You're right. You don't. Oh, to have your skin again." She looks to Louise as if to say, *Am I right?* but this time Louise pretends to be interested in a back issue of *People* magazine. Oh well, let her pout. She'll be back. Faye's salon isn't the only one in town, but it's the best. Her customers are loyal, and her calendar is full. She cannot count on a lot in life, but she can count on that.

Tracy says something that Faye doesn't quite hear. She inclines her head toward the girl. "What, honey?"

"Nothing," Tracy responds as two spots of color rise on her cheeks. Faye remembers this about her. She blushes fast and embarrasses easily.

"Oh, you have to tell me now," Faye prompts, and nudges her playfully, if for no other reason than to get her to lighten up.

She watches as Tracy debates whether to repeat what she said. She looks toward the door of the salon, as if Annie might walk in and catch her. Satisfied that won't happen, she takes a deep breath. "I just said, I don't understand why she wouldn't show up. I mean," she rushes to add, "not for me. But for you." Tracy pauses, sighs. "I mean, considering all you've done."

Faye takes a step back. It's normal for other women—women her age—to comment on all she's done for Annie, what a wonderful person she is to do what she did, the sacrifices she's made for her niece. But not Annie's peers. They always seem oblivious.

"Well," Faye decides to say, "it's her wedding. I've done what any mother would do." She shrugs, hoping the action makes her seem indifferent. "I'm the closest thing she's got," she adds needlessly.

Tracy looks at Faye in the mirror until she meets her eyes. When Faye reluctantly does, Tracy holds her gaze for a moment before speaking again. "I'm not just talking about the wedding," she says. She starts to say more, then closes her mouth with an alarmed look. She has said too much. The moment of bravery is over.

But Faye knows what she meant, what she was trying to say. And she appreciates it. She rests her hand on Tracy's shoulder. "Thank you, honey. That means a lot."

Tracy nods. "It's true."

"I did what anyone would do," she says, though she knows this is not exactly true. She's heard it enough times to know that not everyone would do what she did for Annie. But she is not everyone, and neither was Lydia. She thinks of her dead sister for the briefest of moments; that is all she allows herself anymore. No sense dwelling on the past. There is a wedding to pull off, a life to live in the here and now. When the bride shows up, they will get to it.

◆ ◆ ◆

Annie shows up in time for dinner. The door opens, and she breezes in, calling out, "Hey! I'm here!"

This is what always happens when she pulls one of her disappearing acts. Later, she acts like nothing happened and expects forgiveness. It is part of their unspoken agreement, one that has evolved with time: you recognize that I am damaged goods because of what happened when I was a child. You raise me, and I become the dutiful de facto daughter. On the outside, I will make sure things look perfect, and you will be praised. But when I need to fall apart, you will allow it. You will understand.

Faye wonders if Scott knows about Annie's dark moods, understands her need to come apart every so often. Faye and Clary are accustomed to it; they expect it and recognize the signs and cycles. But Faye fears Annie has kept this part of herself from her fiancé. It is, after all, what you do when you fall in love: you hide who you really are for as long as possible, fearing that if you show your true self, the person you love won't love you anymore. Once, she tried to talk to Annie about this—tentatively broached the subject of Lydia's death (she'd called it *death* and not *murder* to make it sound gentler) and the lingering effects it has had on all of them (she'd included herself and Clary to make it sound less pointed in Annie's direction). But Annie had seen right through her and refused to discuss it.

"That will be my new life," she'd said. "Away from here. Away from all that." Looking at her, Faye could tell she believed it.

"Hey yourself," Faye calls from the kitchen. She hears Annie put her purse and keys on the table in the foyer, then kick off her shoes, just as she's done ever since she could drive a car: *thunk, jingle, clunk clunk.* She will miss those sounds, the sounds that Annie is home, that her chicks are all back in the nest. She can already tell that after the wedding, she will catch herself waiting for that familiar sound sometimes, having momentarily forgotten that this phase of her life has ended. She shakes her head and gives the salad dressing a good shake. She's being maudlin again.

Annie rounds the corner and gives her a wide smile, the one she uses when she's trying to deflect what she knows is coming. In response, Faye raises her eyebrows. "We missed you at the salon today," she says, choosing her words carefully.

"Yeah," Annie says. "Sorry about that. I got . . . tied up . . . with something." She ducks her head and turns the corners of her mouth down, her attempt to look ashamed of herself. "I'm sorry," she adds. "I called Tracy already."

"She seemed kinda mad at you for not showing," Faye says. Good plan: make it look like someone else is mad. But not her.

"Yeah," Annie says. "She said I shouldn't have stood y'all up. I told her it just slipped my mind, and by the time I remembered, it was too late." She holds up her hands in a gesture of innocence. "I've had a lot on my mind lately," she adds.

Faye gives her the salad bowl, and Annie lowers her innocent hands to take it. Without being told, she trots into the dining area off the kitchen to put the bowl on the table. This house was in Annie's father's family. They had allowed Lydia to stay on there to raise Annie after he died in a motorcycle accident. Then, after Lydia died, they'd allowed Faye and Clary to stay to care for Annie "just for a little while." That was twenty-three years ago. But it still doesn't really feel like home.

Sometimes Faye daydreams about what a house of her own choosing might look like. She'd lived in a rented apartment with her husband when she got the call about Lydia and came to fetch her orphaned niece. Of course, back then she'd thought—they'd all thought—she'd get Annie and return to Virginia and her husband. But other than a quick trip to collect her things, she's never gone back other than the occasional forced, quick visit. She'd stayed in this house, raised her daughter and her niece, gotten a job at the salon she eventually bought, and built a life, so to speak. But sometimes she wonders if this life was what she wanted or what she accepted. Any time she tries to really think about it, she gets interrupted by someone who needs something.

"Where's Clary?" Annie calls with her mouth full. Without looking, Faye knows she's eating a cucumber wheel from the salad.

"She's outside in the loft," Faye calls back, gathering the ranch dressing for Clary, the blue cheese for herself, and the Italian vinaigrette for Annie to carry to the dining room table. They are having a light meal of salad and leftover grilled chicken tonight. It's too damn hot outside to eat anything heavier. One of her customers brought her fresh tomatoes and cucumbers from her garden: the first of the season. She'd decided right then and there to make a salad for their supper. She gets to the table and plunks down the three different dressings, a visual of the three different personalities. It would be nice if they all liked the same thing, but that's never happened. Three different flavors of ice cream in the freezer, three different kinds of soda, three different salad dressings.

"She's upset," Faye tells Annie.

Annie looks at her, worried. No one likes to be on Clary's bad side. "At me?"

It is a natural assumption, considering. "No," Faye says, using the tongs to toss the salad one more time, though it doesn't need it. "She lost a dove."

"Oh no!" Annie says. "Did it die? That's so sad."

Faye shrugs. "Don't know if it's dead or not. She can't find it. She did a release at a funeral today—you know Myra McGuirt?"

Annie shakes her head.

"Well, her husband died. So Myra hired Clary to do a release at his funeral today. And the one dove never came back."

"But the others did?" Annie asks. She goes to reach for another cucumber, but Faye puts her hands over the bowl to block her.

"Serve yourself some salad if you're hungry," she scolds. She picks back up with the story. "Apparently so. You know I don't understand all her bird stuff."

All Faye knows is that one day eight years ago, her daughter came home with a wounded bird, determined to nurse it back to health and find whoever owned the thing. She was just nineteen years old and had returned home from a stint of living up in Charlotte, North Carolina, after her high school graduation, her one attempt at independence that didn't last long. Clary eventually returned the bird to its owner, and Faye figured that was that. But the next thing she knew, Clary was begging to build a loft in the backyard and start raising her own doves.

Clary says they're special, but Faye doesn't necessarily agree. She considers her tolerance of her daughter's strange hobby to be enough. Sometimes people pay Clary to release the birds at weddings and funerals; sometimes she has groups of schoolchildren over to learn about them. Faye figures it could be worse. She knows Clary wants her to be proud, to understand what these birds mean to her, but she can't go that far.

When Annie doesn't reach for the tongs, Faye decides to go ahead and serve herself. She's hungry and cannot remember if she ever had lunch today. She had a few Lance crackers midmorning, which is what passes as a meal for her many days. Eating healthy, as Annie is always harping about, is not her strongest suit. But hey, she made a salad for dinner.

"You know what you should do," Faye says. "You should go tell her dinner's ready. Maybe coax her to come in. She can't stay out there looking for him all night."

Annie's big blue eyes grow bigger. "She's been out there all afternoon?"

Faye nods and sits down in front of her bowl of salad. "When she wasn't making missing posters and calling local vets, she's been out there scanning the sky. She's all torn up." Faye adds some strips of grilled chicken to her salad and douses it all with blue cheese.

Annie watches and makes a face. "You know that stuff is terrible for you, right?" she says.

Faye ignores her and takes a big bite. With her mouth full of salad, she says, "Just go talk to her." Thankfully, Annie moves toward the back door, leaving Faye to eat in peace, knowing it won't last very long.

Clary

"I guess you came out here to tell me dinner's ready and I'm supposed to come in," Clary says as she sees her cousin approaching. It's the end of the day, but Annie still looks as fresh and perky as if she just got up. Clary doesn't understand how Annie does it or why she missed out on whatever gene allowed for it. They are related, after all. They even have similar coloring. Their eyes are the same shade of blue. And back when Clary used to know the color of her natural hair, it was blonde like Annie's. When they were little, Faye sometimes even dressed them as twins. But no one ever fell for it. "Friends?" they'd ask, then make the little "aww" face when Faye explained that they were actually cousins.

Annie stands outside the loft and hitches her thumb back toward the house. "Salad," she says. "She used the leftover 7UP chicken she grilled this weekend. But the veggies are fresh from someone's garden." Annie does jazz hands and singsongs the part about the garden, making Clary smile in spite of herself. She's not sure she can eat anything, she's so worried about Mica. Her stomach rumbles as if to say, *I beg to differ*.

"She gave me one of her 'you know what you should do' suggestions."

Clary shakes her head. Her mother's suggestions are never just suggestions. They are commands disguised as suggestions to make them more palatable. At the salon she can say, "You know what you should do . . . ," to a lady in her chair, and the woman will pay rapt attention.

Clary knows Faye believes the same response should happen at home, but it never does.

"She's in there eating alone right now. We're giving her time to reload." Annie makes her voice sound ominous. This is an old joke between them using a line from a movie they once saw. Given time, Faye can come up with a whole new barrage of words, a different slant on an old subject, a brand-new line of inquisition. When they do make it inside, she will start in on one of them. Which one is the only question.

"Hang on," Clary says. Annie's presence there is making her—and the doves—agitated. They eye her through the wire sides of the loft and sidestep on their perches, gauging if she is a predator. "She's no threat," she tells the doves. But as she says it, she remembers their conversation a few days ago and wonders if that is entirely true.

"Faye says you lost one?" Annie asks. Her voice is hesitant, and Clary can tell she's been sent out here to talk about it but doesn't really want to.

"Yeah," Clary answers, but doesn't offer more information. She doesn't want to talk about it with anyone except her vet, an avian specialist in Greenville who is helping her get the word out to other vets that Mica is lost. He's the same vet who helped her unite the bird she found years ago with its owner. And the bird's grateful owner is the one who helped her get started with this hobby that has turned into a little business. It's not enough to support herself—she still has to do odd jobs on the side.

The thought of odd jobs reminds her: she has to drive Miss Minnie tomorrow. That will put a damper on her efforts to look for Mica. She was going to drive to some other towns and hand out flyers to vets and pet stores. There's no telling how far Mica has gone or where he might turn up. She's been so consumed with finding him that she has forgotten everything else.

"Shit," she says, forgetting that Annie is still standing there.

"What's wrong?" Annie asks.

She shakes her head. "Nothing. I just remembered I've gotta work tomorrow. I didn't have to today—Miss Minnie had a doctor's appointment in Greenville—but tomorrow I'm supposed to take her for her drive and fix her supper. And that means I can't look for Mica."

"Mica?" Annie asks, clueless.

"My dove. The one that's missing."

"Oh," Annie says. "I don't know their names."

Clary shrugs. "I don't expect you to."

"Which one was Mica?" Annie asks.

"*Is* Mica," Clary corrects. "He's lost. He's not dead." She hopes it's true.

"Sorry," Annie says, and corrects herself. "Which one *is* Mica?"

"He's the one with the silver tips on his wings. He's a Kentucky White Diamond. I've had him the longest. I got him from the guy who created the breed. I found one of his birds that had gotten lost, and he gave me one to thank me. That's actually what got this"—she gestures at the dove loft Faye let her put up years ago, sheltered in a cluster of trees in the backyard—"all started."

"You've never told me that," Annie says.

Clary shrugs. She doesn't like bringing up that time in their lives, because she knows where it could lead. "Well, you were off at school then," she says, making her voice sound flippant, and prays Annie won't connect the dots and bring up Travis. Annie has been bringing up Travis a lot lately, harping on "doing the right thing." But Clary and Annie disagree on what the right thing is.

"I'll do anything you need for your wedding," Clary had told her when this all first came up. "Just don't ask me to do that. You want to clear your guilty conscience over Cordell Lewis, you go right ahead." She had sniffed indignantly, for effect, hoping she sounded like Scarlett O'Hara, if Scarlett O'Hara had multiple tattoos, lots of piercings, and hair color that doesn't occur in nature. "I didn't do anything bad to Travis Dove—and, I will add, his life has turned out just fine. Why would I go opening a can of worms? Why would you want me to?"

Thankfully, Annie doesn't connect that time with this, and Travis is mercifully left out of the conversation. Clary by no means believes that it won't come up again. "Mica," Annie says instead, and smiles. "Now I understand the name. Silver tips like the mica rocks?"

Clary looks over at her and smiles. She's trying. Clary can see that. "Yeah," she says. "Like we used to collect when we were little."

Annie returns her smile, and it is, as always, brilliant enough to light up the room, or the dusk of the gradually fading day, in this case. It will be night soon. Mica will be out there all alone in the dark. She takes a deep breath to calm herself.

"We thought we were rich, remember?" Annie asks, sounding almost like the little girl she once was.

"Yeah," says Clary. "I remember."

The doves, settled now, make little cooing noises. Birds in the nearby trees join their song. Other than that, there is peace and (mostly) quiet. Until Annie fills it with her words. Annie has never been one to let silence go unfilled. It made sharing a room with her when they were kids unbearable.

"If you need help with Miss Minnie tomorrow, I can help out." She shrugs. "I'm not really doing anything." Her boss recently left and threw the office into turmoil. With the move coming up and the wedding to plan, Annie intended to quit her job in marketing for the grocery store chain anyway, so, rather than going through the transition and adjustment of getting a new boss, she and Scott had decided she'd just leave a bit early. She's supposed to be looking for a new position in Norcross, Georgia, where she will move in with Scott, who accepted a transfer with his job, after the wedding. But Clary has seen no evidence of her looking.

"That would give you time to search for him." Her eyebrows form two arches over her sapphire eyes as she raises them in question. "Right?"

Clary narrows her eyes at her cousin and gives her a knowing smirk. "I don't think you know what you're asking," she says. "Miss Minnie has a route we take every day. We have a routine. She gets real out of sorts if we don't stick to it. I'm not sure she'd take to you showing up to do it. She doesn't know you."

Annie waves her hand in the air, dismissing Clary's argument. "It'll be fine," she says. She grins playfully. "Everyone loves me. Right?" She laughs because this is an old litany of Clary's: how everyone loves Annie, how she gets away with things because of a combination of her tragic past and her cuteness. That cuteness, though, is manufactured. No one knows this as much as Clary, who was there when she created her image, has watched her cultivate it.

The two of them morphed into who they are now under each other's noses. They've seen the many selves they each tried on and discarded through the years before they arrived at these current versions. They each know the parts of those discarded selves they kept, the things they've held on to. For Annie, it is her penchant for disappearing when her dark moods strike. For Clary, it is something else entirely.

She is about to bring up that something else—and their earlier conversation about Travis—when Annie's phone rings: The Dixie Cups singing, "Goin' to the chapel and we're gonna get married." The noise sets the birds off again. The rush of wind created by their startled flapping wings ruffles Clary's hair, and Clary glares at Annie for causing another disturbance. But Annie doesn't notice her cousin's angry eyes. She's too busy looking at her phone to see who's calling. Clary watches her hesitate for a nanosecond, a flash of panic or regret or—something on her face before she hits the button to accept the call.

"Hey, babe," she says, and her voice totally changes, goes soft. She looks over at Clary. *Scott,* she mouths. As if Clary would think she'd call someone else *babe.*

Annie walks far enough away to be out of earshot, and Clary decides to head inside, thinking as she does about whether to let Annie drive Miss Minnie so she can look for Mica. It would be nice to have the time, but would it be worth what it might do to Minnie if she's thrown off her routine? Clary has juggled crazy schedules, worked when she was hungover or even when she was sick, in the name of not disturbing Miss Minnie's routine. Clary wonders if having an unfamiliar person drive instead would affect Minnie, if she would even realize it in her addled mind. Is it the person driving or the drive itself that Miss Minnie enjoys? In the name of finding her dove, Clary decides it's worth rolling the dice. How bad could it be?

◆ ◆ ◆

She takes her place at the table in the same spot she has occupied for as long as she can remember. She glances at Faye on her left and Annie on her right. Every time they sit down together, she knows they are all thinking that this is one of the last times they will be just the three of them. Soon it will be just her and her mother sitting side by side. And, when Annie is there, Scott will be part of the package and, later, Annie and Scott's children. In the coming weeks, something will end, and something new will begin.

Though she is finished with her salad, Faye stays on, watching as the girls eat. It takes her a few minutes, but eventually she poses a question. Clary knows her mother well enough to know she is trying to sound casual but is not quite pulling it off. "Any news on that Cordell Lewis stuff?" She poses the question to the table, but it is directed at Annie, who freezes, her fork still in the air.

"No," Annie responds, her gaze fixed on her fork. Clary shoots a glance at Faye, but Faye isn't looking at her. She's focused on Annie.

"His lawyer's not bothering you, is he?" Faye asks. Clary sees Annie flinch, ever so slightly, and she knows Faye has seen it, too. Whatever Annie says next will be a lie.

"No," she says again.

"Well, I'm glad to hear it. You know what the DA said. We need to keep our mouths shut and let this play out."

"Right," Annie says. "I know." Annie looks over at Clary with a pleading look, begging her with her eyes to somehow change the subject. Every moment that she is silent, Clary knows, Annie sees as a betrayal. But Clary knows her mother will not be deterred. And she also knows that Faye's questions are not random. She either knows Annie has talked to that lawyer or has good reason to suspect that she has.

"I do feel bad, though," Annie adds, surprising Clary. "Like I should maybe speak up." She starts to say more but then stops. Clary imagines she's afraid of giving herself away.

Annie's guilt over Cordell Lewis's imprisonment is a well-known fact. And Clary can understand that. She can imagine how Annie must feel, knowing her testimony at three years old landed all suspicion on Cordell Lewis. The town never really considered anyone else. Without Annie's testimony, they might've gone a different direction, set their sights on another suspect. But small-town justice ruled the day, and whether or not Cordell Lewis did it didn't matter. Someone had to pay for killing a beautiful, young single mother.

"If he gets released, you could buy him a gift card for a restaurant and mail it anonymously," Clary pipes up, trying to be helpful.

Annie makes a face at her.

"What?" she counters. "It's a good suggestion."

Faye gives Clary a look. "No one in this family is buying anything for anyone in that family." Faye shifts her gaze to Annie, who stiffens. "You don't owe them anything. If he didn't do it, then the justice system failed him. Not you."

Clary doesn't think this is entirely true. She thinks that her mother should own up to her part in what happened to Cordell Lewis. Faye was one of the main people who insisted he'd done it. She'd pushed for his prosecution. Though Clary had been only four years old herself and had no memory of that time, she and Annie have pored through the old articles together. When they were teenagers, Clary had helped her cousin do research about the man who went to prison for murdering her mother. He'd always insisted on his innocence. And the word around town is, there's a good possibility that he will be released.

"The timing sucks," Clary says, trying to be sympathetic.

Annie looks at her quizzically.

"So close to your wedding and all," Clary explains.

"Oh yeah." Annie shrugs like it doesn't matter, when of course it does. Who wants to think about something like that at a time like this?

"Well, let's stop talking about it," Faye declares, then stands up, the action an exclamation point at the end of her statement. "I've got something for you," she says.

"What is it?" Annie asks.

"It's a surprise," she says and grins. "Wait right here."

As Faye scurries off to fetch whatever it is, Clary and Annie groan in unison, and thankfully, the tension dissipates. Faye returns, still grinning, then sits back down and slides something over to Annie. Clary sees the edge of what looks like a dishrag underneath her hand. She wonders what her mother is up to.

"I wanted to give you this," Faye tells Annie, smiling shyly. She lifts her hand, and Annie tentatively picks up the material, turning it over as she studies it.

"It's your something blue," Faye explains, though it's really not an explanation at all. Clary recalls Faye digging around in the attic a few days ago, muttering to herself. This must've been what she was searching for. But looking at it, she can't imagine why this relic was worth the effort.

"Was it Grandmama's?" Annie asks. Annie has always been jealous of the silver barrette that was their grandmother's—their mothers' mother. Because Clary was the older of the two, she got the antique silver barrette on her sixteenth birthday. Clary didn't think it was particularly pretty—it wasn't really her style—but as soon as she saw the way Annie looked at it, she pretended it was her prized possession. Sometimes Annie would "borrow" it without permission. Then a fight would ensue, and Faye would threaten to just take the damn barrette back and put an end to it. And around and around it went.

"It was your mother's," Faye says, her voice tight.

Then Clary understands. Faye's sister—and Annie's murdered mother—Lydia has reached mythical status in Faye's mind in the years since her untimely passing.

"It's so pretty," Annie says, but anyone can tell she is lying.

Clary nods along even as she asks, "What is it?"

Annie and Clary both laugh. Faye gives them a look and explains. "It's been in our family for generations. All the brides have carried it. It's a handkerchief." She waggles her fingers, indicating that Annie should hand it back to her. She holds the faded blue scrap of fabric up so they can see that the lace edging has long ago lost its grip on the fabric.

"I bet Miss Minnie can fix that," Clary pipes up.

"I thought Miss Minnie was blind as a bat," Annie says. She means it to be funny, but it comes out sounding harsh. It makes Clary feel defensive of Miss Minnie.

She speaks up on Minnie's behalf. "She is, but she can still make lace. It's called tatting. She's been doing it so long she can do it by feel." Clary remembers Annie's offer to help out with Minnie so she can search for Mica. "You could take it to her tomorrow," she adds.

Annie looks at her, confused for a moment, before she remembers her promise. "Oh yes," she says. "I guess I can! What good timing."

Annie does a good job at feigning excitement, and Clary can tell that, like her, Annie is ready for this forced family togetherness to be over. Annie takes the handkerchief back from Faye and spreads it on the table, running her fingers across it like it really is something precious.

"My something blue," she says, her voice reverent and sad.

They are all silent for a moment, thinking, Clary knows, of Aunt Lydia. There are moments in their little makeshift family where Lydia shows up just as surely as if she has pulled up a seat at the table. It has always been this way. Clary wonders if Annie's marriage will alter things, if, when Annie leaves, Lydia will go with her. Clary wonders who they will miss more.

Annie

After Clary leaves in search of her bird and Faye leaves for the salon, Annie puts the finishing touches on her letter, then emails it off to Tyson Barnes, ignoring the way her heart picks up speed as she hits the little arrow that sends her words off into cyberspace. There is no turning back now.

She thinks about yesterday, how she went to tell her mom what she'd decided to do. She'd filled her in on her talk with the attorney, the news that, with or without her cooperation, Cordell Lewis is getting out of jail. They didn't need her to accomplish that. She'd told her mom that Tyson Barnes wants her to write a letter that basically recants her testimony from back then. He'd said he would read it at Cordell Lewis's final hearing that will take place in a few days, a formality just before he is released.

She'd explained that all that's holding her back is Faye's stern warnings against doing it and pride. To publicly recant her testimony now is to openly admit that she had a part in ruining an innocent man's life. She does not want people to see her that way. But what if, in writing a simple letter, she could give his life back to him—at least what's left of it?

She'd practiced aloud what to say in the letter, hoping that there, in the place where it happened, the right words would come. "How's this, Mom?" she asked the air.

Dear Mr. Barnes,

I am writing this letter to be read in my absence. Though I am unable to add my remarks in person to the hearing that will secure Cordell Lewis's pending release, I would like to extend my support of the release. As the person whose testimony was a key part of his conviction, I would like to go on the record in saying that, in hindsight, I do not think my testimony was credible or reliable. I was three years old at the time of the murder and, by all accounts, was asleep at the time it occurred. Mr. Lewis has given a satisfactory explanation of why I would say that he hurt my mother.

Now that I am old enough to speak for myself, I feel it is my duty to offer these words on behalf of Mr. Lewis and voice my support of his release from what I believe was a false conviction. I sincerely regret my part in this miscarriage of justice and would like to do what I can to make it right.

I understand that there was other DNA discovered at the scene, and that the police never submitted it to be part of Mr. Lewis's defense. As my mother's advocate, I urge the court to test that DNA now and to examine whether someone else could've been the one to murder her on that awful night twenty-three years ago. The town of Ludlow deserves to know if there is a killer in their midst. And I deserve to know who really killed my mother.

Sincerely,

Anne Elizabeth Taft

"How's that?" she asked the clouds, the tree limbs, everything she could see as she lifted her eyes to the sky. But there was no answer. There never was. Tyson Barnes wanted answers, or maybe he just wanted to make a name for himself, searching till he found a cause he could take up and jumping on it when he received Cordell Lewis's sister's impassioned letters begging for help for her brother. He'd found something the media would run with, drawing attention to himself and his career. But in doing so, he had brought attention to Annie at a particularly unwelcome time. She just wanted to get married, to get on with her future to stop being "that poor murdered woman's daughter." She'd spent her life trying to show everyone that she is more than that—and yet it always comes back to it.

She stamped her foot like the three-year-old she used to be, clenched her fists by her sides. "I just wish I could remember," she said aloud. "If I could remember, then maybe none of this would've happened. Was I right when I said it was Uncle Cord? Or is he right when he says I was just confused? Did someone else come to the tent that night? Did I sleep through it all? I just wish you could answer me. I wish you could tell me if I'm doing the right thing in writing this letter. And if I'm not, I hope you'll forgive me."

If someone happened by, it would look like she was talking to herself. But that didn't stop her. It never had. Some people might not understand her returning to this place when she misses her mom, but the place where her mother was killed is also the last place she was ever with her. Sweetness and sadness always seem to come as a pair. So she goes back to this place when she needs to be near her mom, which has been a lot lately. People are mad at her for disappearing yesterday, but she can't explain her urgent need to go to this place, to feel connected to her however she can. They think they understand all she's facing, but they don't. They don't know what it feels like to go visit the place where your mother was murdered and call that "being close to her."

She checks her watch. It's time to go get Miss Minnie. Annie looks at the notice at the top of her laptop screen: MESSAGE SENT. There is no undo button, no take backs. She's done what she promised the attorney she would do. She hopes she's done the right thing.

◆ ◆ ◆

With the air-conditioning in the car on full blast, they are set to go. Miss Minnie is strapped into the passenger seat beside her, still clutching the old handkerchief Annie brought with her, the one that was her mother's. Miss Minnie has been worrying the faded scrap of fabric with her gnarled fingers since Annie handed it to her, but Annie doesn't try to stop her. She is fearful of setting Minnie off. And if that handkerchief is helping to calm her, then let her worry it to shreds. The truth is the old scrap of fabric means nothing to her. She has given it to Minnie to fix just to placate Faye, who seems to need Annie to carry it in her wedding. It's funny the sentimentalities that a wedding brings out. Annie has been having her own sentimental thoughts lately. Kenny's face comes to mind, but she blinks until it fades away. No time for that now.

Annie gives her passenger the side-eye, watching her arthritic movements, doubtful that the old woman can truly make lace with those fingers of hers. But Clary says she can, so it must be true. Miss Minnie's face is turned toward the window, glaring at it like a sullen child. It's clear that, while she is tolerating Annie's presence as Clary's substitute, she is not happy about it.

"Well now, Miss Minnie," Annie says in the brightest voice she can muster, "where shall we go on our afternoon drive?"

Miss Minnie turns and stares at Annie with her cloudy eyes. Clary says that Minnie needs cataract surgery, but at her age, they're more fearful of what the surgery could set off than what she's not able to see. Now Annie wonders what the old woman can make out as she takes her in. The car is silent as Minnie scrutinizes her driver.

"What'd you say your name is, honey?" Minnie croaks, surprising Annie. She has not spoken till now.

"It's Annie. Annie Taft," she says. Minnie says nothing in response, just keeps watching her warily, as though she doesn't quite believe her.

"I'm Clary's cousin," Annie explains.

Still nothing from Minnie.

Annie tries again. "You know Faye? Who does your hair?" Reflexively, Annie tugs on her own hair. She has let it grow long for the wedding, but she plans to cut it right after. She doesn't like her hair so heavy on her neck in the summer. It's like wearing a permanent scarf in this heat. She's warned Scott, who loves her hair long, that a haircut is on the horizon. Scott has expectations.

"Why would you want to do that, honey?" he always asks, truly puzzled. "It's so pretty long."

She always points at his short hair. "Easy for you to say," she counters.

"Glynnis does my hair," Minnie argues, touching her thinning white hair, which is cut in that style that old women wear, the kind that is washed and set and sprayed to death, then worn for a week at a time. Annie has never understood how this works. She could never style her hair just once for a whole week. Though it sounds kind of nice. Easy. Annie spends too much time on her hair. She blames this on being raised by a hairstylist.

Annie knows that Glynnis does not do Minnie's hair, but she does not argue. She just shifts the car into reverse and carefully begins backing down the drive. She's been sternly instructed by Clary: "You ask Minnie where she wants to go, but no matter what she says in response, you take her on the same route." Annie has committed the route to memory after Clary made her repeat it back to her about 452 times this morning:

Take Peppertown Road till it dead-ends into Mill Pond Drive, then follow Mill Pond all the way around (past the entrance to Eden Hill State Park but not the one Annie usually uses) until you come to Fire Alley, which Annie learned from Clary this morning was once the actual alley that ran behind the fire station in town, until the county moved the fire station to its current location. Now Fire Alley goes past a couple of churches and the town ballfields before it circles around till you're back on Peppertown.

"You just go in a big, long circle through the countryside," Clary instructed this morning. "It's easy."

"Sounds like it," Annie assured her. But now, with Miss Minnie sitting expectantly beside her, she's not feeling so confident. Not about the drive itself—she's lived here all her life; she knows these roads by heart—but about the unpredictable dementia patient beside her. She wonders if Clary felt this way at first, if she ever does still. She anticipates the worst that could happen: Minnie freaks out and thrashes around until she causes an accident. She becomes violently ill. She throws herself out of the moving car.

Annie reaches for the controls on her left and presses the button to make sure the doors are all safely locked. She recalls Clary's words: "At some point, she'll start telling you a story. It's always the same story. I've heard it so much I can say it with her. But it passes the time and seems to settle her. So just let her tell it. If she stops talking, sometimes I'll ask a question to keep her going. She kind of snaps back to attention, remembers she has an audience that way. She likes when you act interested."

Annie decides to try that. "Clary said you like to tell stories?" she says to the back of Miss Minnie's head. The old woman is gaping at the scenery like she hasn't seen it a thousand times, like she's being driven through the countryside of a totally new, enthralling place. They could be in England or the African plains, not boring old Ludlow. Annie wishes she could see Ludlow through new eyes. She wonders if she will feel that way when she returns, if Ludlow will become something entirely new to her, if someday she will actually miss this place.

She listens to the sound of the tires on the pavement and the hum of the engine for a while, lulled by the monotony. Clary hasn't prepared her for a scenario in which Minnie says nothing. She seemed certain that Minnie would talk. Annie is a bit taken aback that Minnie is giving her the silent treatment when she regularly regales Clary. An old competitiveness rises up in her. Annie will not come in second to her cousin. So she tries again.

Annie prompts her passenger. "Clary says you like taking this way because it reminds you of a special day?"

Annie glances over to see Minnie's shoulders stiffen in response, but still she says nothing. "Okay, maybe we'll just listen to some music, then?" Annie says brightly. She turns on the radio, and rap music blares from the speakers. Minnie whips her head around faster than Annie would've thought possible. She looks startled and panicked.

"Sorry! Sorry!" Annie says, and quickly punches the button for the all-news channel she forces herself to listen to each morning so she will know something about the state of the world. Scott likes her to be informed, as he calls it. Annie sort of feels that the less she knows about the state of the world, the better. But it helps with their conversations when she can contribute with some degree of knowledgeability. So she listens dutifully and, later, says thoughtful things. It makes Scott happy, and she wants to make Scott happy. She does. Kenny's face flashes in her mind again, and she ignores it again.

The announcer drones on, and driver and passenger let him do the talking for a while. Annie thinks that perhaps they will just finish the ride this way. It won't be Minnie's usual afternoon ride, but it will be good enough. Of course Annie will have to tell Clary that things didn't go as planned, and then hear Clary go on and on about messing up Minnie's routine, but that is none of her concern. At this point she just wants to be done with this boring obligation. She doesn't know why she told Clary she would do this. This is above and beyond the call of duty. No good deed goes unpunished and all that. Clary better find that damn bird of hers.

"And now for the local news," the announcer says. "The top story today is the predicted release of Cordell Lewis, who will await a new trial as a free man, thanks to the efforts of local attorney Tyson Barnes. Lewis has spent twenty-three years in prison for the murder of Lydia Taft, a Ludlow resident who was found murdered after her young daughter was discovered wandering in Eden Hill State Park. That daughter is—" Annie scrambles to turn off the radio just as they pass the entrance to Eden Hill State Park.

When the radio snaps off, she feels Minnie turn from the window to look at her, but Annie keeps her eyes on the road. She wonders if the old woman is looking at her because she abruptly turned off the radio, or if she realizes they are passing the place the announcer just mentioned, or if she is putting together that the reason she turned off the radio is because they were about to start talking about her. She imagines it is not the latter. Minnie has dementia. She couldn't possibly put that together in her addled mind. It's more likely Minnie was just enjoying the dull drone of the announcer's voice and didn't want the radio turned off.

Annie glances over at Minnie, who is back to worrying the hand-kerchief as she, too, stares out the windshield in front of them. They are both looking in the same direction for the first time since they got in the car. Annie waits for her own breathing to return to normal. That news story has rattled her. With Cordell Lewis getting out of prison, she will have to stop listening to the news, no matter what Scott says. She doesn't need to hear people talk about her on the radio. She just wants to get married and get out of this town, leave all this behind her.

They ride another mile in silence before she takes a deep breath and tries one last time to salvage the car ride, just so she can tell Clary things went as planned. She prompts Minnie again. "Clary said you like to talk about a baseball game? And your husband?" She glances over at Minnie to see if she's heard.

Minnie turns and glares at Annie, her head moving on her neck like a ventriloquist's dummy. "My husband is no business of yours, young lady," she spits out. Her cloudy eyes have gone from aged to hard. "You stay away from him. Do you hear?"

Annie's breath is caught in her throat as Miss Minnie continues to stare at her without really seeing her. Minnie's back is pressed against the passenger side door. Her lips move as though she is speaking, but no sound comes from her mouth. Annie wonders what words she is not saying.

She's just an old woman, Annie coaches herself. Don't be ridiculous. Minnie is no one to be afraid of. Take charge of the situation before she gets riled up.

In an effort to calm her passenger, Annie simply says, "It's okay, Minnie. It's Annie, Annie Taft? Clary's cousin?" Ridiculously, she realizes she is pointing at herself and lowers her finger. "Do you know who I am?" she asks, hoping that Minnie's confusion will clear, and she can get her home and tucked in to the couch with the History channel on TV and her bland dinner on her lap, just as Clary instructed. Annie has to hand it to Clary—if this is normal Minnie behavior, she earns every bit of whatever Glynnis pays her.

Miss Minnie narrows her eyes at Annie and clutches the handkerchief to her chest, keeping it away from Annie like a child might. "I know very well who you are," Minnie says. But Annie can see that the old woman isn't looking at her so much as through her. She wonders how she can know who she is if she isn't seeing her at all.

Kenny

She calls because she knows his girlfriend is out of town and she can. This is what Annie does. This is what Annie has always done, always coming back to that one magical night in high school when Clary and Faye went to Virginia for a family funeral and left Annie at home. She'd called him then, too, afraid to spend the night alone. He'd lied to his mother and slept over at Annie's. Their whole relationship had changed that night. At least, as far as he's concerned it did. He can never quite gauge whether Annie was as affected by that night as he was, and he's never been brave enough to ask. Then, and now, he is a fish on her line, and she can reel him in or cast him out, whichever she feels like doing.

He debates not answering at all, giving her a taste of what's to come when she marries the other guy and they can't talk anymore. But then he thinks of the mere weeks they have left before that happens and answers before the call can roll over to voice mail.

"Can I come over?" she asks, breathless.

He rolls his eyes heavenward, searches the ceiling for an answer to this dilemma that has plagued him since middle school: What to do about Annie?

"Are you there?" she asks.

He suppresses a sigh. "Yes." He glances down at his phone. "It's kind of late to be coming over here," he says. This is an excuse, and they both know it.

"Please." She doesn't bother to keep the whine out of her voice.

He wants to say, *Where's your fiancé? Why can't you go to him?* But he knows that if she's calling him, then chances are Scott is out of town. Scott goes out of town often, which is how Annie has continued to hang on to Kenny. Her traveling fiancé plus his traveling girlfriend equals a relationship kept hidden far longer than it should've been. But they've promised: once she's married, that's the end. This makes him far sadder than it should, considering how long he's had to get used to the idea. Annie has been engaged for a year. He thinks of the night she showed up with The Ring on her finger, acting as if it were nothing when it was everything.

"Were you going to tell me or just let me figure it out for myself?" he'd asked her.

She'd covered The Ring with her other hand and looked guilty. "I didn't know which was better," she'd said.

"Come on over," he says now, and sighs loudly, as if he's not happy about this.

"Thank you," she says. And he can hear it in her voice, how relieved she is. He worries about her sometimes, when he's feeling selfless. He worries about what she'll do without him to run to. This loss will primarily be his—he doesn't kid himself about that—but it will be hers, too. She will miss him, but he doesn't think she's fully grasped that yet.

Eight minutes later, she knocks, and he tugs open the door to his apartment, one of four in a small building in the heart of town. He tried to get her to move in when the downstairs unit became available a while back, but she refused. He didn't understand why until she got engaged. Why move out of Faye's when she was just going to move in with Scott. The point is, he thinks, to never live alone.

Annie looks right and left—you never know who's watching in this town—and darts inside.

"You got here fast," he remarks.

"I drive fast when I'm upset," she says. "I need a hug." She throws her arms around him, and he stiffens. He is determined to keep her at arm's length, where she belongs. But Annie has a way of getting past his boundaries.

"What are you upset about?" He steps backward, out of her embrace.

Annie launches into a story about the old lady Clary drives: how she drove her today to help Clary and the woman looked at her strangely and it creeped her out. But of course this is not what Annie is really upset about. There's always what Kenny has come to think of as "the preamble" to their heart-to-hearts. The initial story is always the launching-off point, the part she feels safer telling. After that, she gets to what's really bothering her. Kenny just has to wait it out.

"Also," she says, getting his attention. The word *also* indicates that she's about to get to why she's really there. "I did something I probably shouldn't have."

He shakes his head slowly, wishing he had a twenty-dollar bill for every time he's heard Annie say that exact sentence. "What'd you do that you shouldn't have?" he says, trying to sound noncommittal, bored even. This is the game they play. She pretends she has no one else in the world but him, and he pretends not to care.

"I sent a letter to Cordell Lewis's lawyer. In support of his release."

Her words remind him that Annie is still capable of surprising him. And this fills him with stupid hope. "Everyone told you not to do that."

She folds her arms and cocks her head. "Except you," she reminds him.

"You didn't really ask me my opinion."

"Since when have you ever needed to be asked for your opinion?" she counters, and they both laugh.

They're still standing in his entryway, so he gestures for them to have a seat on his couch. He thinks of what his girlfriend would say if she knew that another woman was here with him, alone. The truth is, his girlfriend doesn't know anything about Annie. Annie had made him promise not to tell her about them. "It's none of her business." She'd pouted. He'd been delighted to hear the jealousy in her words, so he'd agreed. The fact that he has been able to keep this from his girlfriend still astounds him. But he's learned something from it: the trick to keeping a secret is you just have to do it every day, day after day. It's not as hard as people make it out to be. Sure, sometimes your conscience nags at you, but you just find something to distract you when it does.

"How do you feel about it, now that you've sent it?" he asks, though he's not sure he wants to know. He has mixed feelings over what this lawyer is doing, pushing for the release of the man who went to prison for Annie's mother's murder. He thinks of the countless times he's listened to Annie pour out her heart about this man, his conviction, and her role in it. "You were only three years old," he's said more times than he can count. "The adults in your life were the ones responsible for wrongfully convicting him. If he was even wrongfully convicted," he always adds. Because he isn't sure this man didn't do it. There were no other likely suspects. But then again, the town wasted no time taking up their pitchforks and going after the person Annie had pointed at without considering other options. They hadn't exactly looked for another suspect.

Annie thinks for a moment, then swallows before speaking. "There was other DNA in the tent. Male DNA. When Tyson started looking into the case, he dug around and found that the DNA was noted on one of the police forms, but it was never admitted into evidence and never turned over to Lewis's attorney. He proved they intentionally left out that evidence, which is getting Lewis a new trial based on something called a Brady violation." She looks at Kenny. "In other words, even without my support, Tyson says he's going to get out."

Kenny feels inexplicable jealousy at Annie's use of the lawyer's first name, as if they're pals now. He pictures a guy who looks like a southern banker, dressed in a ridiculous seersucker suit that Annie probably finds charming, sees her sitting close to him as they go over some legal brief. Their hands touch by accident, then linger for a second too long. He sees this guy, this Tyson Barnes, who's been all over the paper since he started this controversial crusade, being the one who stops Annie's wedding when Kenny himself cannot.

"So." He clears his throat and his mind at the same time. Focus, he has to focus. "That's good. Right?"

"I just wanted my conscience to be clear," she says. She tucks her legs underneath her as he watches, traces the curve of her calf muscle with his eyes, then forces himself to look back at her face. Friends. They are friends. Best friends, even. Secret best friends, as she always says. He has this part of her, this part no one else has, a secret side of herself that she gives only to him. In some ways, it's more than her own husband will get. It is theirs alone. He must learn to be satisfied with that. And yet, as the wedding draws closer, she's moving further away. And soon he will lose her altogether. He isn't sure he can handle that.

He raises his eyebrows. "Well, if it did clear your conscience . . ." He lets the words hang in the air. Annie has struggled with this for as long as he's known her. He wants her to be free of this. He wants her to be free of a lot of things. Scott and that ring, for starters.

She sighs and rests her head against the back of the couch, looking hard at him with those blue eyes of hers. "But what if I'm wrong? What if I've let time confuse me, and I was actually right when I was three? What if I'm helping free the man who murdered my mom?"

He looks down at his hands, resting on his knees. "Is that what you really think?" he asks.

"I don't know what I think!" she hollers, startling him. He looks back at her just as she launches herself into him, knocking him into the couch's armrest. With her face buried in his chest, she says, "And besides, I already did it. It's out there now."

He feels the nearness of her, feels her breathe in and out as she waits for his response. He knows she wants reassurance, but he is silent as he considers how to respond. He will not lecture her like Faye or tease her like Clary. He will not take charge like Scott. But what does that leave him with?

"Please tell me I did the right thing," she says, her face still buried in his chest. He wishes they could stay that way forever.

He wraps his arms around her, kisses the top of her head as tears fill his eyes. He is glad she cannot see him right now. "I can't do that," he says sadly. "No one can."

"I know," she says, and her voice is very small. "But can I just stay here awhile, with you?"

And he says okay. Of course. She can stay as long as she wants.

MAY 28

Four Days until the Wedding

Laurel

She stands at the prison gate and waits for Cordell Lewis to walk through. There aren't as many people here as she would expect, considering the way everyone's been fussing about the news of his release. She would've expected a throng of reporters, a gathering of relatives and friends with signs that say WELCOME HOME, maybe even some protesters with signs of their own. She'd expected a scene but has happened upon a quiet affair.

A reporter from the Greenville paper is there, and one from the Spartanburg paper. They stand awkwardly together, pretending they wouldn't step over the other to get at Cordell Lewis, given the chance. They make the smallest of small talk, keeping their words at one-syllable responses, passing the time and doing their best to ignore the heat. This is taking longer than it should, and Laurel is daydreaming about going to the pool after she writes up the story, maybe even ordering a Tom Collins or a margarita from the bar to sip. She's spent most of her adult life pretending her family doesn't have money, that she didn't grow up with all the trappings of a privileged southern girl's life. Today she intends to own it outright, if just for a few hours.

If they'd get this show on the road, she thinks, and as she does, she thinks of her grandmother, who used to say that all the time. "Let's get this show on the road, Glynnis," Minnie Porter, or Miss Minnie as everyone calls her, would pronounce, and that meant it was time to move. At the thought of her grandmother, a small wave of guilt washes over Laurel. She's gone to see her only once since she's been home. She keeps telling herself she's too busy, but the truth is, she just doesn't like seeing her grandmother as she is now. Once upon a time, Minnie Porter ruled this town, deciding people's social standing with one word from her lips. Now she's a sad, confused old woman who stares at the TV until she falls asleep sitting up every night, a line of spittle snaking its way out the corner of her wide-open mouth. Every afternoon, Clary Wilkins—the weirdo—drives her grandmother along the same route, then feeds her supper. Laurel supposes she should feel bad that Clary is being paid to do what probably should be done by her own family. But they're all busy with their own lives. And she's sure Clary needs the money.

It strikes her then—how odd it is that she's standing here thinking about Clary as she's waiting for the man who went to prison for her aunt's murder to walk out the prison gates. She wonders briefly how Lydia Taft's family feels about this. Of course, she'd have to get one of them to talk in order to find out. And Annie never has returned her calls since her no-show at the restaurant. But she keeps faithfully trying, enduring the brush-off.

She shakes her head, uses the toe of her shoe to kick at a loose piece of gravel in the asphalt, which is radiating heat in waves that undulate in the air. She's definitely going to the pool as soon as she files this story for Damon. Ugh. Damon. There's someone else she's got to contend with now that she's back. She needs to write that book about Annie's mom—and now about Cordell Lewis's release—make her mark in the writing world somehow, and get out of here again. Preferably soon. Preferably for good this time.

A man begins to sidestep his way toward her. She recognizes him immediately and feels slightly nervous as he approaches. She has always respected and feared lawyers, as if they possess something she never could, some special insight into truth and justice, a gift bestowed on them at birth, like a pitching arm or a brilliant mind. Laurel likes the news, but she wouldn't want to legislate it. The responsibility would scare her. Just look at the reason they're here today. A man's life is in this man's hands. Whether she reports it correctly or not ultimately won't matter. Whether Tyson Barnes does his job will.

Tyson Barnes, though, seems unfazed by the weight of what he is doing. He grins and points at her. "I know you," he says, his voice affable. She can almost feel her mother's hand on her back, pushing her toward him. *He would be perfect,* her mother's voice inside her head says.

She silences her mother in her mind and finds it in herself to smile. "You do?" she asks. She can see that he is a man who will respond to flirting. She will do what it takes if it earns her a good quote for this story.

"You're the new reporter for the *Ledger*," he says. "I know your dad."

She rolls her eyes. "Everyone knows my dad."

He lifts his eyebrows and intones in mock seriousness, "You're from a prominent local family."

She laughs in spite of herself. "Well, that's sort of a dubious honor." She sniffs. "A prominent Ludlow family is sort of an oxymoron, isn't it?"

His eyes stray toward the still-shut gates that presumably Cordell Lewis will stroll through momentarily. She watches Barnes's face to determine if he's worried. But he seems confident. Laurel wonders if Tyson Barnes is ever not confident. "I guess if you're here, then I'm in the right place."

He inhales deeply, and she sees it—the slightest flicker of doubt. It is gone nearly instantaneously. He turns toward her. "Yep. Big story, lots of time invested in this one."

"And you really don't think he did it?"

This time there is no flicker of doubt. "No. Not for a minute."

"And you have no qualms about his being released today?"

Tyson gives her the side-eye. "Is this on the record, or are we just shooting the shit?"

Laurel, feeling brave, replies, "On the record." She pretends to search for a pen as if she's going to take notes, but it's not necessary. She will remember this conversation.

He cocks his head, considering what to say if it's going to be quoted in black and white. "No qualms whatsoever. This is justice you're seeing here today. Delayed justice, to be sure. But justice all the same. It's time he got some." His eyes stray toward the gates again, as if willing Cordell Lewis to appear. "He's a victim just as much as the victim herself."

"A victim of what?" Laurel hears herself challenge.

"Small-town justice," Tyson responds quickly. "An inept police force gunning for someone to pin a murder on, not taking the time to do their due diligence. He might've been the first suspect, but he shouldn't have been the only suspect. They never looked any further, and they should've."

She watches as color rises in his cheeks, sees that he is in this for far more than glory or notoriety. Tyson Barnes is a man who believes in his cause. "Well, you're making it right today," she says.

He nods, agreeing with her. She sees it again, though, that barest flicker of doubt. "I hope so," he says.

"There he is," she hears the reporter from Greenville say to his cameraman as they begin to move forward in one practiced, synchronized motion. The pronouncement spurs Tyson Barnes into action. He forgets that she exists as he pushes forward to intercept his client before the hordes get to him. Laurel watches the whole thing from a safe distance, almost forgetting to lift her camera and snap a photo of what is playing out in front of her.

Cordell Lewis, tall and bulky in the old photos Laurel has seen, seems to have shrunk in prison. He looks slight and shriveled as he blinks in the bright sunlight, scanning the few faces gathered there for familiar ones. His gaze flickers across her, and their eyes meet for a fraction of a second before he looks elsewhere, in the direction of someone calling his name. She feels a prickle along the back of her neck. Did she just look into the eyes of a murderer? Is she watching a killer walk out of jail, exonerated by an opportunistic attorney with a smart angle? Or did she just look into the beleaguered face of a broken man who took the fall for someone else's crime?

Annie

She isn't normally here at night. She usually comes only in the day. She hadn't intended to end up here, but here she is, alone and afraid. Large, driving summer raindrops fall all around her, pelting her in the head and running into her eyes. This wasn't the way it was supposed to go. The evening she'd planned has unraveled. One last time, she'd thought. One last, innocent moment together. Then new life ahead.

She looks over her shoulder to make sure no one is coming as she stands in the clearing, steps away from, based on what Hal York has always said, the spot where they found her mother twenty-three years ago, cold and still on a chilly morning in Eden Hill State Park.

"My mommy's sleeping," her three-year-old self had told Hal. "I'm hungry, but she won't get me any breakfast." Hal York said he'd found a Pop-Tart wrapper she'd tried unsuccessfully to tear into before she went off in search of help. Hal told her that was what got to him the most: that ravaged, but unopened, Pop-Tart wrapper, the Pop-Tart inside it smashed and crumbled by determined three-year-old hands. It had told Hal York all the story he needed to know. It had set him off in search of a monster who would kill a young single mom, then leave her little girl to fend for herself in the cold, dark woods.

"I think I've made a mistake, Mom," Annie says now. "I think I've messed up for real this time. Cordell Lewis got out this morning, and I think I saw him this afternoon in town, watching me. So I went to talk to Kenny because he always makes me feel better, you know? Safer? And I can tell him anything without him trying to fix it or take control of it. He just, you know, listens."

Her voice breaks, and she cannot tell if it's because tonight Kenny didn't listen like he usually does or because, as of tonight, she cannot go to Kenny anymore. She won't have him around to talk to. It's the deal they made. But the time has run out so much faster than she counted on. "It's the end of an era," Kenny had said tonight, trying to be funny. But it isn't funny.

"But tonight he didn't want to listen to me. He didn't want to talk about Cordell Lewis or what he called 'my unfounded delusions.' He told me he wants . . . more." Annie pauses, thinks about what Kenny brought up, about that one night all those years ago that they spent together. Did she think about it ever? Didn't it change things for her? Because it did for him.

"Why do guys always want more?" she asks her mom. "This is why I need you to talk to—not Faye and not Clary and not Scott and not even Kenny. I need my mom! I need to ask you about relationships and who I should marry—the guy who knows I come here or the guy I would never tell about that?" She pauses, straining her ears to listen for approaching footsteps. She knows Kenny will eventually show up—he just doesn't know the way as well as she does, especially in the darkness and rain.

What if, now that he's out, Cordell Lewis decides to come back to the scene of the crime? What if he finds her there and gets angry? She tries not to give herself over to her unfounded delusions. She takes a few deep breaths.

"Kenny was supposed to be my friend—so why did he have to ruin things tonight? Why do they push like they do?" She stops talking as a realization dawns on her.

"Is that what happened to you, Mom? Did someone want more than you were willing to give? Did it set them off?" She drops her head as if she is praying, but she's only collecting herself, centering herself. She looks up again, at the empty spot where she imagines her mother is sitting, unseen but there.

"I think he's really mad at me. So I ran off. I was hurt and angry but also a little scared. I've never seen him like that before."

"ANNNNIIIEEEE!" She hears Kenny calling for her, his voice nearly drowned out by the pounding rain. The voice calls again. Then again, sounding closer. She thinks it's Kenny, but the closer it gets, the less certain she becomes. What if it's Cordell Lewis? Or Scott? Her heart is pounding so hard in her chest she's not sure she can run, but she feels she must. She must find somewhere safe to hide until whoever it is gives up and goes home. She can't talk to Kenny right now, not after what he said. She's never seen him so angry. He frightened her. She'll hide for a while, then go back home, invent something to tell Faye. Her lies are starting to pile up. She has lied to Tracy, lied to Scott, lied to Faye and Clary. She has lied to herself. One thing she knows about lies—once they start to stack up, they can topple over, crushing you under the weight of them.

"I've gotta go now, Mom. But I'll come back." She starts to run away but turns back. "Who knows, maybe the next time I come here, I'll be an old married woman." She smiles, turns, and runs.

MAY 29

ARRIVAL DAY

THREE DAYS UNTIL THE WEDDING

Faye

She's finishing with a customer when she looks up to see Laurel Haines milling around in the waiting area. She averts her gaze before Laurel realizes she's seen her, hoping in vain that Laurel is simply here to get her hair done. She is in no mood for an encounter with that girl right now, not when she can't find Annie and doesn't know what she'd say to Laurel if she asks. She glances back at Laurel. *When* she asks.

Sure enough, as soon as her customer is up front paying, Laurel appears at Faye's side as she's sweeping away the hair.

"Hi, um, Mrs. Wilkins?" Laurel ventures. She is standing by Faye's elbow, annoyingly close. Faye can smell the determination on her like alcohol on a barfly.

Faye raises her eyes to look at Laurel, trying to reconcile this girl with the one who went to high school with Annie. She recalls that in high school, Laurel made her mother, Glynnis, take her all the way to Greenville to get her hair done because "no one in Ludlow can do it right." Faye is every bit the hairstylist of anyone in Greenville, but Laurel never gave her a chance to prove it. It's hard not to hold a grudge.

"Did you want an appointment? If so, she can help you," Faye says, and points to Kelsey, perched on a stool at the front desk, her face in her phone as usual. No matter how many times she's asked that girl not to be on her phone during work hours, Kelsey doesn't listen. Kelsey replaced Clary when it was clear that daughter working for mother wasn't going to work out. Clary may not've liked Faye's rules, but at least she had grudgingly abided by them.

"Kelsey!" Faye hollers across the room. Laurel jumps a little when she does. When Kelsey looks up, the expression on Faye's face makes Kelsey put down her phone. She all but drops it.

"No—I—" Laurel blanches and fumbles for her words, leaving Faye to wonder just how good a reporter she is. Glynnis has told Faye that Laurel has been "let go" from several papers who "had to downsize." Glynnis blames this on the state of the newspaper industry, but perhaps it's the girl herself. Faye studies her, recalling what a go-getter she was in high school. Faye doubts she has slipped that much in the intervening years. Newspapers are failing, and Laurel is probably just a victim of that.

No matter what caused her return, Laurel has moved back to Ludlow and is now a reporter for the *Ludlow Ledger*, the town paper run by one of Faye's least favorite people, Tad Collins. When she first got to Ludlow, Tad took her out for drinks, ostensibly to welcome her to town. Faye, grieving and in shock, had accepted his invitation, then proceeded to quickly drink two drinks on a day she'd barely eaten a thing and get just tipsy enough to confide in him about Lydia's murder, foolishly believing he was being a friend. This, she often reminded herself after that, is why she shouldn't drink. Everything she said ended up on the front page of the paper the next day. The two have hardly spoken since.

"I was wondering if you could answer some questions about Annie's upcoming wedding," Laurel says. Though she gets all the words out this time, Faye can hear the nerves in her voice. She decides to use this to her advantage.

"I think those would be questions for Annie, don't you?" Faye stops sweeping and strikes an imperious pose, the broom in her hand notwithstanding. "What you should do is speak directly to her."

"Well, see, um, that's the problem. I can't seem to get ahold of her."

Join the club, Faye thinks but doesn't say. Instead she raises her eyebrows. "Well, I guess you should keep trying," she says. She's heard that she can be intimidating and is hoping that's true right now. "Surely you'll catch up with her eventually."

"But the paper is running a story on it tomorrow," Laurel says. "I really just need a quote or something now." She looks at Faye and straightens her back as she holds her gaze. Faye watches as the young woman finds the extra bit of courage she needs. "This wedding matters to the town. I mean, Travis Dove is returning to perform the ceremony, and of course this town loves Annie."

Faye hears the way Laurel's voice changes as she speaks of how the town loves Annie. She's right. It does. Its citizens rallied around the orphaned child, rooted for her to move forward and do well after her mother's death. Ludlow isn't a town where murders happen, and Lydia's altered it forever. The town needed a happy ending to come out of it, and this wedding is what they've been waiting for. Annie is Cinderella, and the town is her fairy godmother, only too happy to escort her into the arms of her waiting prince. Faye looks at Laurel, who is more like the jealous stepsister in the scenario—one who has been forced to chronicle the blessed event.

"Tell you what," Faye says. "If—I mean, *when*—I talk to her, I'll tell her to call you right away. I'll make sure she knows time is of the essence." She smiles sweetly at Laurel and feels the tiniest bit sorry for her. It must be hard, coming back here a failure, settling for working for a small-town newspaper when once you had dreams of the *New York Times*. Faye understands this better than most, how life can surprise—and disappoint—you.

"But now I've got a customer waiting for me," she says, and points to the waiting area where Myra McGuirt sits with an untouched back issue of *Southern Living* on her lap, watching them. She waves Myra over, ending the conversation so that Laurel has no choice but to show herself out.

Myra is far overdue because of Willie dying, but Faye says nothing about the shape her hair is in. She just fusses over her, then listens as Myra recounts the story about Clary's dove flying back in the funeral tent and looking at her one last time before flying off, as if Willie himself were saying one last goodbye. Faye blinks back tears as she listens, incredulous. Faye wonders if that bird is the one that never came back. Clary hasn't told her. Clary, she suspects, has given up on the missing dove. Maybe, Faye thinks, that bird really did fly up to heaven with Willie and just decided not to come back.

"I'm sorry to go on and on," Myra says. "I'm sure you already heard all about it from Clary." The tears in Myra's eyes threaten to spill over, so Faye surreptitiously hands her a tissue.

"She didn't tell me a thing," Faye says, her eyes focused on Myra's hair and not her face. "You know how kids can be."

"Well, I'm just so glad I had her do the release. It was . . . unforgettable. She's got a gift with those birds, I tell you." Faye has never considered what Clary does with the doves as a gift. She paid to put in that loft for the birds and patted herself on the back for having done so. Other than a stray comment here and there, or the sound of the back door opening and shutting as Clary goes out to tend to them, the birds don't cross her mind much. She should ask more questions, take more interest. Maybe Clary does have a gift, and she's missed it.

Somehow, bless her, Myra knows to change the subject. "So, how are wedding plans coming? What's it now? A few days away? I can't believe you're here working!"

"Well, you know my regulars would kill me if I didn't figure a way to keep up. Today's my last day, though. Tomorrow we have the bridesmaids' luncheon. Then the rehearsal the next day, and then the big event is Saturday!"

"You're a good one to hang in there this long. I've been the mother of the bride before, though that was many years ago. Weddings are so much more a to-do now than when my Robin got married."

Faye does not correct Myra, does not say that she's not the mother of the bride. Not really. She just agrees with Myra about how much work it is, then tells her how much work Annie has done herself. She does not say that, once again, Annie has gone MIA. The thought makes Faye's blood pressure rise. The insensitivity!

On the counter, Faye's phone buzzes, and she hopes that, once she's done with Myra and can check it, it will be Annie finally making contact.

"Any nerves for the bride?" Myra asks, as if reading Faye's thoughts.

"Oh no," Faye lies to Myra McGuirt, the recent widow. "She can't wait. This is the happiest time of her life." The truth is Annie hasn't been herself ever since all the Cordell Lewis business started up, ever since Glynnis's daughter started sniffing around for a story, ever since her last disappearing act. Faye feels certain that if she were to go right now to the place in the park where Lydia was found, she would find her niece. But she has not done that. Even though Annie thinks it's a secret, Faye knows Annie goes there, rather than to the cemetery, to feel close to her mother. And she's never impinged on that. But if Annie doesn't surface soon, she might be forced to.

"So no doubts about moving away from here? That's a big change for her," Myra observes. Faye does not want to talk about Annie moving away, but Myra is forcing her to with all her questions. Because Myra is newly widowed, Faye makes herself be gracious.

"We've talked a lot about it. But she says she's sure." Faye can hear the earnestness in her voice, as if Myra isn't the only one she's trying to convince. The truth is, whenever Faye has tried to broach the subject of Annie moving with Scott, Annie has argued with her, then quickly changed the subject. "She seems to think that a new town, a fresh start, will be good for her."

"Well, I imagine with that man out and roaming the streets . . ." Myra lowers her voice. The subject of Cordell Lewis's innocence or guilt is a hot topic of debate in town these days, and Myra has the good sense not to invite other customers into the debate. "What I'm saying is, she might feel safer somewhere else."

"Yes," is all Faye says. Finished with Myra's hair, she spins her around in the chair to see her reflection in the mirror.

"Oh, I look so much better!" Myra exclaims. But then a look comes over the older woman's face, her mouth crumpling slightly. "But I don't know for who now," she adds quietly. Faye thinks again about Clary's dove coming back to look at Myra one last time.

"For yourself," she says, and gives Myra's shoulder a little squeeze. She winks at her in the mirror before sending Myra to pay up front. Faye turns to her phone to see who called. It wasn't Annie. It was Scott. She hits "Redial" as fast as she can.

"Scott?" she asks as soon as she hears his voice. "Is she with you?" It is only when she hears the desperate tone in her voice that she realizes just how worried she really is. She's tried all morning to tell herself otherwise.

"N-no," Scott says. "I, uh, I was trying to find out if maybe she was with you." Scott's voice sounds different. Strained, uncertain. Far from the confident young man with the world by the tail he usually is, at least around her.

"Scott," Faye says, making her voice sound even and measured, restraining it from launching into the louder, higher pitch that threatens.

She has customers in the store, all only too happy to pick up on some good gossip. She turns her back to the salon. "When was the last time you heard from Annie?"

"It was, uh, yesterday afternoon? Evening? Before she went to Tracy's. She said she probably wouldn't be answering her phone because she, uh, wanted some girl time."

This was the same thing Annie had told Faye and Clary. Faye sensed that Clary was hurt that she wasn't included in the "girl time," but she hadn't pushed Clary to admit it.

"Do you think she really went to Tracy's last night?" Scott asks, and in his voice is not concern but barely restrained jealousy. "Do you think she was somewhere else?"

This is exactly what Faye is thinking, but she doesn't tell Scott that. No sense fueling his jealousy, though what that boy would have to be jealous about she doesn't know. He's the total package, which is exactly how Annie described him before she brought him home the first time. Faye can still picture the two of them standing in the den, holding hands, Annie gazing up at him adoringly. They already looked like they belonged on top of a wedding cake.

"I just thought, you know, if she was going to tell anyone the truth, it would be you," he continues.

Faye is flattered, no matter how untrue his statement is.

"If you know something, Faye, please tell me," he says.

"I don't," she breathes. "I wish I did, but I don't." She grasps at something she can say, something . . . productive. "What you should do is maybe call some of her work friends or just the girls she runs around with who I don't know very well. Anyone you can think of—okay?"

"Of course, sure," Scott says.

"I'll call Tracy right now. And I'll try Clary," she says, because she doesn't know anything else to say. And then she thinks of someone else she should call, someone she'd like to see right about now. Someone who always knows what to say to reassure her. "I'll call Hal York, too," she says, more to herself than to him.

"The sheriff?" Scott's voice goes up a notch on the word *sheriff*, making him sound like a boy whose voice is changing. "You really think that's necessary?"

"He's an old friend," she explains. "He'll know what to do."

She hopes she's right.

Laurel

After being dismissed by Faye Wilkins, Laurel walks down Main Street in a huff, making her way back to the *Ledger*'s office. She stands for a moment in front of the building that houses the paper before going in. The nondescript one-story beige rectangle looks more like the site of some government office than a newspaper office. If not for the sign outside stating that it's the town paper, no one would ever guess. When she'd walked in for her first "interview" (though her employment had already been prearranged between her parents and Tad Collins before she even arrived in town), she'd hoped that the bland exterior hid a bustling, vibrant interior, like the newsrooms she was used to. Instead, it housed a small, beleaguered staff and the lingering smell of burned coffee.

Still, she's doing what she can, for her part, to raise the *Ledger*'s profile, to make it more like a real paper. She's created them a Facebook page, put them on Twitter, and nosed out any hope of real news in this town. Never mind that the closest she's gotten to going viral is more than a thousand views of a video she posted of Dewey, the office cat, and several hundred shares of her article on Pearl Bost, a local resident who became the oldest living resident of South Carolina when she celebrated her recent birthday at 114 years old.

She looks back at her car and debates what to do. Damon doesn't expect her back. He expects her to interview Annie Taft's aunt and then write up the interview and send it to him. But there'd been no interview. And the last thing she wants to do is go inside and admit to Damon Collins that she has failed at even this small task.

She still can't believe that Damon Collins is her boss. She thinks of the time they were at the country club pool when she was thirteen and Damon was twelve. Their parents were sitting across the pool, drinking cocktails, gossiping, and ignoring their children. She hadn't felt like swimming, sitting instead on a chaise longue reading a book, fully dressed, sipping a Shirley Temple. When she got up to go to the bathroom, Damon had pushed her in. She'd been dressed all in white, and everyone could see through her clothes when she emerged from the swimming pool dripping wet. She'd been wearing a training bra, which was now visible through her soaked clothes. Damon had pointed and laughed and not gotten in any trouble at all. Now Laurel is expected to forget all that and pretend that he is her superior.

Though his father has put him in charge of the paper to give him something to do (much the same as Laurel's parents have insisted she work at the paper since she has come back to town), his father is the real boss, calling the shots from a golf cart at the same country club where Damon pushed her into the pool. Damon is still a brat—spoiled, entitled, and not the least bit interested in the news. He's playing a game, placating his father and biding his time until he can make his move. Though Laurel can't fathom what that move would be. Damon doesn't seem to care about anything beyond reliving his fraternity days. Which were, according to him, *epic*.

She decides to go ahead and tell him Faye shut her out and walks toward the building. She tugs open the door with more force than necessary and marches past the other cubicles to Damon's office, the only one with a door. But Damon never closes his door, so she is free to barge right in and get it over with. She pushes her sunglasses up on top of her head so he can see her eyes. But he doesn't bother to look up at her.

"I'm actually busy here, Haines," he says, his eyes on his laptop computer screen. She glances down to see what he's busy with. Facebook. It figures. But of course not the *Ledger*'s Facebook page. He is on the page for his favorite hangout, Hops Haven. Which also figures. When he's not at the office or sleeping, he's at Hops Haven. Or just "Hops," as he calls it. Damon could do so much with his life, but he is content to do the bare minimum. He has no dreams that she can see. Laurel, however, has lots of dreams, lists of them. Dreams that go far beyond this small town and this hardly-worthy-of-the-name newspaper. The fact that she's ended up back in Ludlow is merely a small detour. That's what she tells herself.

"Just wanted to update you: I got the brush-off from Faye Wilkins."

Damon gives her the side-eye but lets it go. "I'm surprised you couldn't sweet-talk her into talking, bat those pretty eyes at her."

"She hardly looked at me long enough for me to bat my eyes," Laurel retorts, ignoring his attempt at flirting. Like her parents, Damon seems to have forgotten how much they hated each other as kids. "She was too busy showing me the door," she grouses.

Damon drops his eyes back to the computer. "All I ever hear from you is how you want to be this great investigative reporter, win the Pulitzer and shit. And you're gonna let a hairstylist put you off? It's not looking too good for you if that's the case."

She starts to argue, but then she realizes he's right. Damon being right about something makes her angrier than being assigned a little story about this town's answer to a society wedding. What she really wants to do is write more about Cordell Lewis's release, which to her is a much bigger story than this stupid wedding. If she could talk to Annie, reestablish a relationship with her, she could write this book she's been making notes about.

"Might want to find another angle," Damon advises. "Someone other than the aunt, maybe?" He glances up from the computer long enough to wink at her, which makes her wonder if she could file for sexual harassment. Surely a male boss winking at a female employee is wrong. But who would she tell? It's not like the *Ledger* has a human resources department.

"Fine," she says, turns on her heel, and walks out, half expecting him to call out to her, but he doesn't. She sits down at her desk, rests her palms on the cool surface, and takes a moment to recalibrate. She will prove she can do this. And maybe in the process, she'll get information for her book.

She pulls up Facebook on her laptop and turns the screen so no one can see what she's doing, even if she is actually using the site for research. It's not like anyone is paying attention. Damon is in his office goofing off, and the only other people in the building are Margaret, the admin person, and Gary, who sells ads, which is a joke. The same businesses run the same ads in the same spots and have since about 1983.

For lack of a better idea, she sighs and types Annie's name and "Ludlow, SC" into the search bar and waits to see Annie's name and smiling face. Annie has her privacy controls pretty tight, because that's all Laurel can see. Though she has requested Annie as a friend, Annie hasn't accepted yet. With everything going on, she imagines Annie is leery of old friends in the media trying to be her friend, in real life or online. Though she resents Annie dodging her, she also understands it and knows if it were her, she would likely do the same.

She studies Annie's photo, willing herself to think of who she could talk to next. But as she looks at Annie's smiling face, the one thing she thinks of is how hard it must be having all this stirred up at the same time she's getting married, the happiest time of your life overshadowed by the release of the man who may or may not have murdered your mother. Having both grown up with it and now covering the newest developments, Laurel knows the story all too well.

Laurel finds news stories and scans one after the other, eager to understand the scope of what has transpired, to perhaps put the events in some sort of context. Annie was three years old when her young mother, Lydia Taft, was murdered. Annie was found toddling down a hiking trail in Eden Hill State Park, hungry and dirty and still wearing pajamas, though it was nearing lunchtime. The police later found her mother in a nearby tent, strangled, her body cold. Though a three-year-old should never have been questioned and certainly not relied on, the precocious only child spoke clearly, and with certainty, telling a story about camping with Uncle Cord, a man the police would later learn was the name she used for her mother's on-again, off-again boyfriend, Cordell Lewis. The fact that the couple was "off again" at the time of Lydia's murder raised immediate suspicions.

The police went after Lewis and never considered another suspect. Even though Lydia Taft's best friend, Susan Reed, said Lydia had confided in her that she'd been carrying on with a married man whose wife was growing suspicious, which should've been investigated. By then it didn't matter. With Faye Wilkins and a young officer, Hal York—now the Ludlow sheriff—pushing for it, the authorities built a case against Cordell Lewis, a gentle giant who never once asked for a lawyer when questioned. Why would he fear being convicted when he hadn't done it? And yet, Annie's testimony, which was taped—you could watch grainy footage from one of those true-crime shows of a little girl in a pink-checked dress with a blonde ponytail—asserted that it was indeed Uncle Cord who'd taken them camping and Uncle Cord who'd hurt Mommy.

Lewis had an explanation for that—earlier in the night, he'd come by to help Lydia set up the tent, never intending to stay the night. The night was to be a special time between Lydia and her daughter—no boys allowed, Lewis claimed. But he had helped her set up the site, making sure—in a twist of irony—that the two would be safe. He and Lydia had been playing around, tickling and play fighting, and he'd grabbed Lydia a little too hard. Lydia had cried out, and Annie had been concerned. That's what the child meant when she said he took them camping and he hurt Mommy. He'd insisted on this story, and later so did his attorney, when he finally got smart and asked for one.

But Lewis had never stood a chance. Justice may have been swift, but it was blind to anyone else but him. And if the people with the pitchforks were satisfied, then that was good enough. Laurel read quotes from his family, the people who'd loved and stood by him for two decades, declaring his innocence even as other people called them names and shunned them. They finally persuaded the state's Innocence Inquiry Commission to take up his case.

Lewis had served twenty-three years of his life sentence when the Innocence Inquiry Commission attorney, Tyson Barnes, went before a judge earlier this year, citing that the prosecution hadn't turned over evidence of DNA found at the scene that didn't match the defendant. This past week, with the support of the victim's daughter, the conviction was overturned, and Cordell Lewis was released yesterday. Though he could be retried, the new DA has admitted they likely won't pursue a new trial. What's left of Cordell Lewis's life remains ahead of him.

This piece on Annie's wedding is becoming more than a story. Laurel can feel her brain making connections between the backstory of Annie's life and the new story of her wedding. She could make something of this, and it could be good. She knows this intuitively, before she has written a word. She feels herself leaning forward, leaning into the story. She recognizes it, the prickle right where her hair ends and her neck begins, the feeling of her heart going out of her body and toward something else, something that simply says *more*. She has forgotten this feeling—this pure, simple love of the story. All she knows right now is that she is not going to let Faye Wilkins's rejection stop her from seeing what she can do to go deeper.

She thinks for a moment. Who else is close to Annie Taft; who else could she talk to? Annie isn't responding to her calls, not that Laurel expected her to after the last time. She pulls up Annie's limited profile again, sees the thumbnail photo of her there, standing beside a man. Her fiancé. Laurel finds his name in her notes: Scott Hanson. She scrolls back up to the top of the screen and enters his name into the Facebook search bar. She knows he lives in Greenville, so she enters that, too, to try to narrow it down. Several results come back, and she peers at the tiny faces, hoping to match the face in Annie's shot to one of the faces there. She sees a photo matching Annie's profile picture and knows she's found the right guy.

Scott's profile is not as limited as Annie's. She checks out his "About Me" page as she debates whether to message him through Facebook or try to approach him another way. She glances around the mostly empty office, then back at the page, blinking from Scott's and Annie's smiling faces to the tiny bit of information about himself he's allowed the world to see. She is just about to give the message idea a try when she sees something under his list of groups: the name of a very familiar fraternity, from a very familiar school.

She looks over at Damon's office, sees the obnoxious orange tiger hanging on his open door, a literal sign that she's on the right track. She stands up and navigates the desks, coffee station, and printers, propelled by excitement but also a bit of anger that Damon didn't suggest approaching Scott Hanson in the first place. He obviously knows him, their being fraternity brothers and all. She strides into his office for the second time that day and speaks before he can acknowledge her.

"Why didn't you tell me that Annie's fiancé is one of your fraternity brothers?"

He looks up from his laptop but not before shifting it so that she can't see what he's looking at. Probably porn. Or one of his stupid video games. He is a manboy, but right now he's the person who can help her with this story. A story he gave her.

"I mean, you assign me this story, then send me off to talk to the aunt without ever suggesting this other option. Which sounds like a *better* option to me. How long were you going to let me dangle like that?"

Damon yawns, bored with all this. "Look, yes, he's technically my fraternity brother, but he was older than me, so it's not like we were good friends. I know him, but I don't *know him* know him. I don't have his number or anything. We're not buds." The way he says *buds* makes him sound like an imbecile. Because Damon has buds, and he is actually proud of it.

She puts her hand on her hip. "I bet you have his email. Or could get it," she counters.

The look on his face tells her she's hit her mark.

"Send it to me."

"It's not something I should do," he says. "I shouldn't do something for a colleague that would infringe on a brother's privacy."

He sounds like he's reciting from a memorized list of rules. She gives him a look that says, *I'm not buying it.*

"Especially not at a time like this," he protests further. "I mean, the dude's getting married in what? Three days?"

She narrows her eyes at him and ignores his question. "So you mean it's okay if I go bug the bride's aunt, who's basically like her mother"— the video of three-year-old Annie talking to police with Faye standing beside her plays in Laurel's mind—"who's putting on this entire wedding, I will add, in the name of getting a story. But it's not okay if I email her fiancé? I need to talk to someone associated with this wedding. So . . ." On the wall beside Damon, her eyes land on a framed newspaper cartoon of a tiger eating a chicken bone. "Throw me a bone here," she finishes her plea.

Damon closes the computer a little too forcefully, no longer in the mood for a nice fake gun battle or some naked women, she supposes. He pulls out his phone and begins punching buttons. She waits patiently, hoping he's doing what she wants him to do instead of merely trying to ignore her. Outside the room, in the open space where her cubicle is, she hears her phone go off, indicating she has a new message.

"I didn't just do that," Damon says. "Okay?"

"Do what?" she agrees readily. "A reporter never reveals her sources anyway."

"Yeah, well I'm guessing this one ain't gonna be too hard to figure out."

She stops in the doorway long enough to thank him.

"Nice investigative work, Haines," Damon calls.

She smiles in response and goes to get her phone, appreciating his attagirl, wishing all the while that it didn't make her feel the tiniest bit better.

Faye

She is drinking alone when Hal arrives. He moves cautiously toward her, like she imagines he would approach an armed suspect. When he raises his arm to point to the open champagne bottle on the coffee table in front of her, his movements are robotic, calculated.

"Celebrating something?" he asks, then flashes a weak smile.

She shrugs. "It was the only alcohol I had in the house."

Faye is not typically a drinker. Her parents were both alcoholics, and she fears becoming like them. But Annie is missing three days before her wedding, and Faye is getting more and more worried. She can't stop her mind from circling back to the fear that this time her disappearing act is something more, something bad. If ever there was a time for self-medicating, this is it. When she'd spied the bottle chilling in the fridge, she'd popped the cork in desperation without putting too much thought into it. A customer gave it to her a few days ago in honor of Annie's wedding. It was to be used for that. Now she wonders if drinking it beforehand has jinxed things somehow.

Hal takes a seat beside her but leaves the width of a whole person between them. This is how it always is with them. They literally keep their distance. It is not something they've needed to discuss in a long time. It's just the way things have to be. She looks at him and raises the glass and her eyebrows in unison. He shakes his head and points at his name badge. He is here on official business, investigating a potential missing person. He is not here as a friend. But of course he is always there as a friend—wasn't that what they'd promised each other all those years ago?

She would like it if he would drink a glass with her. If for no other reason than she would no longer be drinking alone. She thinks about Clary coming home to this: her mother and the sheriff sitting on the couch drinking champagne at four in the afternoon. She wonders if at this point it would even seem strange to her daughter. Hal York was a fixture of her childhood, their family friend, the first person Faye met when she arrived in Ludlow to collect Annie. She had been, come to think of it, exactly Annie's age now: twenty-six years old.

Faye can still picture it, the way Annie wrapped her three-year-old self around Hal, clinging to him like a baby monkey, refusing to let go when he tried to hand her off to Faye. As they'd stood there awkwardly with this child between them, it had already felt like they shared Annie, that she was their child. She takes another sip of champagne and feels that bad feeling again. Annie is there, in that space they've left between them.

"I want you to talk to Cordell Lewis first thing," she instructs him.

"I'm not going to go talk to Cordell Lewis yet," he says. "That's presumptuous. The guy just got out of prison for a crime he likely didn't commit. If I go beating on his door making insinuations, that hotshot lawyer of his will have my ass."

She raises her eyebrows at him over the glass; she will not be deterred by Hal or Cordell Lewis's hotshot lawyer. "Annie helped send him to prison for that crime he likely didn't commit. I think that would be an excellent reason to question him, seeing as how she's missing."

"She's not missing," he argues. "That's also presumptuous. We'll find her. And when we do, we'll find out that there's a perfectly good explanation for where she is."

"Then you tell me why no one can get ahold of her!" Her voice is loud in the quiet of the house.

Hal inhales deeply, tries a different tack. "She hasn't spoken to anyone since . . . when?"

"Yesterday," Faye answers dully, hating the word as she speaks it. "And her phone's d—" She stops herself. "Shut off. When I call, it just goes straight to voice mail." For Christmas this past year, she'd gotten both Clary and Annie portable chargers so they could stop claiming that their phones were dead when they wanted to ignore her. It hadn't done much good.

"And you weren't worried when she didn't come home last night?"

Faye shakes her head emphatically. "She told me she was spending the night over at Tracy's house. They were going to give each other pedicures and watch *Father of the Bride*." She feels like she's talking about Annie the teenager not Annie the grown woman.

"But Tracy says she was never there?"

Faye shakes her head and sets down the glass. "She lied about that, I guess."

"But why would she lie? Did you check with Scott?"

"Of course I checked with Scott!" she answers, defensive. "He called me, actually. He thought she was with Tracy, too."

"When is the last time he spoke with her?"

"He said it was yesterday evening; I didn't press for a specific time. She told him the same story about pedicures and *Father of the Bride*. He said he usually checks her location if she's out, but he didn't last night. He said he texted her a few times, and she didn't respond. But he just thought she wanted some girl time before the wedding hoopla started."

Hal has his detective face on. "And you don't think it's weird that he checks her location?"

"I guess not." She shrugs. "How would I know? That's how they all are now. They keep constant tabs on each other and think it's normal to know each other's every move. When we were growing up it was, 'Love means never having to say you're sorry.' Now it's, 'Love means never being out of touch with your significant other.' You mean you don't keep tabs on your wife everywhere she goes?"

He gives her a look that says she should know that he doesn't. "I don't care if they think it's normal. I think it's weird," he says, moving the subject away from his wife, as he always does. "Why would he check her location unless he doesn't believe she is where she says she is?"

"Last night he apparently did believe her. And look where that's got us." Faye shakes her head. "He said he's been concerned about her, what with Cordell Lewis getting out and all. It's like I said earlier—"

Hal interrupts her before she can start in on Cordell Lewis again. "I just don't understand her need to lie."

She hears his words, thinking of the lies they've told through the years: to other people and to each other. Sometimes, she thinks, there is a need to lie.

"It's probably nothing," Faye tells herself as much as him. "Just her usual shenanigans, made larger by the fact that she's due to get married." She looks at Hal. "Maybe she's got cold feet?" She begs him with her eyes to say, yes, that's probably it. But he hesitates before doing so. And in that hesitation are all her greatest fears.

He reaches across the appropriate space they have left between them, putting his large hand on her bare leg. His skin in contact with hers is a no-no, breaking the rules they established for themselves all those years ago. But in the moment, Faye doesn't care about the rules. She places her hand atop his, feels the heat of his skin radiating through hers. She swallows, forces herself to smile at him. She will not tend toward the dramatic. She will not be a hysterical woman. She will not assume the worst. "We'll find her," she says to Hal, her best friend and the man she's loved for far longer than she likes to admit.

"Yes," he says. He gives her an earnest, kind look in return, and it makes her love him all the more. She knows this is wrong, but she cannot let him go. She reaches to pour herself some more champagne, then raises her glass in a toast to hope.

Clary

For the first time since she lost Mica, she doesn't go straight to the dove loft when she comes home to see if he has returned. She just walks into the house, mentally preparing herself for all the duties her mother will undoubtedly throw at her as soon as she lays eyes on her. She's ignored her calls today, and she's sure she'll get an earful for that. It is go time as far as the wedding is concerned. This is the day they've all been waiting for. Or dreading, depending on who's talking.

When she gets inside the door, she sees her mother waiting there for her, perched on the couch with a champagne glass in her hands, of all things. She springs into a standing position as she realizes that it's Clary, and not Annie, coming in the door. "Is she with you?" she asks, craning her head to see past Clary, willing the door to open a second time.

"Why would she be with me?" Clary tries to leave the sneer out of her voice, but it's still there, squatting inside her mind beside the anger that has simmered ever since the moment she hung up on her cousin.

"This could've been avoided, you know," she'd said to Annie before she'd hung up. "Pastor Melton would've done just fine to perform the ceremony. But oh no, you just had to get Travis the Superstar to come riding back into town."

Annie had spoken firmly, but lovingly, in response to Clary, as if she were the patient parent and Clary the stubborn, petulant child. Clary hates when she does that.

"Travis and I are old friends," Annie explained, as if Clary didn't know that, as if Clary wasn't Travis's friend way before Annie ever deigned to talk to him. "He's a very popular preacher, and it's an honor that he's coming back here to do this for us." Then she'd added, "He has more than a million Instagram followers." That was when Clary had hung up on her, an exclamation point at the end of Annie's sentence.

Faye snaps her fingers in Clary's face, bringing her back to the present. "Clary!" she says. "You're not paying a bit of attention! We are in crisis mode here!"

"When are we not in crisis mode, Mom?" Clary asks with a deep sigh. She is already bone weary of this wedding, and it hasn't even started yet. She drops her purse on the table in the foyer and heads toward the kitchen at the back of the house. She points to the glass still clasped in Faye's hand. "Is there more of that?" she asks. Her mother doesn't usually keep alcohol in the house, so she's going to take advantage of this while she can. She could use a drink.

"Clary!" Faye says, her voice rising louder. "Now is not the time to be making jokes!"

Clary hears the desperation in her mother's voice, that voice that says, *Make sure your seat belts are buckled and you know where the oxygen masks are located, because this is no longer normal turbulence.* She stops walking and turns to look back at her mother.

"What?" she asks.

"No one can find her," Faye says. "Best we can tell, no one's heard from her since yesterday afternoon." Yesterday afternoon was when Clary had hung up on Annie.

"Tracy," she says, a memory of what Annie had said coming to her. "She's with Tracy." She'd been glad Annie would be out of her hair for the night.

Faye shakes her head grimly. "She lied," she says. Now she is the one who sounds bone weary.

"Lied?" Clary asks. "Why in the world—"

Faye shakes her head harder. "We don't know."

Clary narrows her eyes at her mother. "Who is 'we'?"

Faye shrugs. "Tracy. Scott. Hal."

"You called Hal York?" Clary asks, looking around as if Hal is there, and she has somehow overlooked him.

"Of course I did!" Faye says. She is gesturing with the champagne glass, and Clary fears the liquid is going to slosh right out. "Annie is missing and that jackwad is out of prison and she's about to get married and . . . I had to!"

Clary feels the need to take charge. "Mom," she says, keeping her voice level. "I'm sure she's just fine. She's probably taking some time for herself. You know, getting ready for her big day."

She's surprised at herself. Her voice sounds so gentle and rational. She's not usually the calm one. "Is Hal going to talk to Cordell Lewis?" she asks.

"He said not yet, that there's no reason to suspect him." Faye sniffs. "He said it would be pretty dumb of Lewis to do something like that so soon after getting out of prison. But I say, maybe he just snapped." Faye eyes Clary. "People do snap, you know."

Clary takes in the look on Faye's face and wonders if her mother isn't close to snapping herself. When they do find Annie, she's going to tell her how selfish it was of her to put Faye through this. She could've called. It would've saved them all a lot of needless stress and drama. She wonders if this is somehow Annie's way of punishing her for hanging up on her. But that seems extreme even for Annie.

"What does Scott say?" Clary asks, thinking perhaps she should talk to him even though Faye already has. Maybe there's something he's not telling Faye. Faye is not Annie's mother, but she's the closest thing she's got. And there are things you don't tell parents. Maybe he and Annie spent the night together, and Annie lied about it. And now maybe Scott is lying, too. Is Scott a good liar? She doesn't know. In her mind, Scott is a cardboard cutout of a man, placed in the spot in Annie's life that said

Groom Goes Here. It was time for Annie to get married, and he appeared. Clary never asked many questions. Maybe she should have. It occurs to her that she barely knows Scott Hanson.

Faye shakes her head again. "He's as clueless as we are."

Clary racks her brain for anything Annie might've said recently, any clue as to where she could be. She thinks of the silence between them after she hung up. Usually Annie would wait a few hours and then call her back, ostensibly just to pester her some more but mostly to make sure they were going to be okay. She never could stand for there to be friction between them. Clary could let it drag on far longer, but Annie was compelled to fix things. It's not like Annie to stay out of Clary's hair for this long. The fact that she has is concerning, now that she thinks about it.

"Scott said, 'If she was going to tell anyone, she'd have told you.'" Faye rolls her eyes. "Like I said, he's clueless. Neither of you girls tell me a blessed thing."

Faye is correct, but Clary doesn't say so. Instead she says, "Mom, she's just been spacey lately. This isn't the first time she's gone missing. I mean, the day Mica went missing, no one could find her the whole day. And she never told anyone what that was about." As she thinks about Mica going missing, she recalls Annie volunteering to drive Minnie for her so she could look for him, which makes her feel worse about having hung up on her. Even if Annie was trying to strong-arm her into having a conversation with her ex she never intended to have.

"Maybe," she says hopefully to Faye, "she's got a secret lover. Maybe she's thinking about calling off the wedding."

Faye shoves her, but lightly. "Clary, stop it," she says.

"Well, think about it, Mom. She's out to lunch half the time. She avoids eye contact sometimes. She keeps mysteriously going missing with no explanation. I mean, it could be."

"She's just caught up with her wedding. It can be all-consuming. You wouldn't understand."

"Gee, thanks, Mom."

"Oh, honey, I didn't mean it that way. I'm sorry." She reaches for Clary with her free hand, her other hand still clutching that glass of champagne.

"It's fine," Clary says, even though the comment does sting. Mostly because Faye is right. Clary doesn't understand. And she is starting to think she never will. Not that it matters, she tells herself. She doesn't need a man to be happy. She isn't a Disney princess who needs to be rescued. She's a strong, capable woman who can take care of herself.

"The truth is," Faye says, "if she were going to tell someone the truth, it would be you."

Clary considers this. Annie certainly knows her secrets, but does Clary really know Annie's? She feels Faye's eyes upon her and comes up with an answer quickly, one that she hopes will calm Faye's nerves some. "I doubt Annie has any secrets, Mom. Her life's a pretty open book. She's everyone's darling. She's overcome her hard past. And now she's getting married."

Faye looks dubious.

"She is! Annie is getting married in three days." She reaches for the glass in her mother's hand and takes it from her. Faye watches as she turns it up, tossing back the last of the champagne. Though it has gone warm and flat in Faye's anxious grip, Clary swallows it all.

Kenny

He is walking the mile and a half home from Hops Haven. Well, *weaving* would be a better term for what he is doing. He is trying to sober up, hoping the walk will help him. His girlfriend will be there when he gets to his apartment. She has texted him to say she's back from her trip and what should they do for dinner. She can't wait to see him. But she doesn't know what she is saying. When she sees him, she will be angry. She will take one look at him and know he is drunk. She will ask him why he was drinking on a Wednesday afternoon. On a workday. To his girlfriend, workdays are sacred.

He cannot tell her it is because of Annie, because of what happened last night. He was supposed to work from home today, but he couldn't be there, alone with the memories and regret. Somehow he ended up at Hops Haven, sitting at a table with his laptop open as if he was working but drinking beer after beer instead. He just sat there thinking. And drinking. He cannot tell his girlfriend the truth about any of it. He has made a promise. Annie is his secret best friend. Even now, after everything that has happened. He cannot tell anyone the truth.

He walks along the familiar streets of the town of Ludlow, angry that he is still walking them all these years later. It is not his hometown; he was not born here like most of the other Ludlow residents. But he has been here since the seventh grade when his parents divorced and his mom relocated them. Long enough to call it home.

He thinks of his younger self, with all his plans and dreams. The sky was his limit, as his guidance counselor told him in high school. He could go to college; he was plenty smart enough. That wasn't bragging, just a fact about him, the same as the fact that he has brown hair and hazel eyes and a metabolism that lets him eat just about anything he wants and not gain weight. After college, he would go somewhere where no one knew him, where no one decided things about him like the people here had.

But he hadn't done any of those things. He'd stayed right here. He kicks at a tuft of grass growing within the sidewalk cracks, angry at it for being a tuft of grass in this town, on this sidewalk. But his balance is off because of the beers, and the kicking action causes him to stumble.

He reaches out to steady himself, but there is nothing around but air. He staggers but eventually rights himself. He stands on the sidewalk and takes a few deep breaths, his hands braced on his knees as he studies the cracks in the sidewalk. Step on a crack, he thinks, break your mama's back. That's it, right there, he thinks. The reason he won't leave this town even with Annie gone.

Forget breaking your mama's back—his leaving would break his mama's heart. And he can't bear to do so. He is all she has left. So he stays. He changes her light bulbs so she doesn't have to climb on a stepladder to do it. He takes her to get a barbecue sandwich for supper at Brooks' Barbecue once a week. He comes over in time to have breakfast with her on Christmas morning and buys her a corsage, which she proudly wears to church, on Mother's Day. He takes her car in for servicing. And he sits beside her in church on Sundays while her aging friends cluck about what a good son he is and how they wish their sons were so attentive.

That he has found a girl who puts up with his relationship with his mom is nothing short of a miracle. A pretty girl, a girl who has a good job, also in IT, so they have that in common. A girl who actually understands what he does and doesn't just nod vacantly when he tries to explain about a problem he had with siphoning data off a back-end database. A girl who doesn't gripe about the times when he is silent, who doesn't insist he constantly share how he feels. A girl who knows what it is to feel awkward around other people, because she is sometimes awkward herself. A girl who thinks that his devotion as a son is an indicator of what his devotion as a husband will be. And yet he has not asked her to marry him. He hasn't put a ring on it, as the song says.

Like Annie intends to do.

His mind goes back to last night, even though he has spent the better part of the day trying to keep it from doing so. He recalls the look on her face, that one that made her look like everyone else and not the girl he loves. He feels the rage that welled up inside him, unbidden and uncontrolled. She saw it at the same time he felt it. Then he sees her running away from him.

Now she does not answer his calls. And the clock is ticking until she gets married and they can't be secret best friends, or anything else, anymore. He fears that last night was actually the end for them, that their longtime friendship is over sooner than he expected it to be. He thought he had more time. But isn't that what everyone always thinks?

A car goes by, and he looks up, feeling caught, feeling guilty, an old feeling he's spent his adult life trying to outrun. But he isn't that fast. He never was. He blinks as he watches Hal York's truck drive slowly past him. York spots him, and Kenny does his best to stand up straight and meet the sheriff's eyes until he is all the way past him. "Just look people in the eye," Annie used to say to him. "I know you're shy, but people don't know that. They think you're hiding something. Can you do that? For me?" She'd made him promise he would. She was always asking him to do hard things. And now she's asking him to do the hardest thing he's ever done, to let her go.

When Hal's truck disappears, Kenny begins walking again, thinking that perhaps he will suggest to his girlfriend that they leave town. He can't stay around to witness the festivities, the arrivals, the talk around town. He thinks of where they could go. Somewhere pretty and romantic like Charleston, with enough trappings to distract them both. He has the money to go most anywhere. He doesn't spend much because he's been saving for a life he will never have. It is long past time to let that life go and try to find a new one. He will tell his girlfriend it will be a getaway. Which is exactly what it is. He will get away from all this. He will get away and try his best not to look back.

His girlfriend falls for it, never the wiser. She doesn't even seem to notice he's drunk, probably because the sight of Hal York helped sober him up. She claps her hands together and gives him a big kiss, tells him he is the sweetest man she's ever known and that she's the luckiest girl in the world. He agrees with her even though it is nowhere near true. Instead he fetches them both a beer and sits beside her on the couch to look together at the computer to see where they should go. He feels happy, relieved. He will get out of here while the getting's good. His mother will be fine for a weekend. She can go to church with someone else this Sunday. It won't kill her.

They do decide to go to Charleston, which isn't far enough away for him, but there isn't time to arrange much else, and his girlfriend has to be back in time to prepare for the week. He leans over and kisses her when she says that, because she is so responsible, so solid and good. Not like Annie, with her whims and frivolity, always proposing the most preposterous things and expecting him to go along with them. "Let's drive to Greenville and walk by the river!" she would say, and then expect him to jump up and do it no matter what else he might have going on. She used to love to walk by that river. Now they'll never get to do that again.

"Let's go tonight," he says. He nibbles on her earlobe because he knows that drives her crazy, and he wants to drive her a little bit crazy, keep her distracted and unbalanced. He will keep her busy, take her to do anything her little heart desires. He will make the time pass by in a blur for them both.

But she pulls away and shuts the computer, giving him a sideways glance. "You know I can't do that," she says, scolding him like a child. "I've got work tomorrow. And besides, I just got home. I've got sixty-four emails in my inbox and two reports to write before I can even think of leaving. The earliest I can get away is tomorrow, late afternoon." She kisses his cheek. "We can both work from home tomorrow morning, though."

He rubs his hands along his thighs, dries his clammy palms on his shorts. He feels antsy, anxious. He takes a long pull from his beer and feels his girlfriend's eyes watching him do it. He has to act normal. He sets the beer down and gives her a smile. "Sure, yeah," he says. "Of course. We'll leave tomorrow afternoon. Say around four? It'll be a nice long weekend."

She smiles back, and he can see she is reassured, that things are fine again. He feels relief wash over him. They will leave town in less than twenty-four hours, and he will escape all this; he will put Annie Taft out of his mind.

Laurel

As she waits for a reply from Annie Taft's fiancé, she works on her research into Annie Taft's mother's murder. She pulls up the articles from the *Ludlow Ledger* in the days and months after the murder and pores over each one again and again, curiosity compelling her, losing track of time until she looks up to find she is alone in the office and the sun is making its descent in the sky. She eats stale popcorn at her desk and calls it supper, enjoying the quiet dimness of the office. When the sky becomes full dark, she gives up on hearing from Scott Hanson and goes home, hoping her parents will have turned in for the night. Instead she finds her mother sitting at the kitchen table, dealing herself a hand of solitaire.

The sight makes Laurel feel both sad and afraid at the same time: sad for her mother, whose life seems so lonely, so *solitary*, even in the midst of her marriage and social standing and various committees she serves on. More than that, she is afraid that her own life will turn out much the same, which seems to be her mother's sole intent since she arrived home. Glynnis keeps mentioning the few eligible young men in town or friends of friends whose sons live in Greenville and wouldn't mind meeting a smart, pretty young woman from Ludlow. She could stay at the paper, settle down, and would that be so bad?

Yes, yes, it would, Laurel does not say. She just changes the subject, asks after her grandmother, or acts interested in one of Glynnis's pet projects, which is usually enough to distract her mother for a while.

When Glynnis sees Laurel, she lays her cards on the table and reaches for today's paper, folded beside her. She holds it up, pointing at the headline of the article Laurel wrote about the town's reaction to Cordell Lewis's release, specifically on the division between those who think he deserves to be released and those who think he deserves worse than he got. Laurel had had to basically threaten to quit if Damon didn't let her run with the idea. Ludlow doesn't like calling attention to its conflicts and scandals. She'd done man-on-the-street interviews and enjoyed it, collecting quotes and drawing conclusions. At first she'd used her voice recorder, but when the third person called her "fancy" or "highfalutin," she'd stowed it in her purse and resorted to pen and paper, frantically scribbling down the words of her fellow citizens.

"I say the needle would be too kind for the likes of him," one man said to her. He'd been standing outside Hops Haven when she randomly asked his opinion. He'd looked kind and gentle, but his response had been far from it. When she'd asked for his name, she'd expected him to say he preferred to remain anonymous, but he'd proudly given it to her, even spelled it to make sure she got it right.

Damon had grudgingly agreed to run the article this morning, then hit her with the wedding story assignment. Laurel felt certain it was his way of putting her back in her place, a reminder of what she was hired to do, a subtle hint that she wasn't so great after all. She can't help but think that Damon secretly likes this, getting a front-row seat for her downfall. She used to tell anyone who would listen that she was going to travel the world someday, that she was going to interview famous people. She'd been so vocal, so obnoxious about it. Why hadn't someone told her to just shut up already? Why hadn't someone warned her that life had a way of tearing down your dreams, so you better keep them to yourself lest you have to eat a very public serving of crow at twenty-six years old?

There was no way to take it all back now. She just hoped that, with time, people would forget about her stupid dreams. She had. If Glynnis hadn't signed her up for this job, she'd be spending her afternoons at the country club pool, reading and coming up with a whole new dream. A dream for grown-up Laurel—forget that kid with her head full of nonsense. Maybe she would do what her mother wanted and find some rich guy, marry him, have some kids, and take up bridge. Did people even play bridge anymore? Tennis might be better. She'd seen some women in white skirts chasing the little yellow ball at the club just the other day. Never mind that she'd never been particularly athletic. She always thought she'd interview the athletes, not be one.

Glynnis gives her a thumbs-up and grins, nodding in the direction of the newspaper. "Way to go, honey!" she says, her eyes wide and bright. Laurel knows that Glynnis couldn't care less about the news, unless it's a particularly juicy piece of gossip about one of the women she calls her friends. She is only pretending to care for Laurel's sake. Appreciating her effort, Laurel pats her mother's shoulder and kisses the top of her head.

"Thanks, Mom," she says, then yawns loudly for effect. "I'm wiped out. Just gonna head straight to bed."

She leaves the room before Glynnis can say more. Though she appreciates her mother's attempt at support, the last thing she wants right now is to discuss the newspaper with her. Her mother had thought she was doing the right thing in getting the job for Laurel, who hadn't the heart to tell her she'd learned something valuable in her time out in the big, wide world: she isn't cut out for journalism. She isn't any good. You can have a dream all you want, but if you don't have the talent to go with it, the dream isn't going to get you very far.

"You weren't fired," Glynnis had always corrected her. "You were let go."

"It's semantics, Mom," she'd argued. As she spoke, she'd felt the pain in her throat that came with keeping her tears bottled up. "If they really thought I was worth keeping, they'd have kept me."

Glynnis had acted like she hadn't heard her daughter, expounding on what a good opportunity this job with the *Ledger* was. "It's in your *field*, honey," she'd said, clearly proud of herself. She'd sprung this news on Laurel the day she got home, the tone of her voice telling Laurel all she needed to know about the stipulations of this new living arrangement. She would be allowed to move back home at age twenty-six, but she'd earn her keep by working for the Collins family, which included their son. As her boss. She didn't find out that part till the day she started, and by then she was already there, wearing a dress her mother bought her for her first day and holding a lunch her mother had packed her. It was the first day of kindergarten 2.0. Damon had lost no time in teasing her about that, quickly proving he was still just as annoying as he'd been as a little kid.

"Lemme see," he'd teased, making a grab for the bag as she deftly moved it out of reach. Good thing her reflexes where Damon was concerned were still on point. Undaunted, he'd kept trying. "What'd she pack for you? I bet she cut the crusts off. Come *onnnn*. Just lemme see if she cut the crusts off."

Then he pretended to pout that Glynnis hadn't made him a lunch, too. Laurel had fought the urge to run screaming from the building, from the town, from the entire state of South Carolina.

When she was a little girl, she thought that people lived where they decided to live and did the job they decided to do. She'd thought the hardest part was deciding, and she couldn't figure out for the life of her why some people made the decisions they did. She'd told everyone that she'd decided not to live in Ludlow when she grew up. She'd decided to see the world. As if that settled it.

She walks through the den, edging past her father, who looks momentarily displeased when she crosses in front of his view of the TV. She mumbles a "Hey, Daddy" and hears his grunt in return as she climbs the stairs, her feet carrying her away from her parents' mundane existence and into the sanctuary of her bedroom. She slips inside, reaches for the light switch, and closes the door behind her. Golden light from an out-of-date fixture illuminates her walls, covered in her collection of newspaper clippings, the pulpy paper gone yellow and thin over the years. She has the headlines from 9/11, Sandy Hook, Obama's election, the killing of Osama bin Laden, Prince's and Michael Jackson's deaths. There are the smaller stories, too, the ones that mattered only to people in this town, to her: the year her high school football team won the state championship, the headline about a classmate killed in a car accident one rainy night.

She'd discovered a passion for news when she was eight years old, in the third grade. A boy in her class got cancer and needed a bone marrow transplant. The class decided to all get tested to see if any of them was a match. The story became news, covered first in the town paper and then spreading to larger outlets, until it became a nationwide story. Before they knew it, Mrs. Wiley's third grade class became the national poster children for the need for bone marrow donors. They were in papers clear up to New Jersey and as far west as Santa Fe. TV stations came to interview them, showing footage of them healthy, playing and running on the playground, juxtaposed with film of the sick boy limping down a hospital hallway, clutching an IV pole, his skinny body clearly ravaged by the cancer.

But all that coverage was not what forever changed Laurel. That came later, when a woman in Manteo, North Carolina, read the story, was inspired to get typed, and became the match for her classmate. Danny, who came back to school the following year, is still alive. Laurel ran into him not so long ago in the Walgreens. He's getting married, he told her. He's got a job as an electrician.

Her phone buzzes in her pocket, and she fishes it out, confused. No one calls her this late. She doesn't really have any friends here in Ludlow—hasn't made the effort, to be honest. It's as if making friends will mean her return is permanent. She prefers to perpetuate the illusion that this time at home is just a pit stop. Yeah, right. Just like the amputation in the Monty Python movie was just a flesh wound.

She grimaces when she sees Damon's number on the screen. It's awfully late to be calling her and definitely not professional. She will scold him if this is for something stupid. Maybe he's drunk and has dialed her by mistake. He's probably trying to hook up with someone, looking for a booty call, and hit Laurel's name instead of some chick named Laura or Lauren. Though she thinks he looks like exactly what he is—an overgrown frat boy—he definitely has his share of interested girls, based on his Instagram feed. Not that Laurel cares. The only reason she's even seen his Insta feed is because of the social media work she's been doing for the paper, trying to bring them into the twenty-first century and not stuck in the eighties forever. She had to tag him in a post one time, and she had the paper follow him, just for good measure.

"Hello?" She answers the call just before it rolls over to voice mail.

"Laurel?" Damon asks, surprising her with the admission that he knows who he has called.

"Yes?" she asks, intrigued now. She braces herself for exactly why he has called.

"Sorry for calling so late," he says, sounding like a grown-up. "But I wanted to tell you about a rumor I heard. Thought you might want to look into it."

"Okay . . . ," she says. The word *rumor* piques her interest. If he tells her the rumor is that the library is moving the book sale to another date, she will throw her phone across the room.

"Word on the street is that you aren't the only person who can't get ahold of Annie Taft. No one can."

She thinks about this, about how Faye spoke to her today, how frazzled and prickly she acted. Maybe it wasn't because she didn't like a reporter asking questions about the wedding. Maybe it was because Faye was worried about her niece because she couldn't find her.

"I think you should poke around tomorrow, see if you can find out anything. If Annie Taft is really and truly missing, we have the makings of quite a story."

"Maybe she's just a runaway bride," Laurel says, trying for a rational explanation. She's heard this happens. Hell, they even made a movie about it. She pictures Julia Roberts riding that horse in a wedding dress, but in her mind it's Annie on the horse, Annie making her getaway. But what would make Annie want to run? By all accounts, she's marrying a great guy and having a beautiful wedding. But if there's anything Laurel knows, it's that nothing is ever as it seems.

There is a pause as Damon thinks this over. "Maybe so, but maybe that's a story in itself."

Laurel tries to think if it would be appropriate to write about Annie being a runaway bride. It's not exactly the stuff of front page news, unless it had something to do with Lewis's release—then it would be: *Bride Cancels Wedding in Wake of Suspected Murderer's Release.*

"Yeah, maybe," she says. "Either way, I'll look into it first thing in the morning."

"Good deal," Damon says. "Sorry for calling so late. I just couldn't stop thinking about it, and I thought you'd want to know. You know, so you can think up a game plan then hit the ground running in the morning," he says. He laughs, but it is not the laugh of a sneaky, mischievous boy. It is the laugh of a peer, one she spends more time with than anyone else, if she's honest. "I know how you are," he says.

"Yeah," she says, "I guess you do." And the realization hits her that this is actually true. Suddenly she feels vulnerable, self-conscious, like he is in the room with her and can see the newspaper clippings on her walls, the mascara smeared under her eyes.

"Thanks for letting me know," she says, anxious to be off the phone, to end this call that feels different than their usual conversations. She wants to go back to the way things were this afternoon in the office when she was yelling at him about Annie's fiancé. Come to think of it, Annie's fiancé hadn't replied to her email. Wait a minute.

"How'd you come by this information?" she asks Damon. "Who told you no one can find Annie?"

"I might've taken your advice and capitalized on a little brotherly love," he says, and chuckles. And though he definitely still has a streak of mischievous boy in him, she's happy that this time he's used it for good.

"At least he talked to you. He never replied to me," she says glumly.

"Because I told him he didn't have to. He's pretty upset, so I said I'd pass along what was happening. So now you are, officially, informed. And he said he'd keep us informed, too."

"Us?" she asks.

"I figured we'd work on this one together, since I'm kind of involved now."

Great, she thinks. "Oh," she says.

"Don't sound so thrilled," he says.

"No, it's fine, I'm just, um, used to working alone."

"It'll be fun," he says. "You'll see. So, I'll see you tomorrow, partner?"

"Yes," she says, willing her voice to express more excitement than she feels, unable to keep her teeth from clenching at his use of the word *partner*. What has she gotten herself into?

Clary

She wakes to the low murmur of voices coming from the den and realizes she has fallen asleep waiting on her mother to return from driving around, looking for Annie. "I can't just sit here anymore," Faye had announced as she picked up her keys and left.

It was too late and too dark to do much good, but she didn't give Clary time to point that out. Besides, she understood. When Mica had first gone missing, she'd searched in the dark, hoping his white and silver feathers would shine brightly against the black night. But of course that hadn't happened.

A half hour after her mother left, Clary had checked on the doves, then stretched out across her bed to wait for Faye to return. She'd fallen asleep. Now, groggy and disoriented, Clary sits up and looks around her dark bedroom, grabs her phone to check the time, hoping that there will be a missed call or text from Annie, that this will all be over. But it is 11:13 p.m., there's nothing from Annie, and there are strange voices out in the den. She knows that it's not over.

A foreboding feeling nags at her: this will not be like the other times her cousin has pulled her disappearing act, that Annie will not come strolling in the front door, drop her keys, kick off her shoes, and announce, "Hey, I'm here!" the phrase in itself an admission: *you can stop looking for me because I'm here now.* Clary fears that, like Mica, this time Annie isn't coming back.

She does her best to push the negative thought from her mind, slips from her bed, and pads into the den, straining to discern the voices. One is male; two are female. She peers around the corner to check if her hunch is right. It is: Scott is there, along with her mom and Tracy Douglas, Annie's best friend. Clary knows she must look like a hot mess but doesn't care if these three see, so she walks into the room.

"Oh, Clary," her mother says when she sees her. She starts to rise, but Clary waves at her to sit back down. She can see exhaustion in her mother's eyes. The poor woman has to be beyond tired. She goes over to where Faye is sitting and plops down beside her, rests her head on her shoulder as she feels her mom's arm slip around her. Faye's affections are rare and fleeting; Clary has learned to soak them in when she can get them. She is still like a child in that way, always straining for her mother's touch. But Faye is tough and reserved; she was never a touchy-feely mom. Faye is just the way she is. Clary accepts that, but sometimes she wishes it were different.

"Why didn't you guys wake me up when you got in?" she asks, hearing the note of accusation in her voice. In not being a part of this conversation, she is already behind, already on the outside. She eyes Tracy, feeling the old jealousy she once felt—the unspoken rivalry between them for Annie's attention—crop up unexpectedly. She thought they'd all outgrown that.

Faye presses her mouth to Clary's temple in what passes for a kiss, then rises. "There's nothing to tell. We're just guessing at this point," she says as she crosses the den toward the kitchen. "I'm making coffee; who wants some?"

Scott and Tracy both raise their hands, even though Faye's back is turned and she can't see them respond to her question. Clary sees them eye each other and smile at their mutual gaffe. In unison, they both say, "Me," and then smile at each other again. Clary refrains from rolling her eyes at the two of them and their chumminess. She rises and follows her mother into the kitchen to help make coffee, though Faye doesn't need help to do this most basic of tasks.

"If I didn't know better, I'd say Tracy has herself a schoolgirl crush," Clary remarks.

Faye pauses long enough to shrug. "Doesn't surprise me. Tracy's always wanted what Annie had."

"Yeah, I guess you're right. Still, though . . ." She stands awkwardly, moving out of the way when her mother shoos her. Their galley kitchen isn't large. Faye has always complained about it. "Anything more from Hal?" she asks, just to fill the silence as Faye measures grounds into the machine.

Faye stops what she's doing and asks, "You?" She raises the scoop to indicate what she means.

Clary does not want coffee this late at night. She wants to go back to sleep. But she suspects that's not going to happen. Not with Tracy and Scott here and her cousin missing. It would be rude and insensitive to go back to bed. She shrugs. "Sure."

Faye looks at her. "Hal is investigating," she says, her words succinct, telling Clary all she needs to know. Nothing has changed; it's a waiting game.

"Why's Scott here?" she asks, because, though she has nothing against Scott, she feels inexplicably angry with him, as if he should've prevented this somehow.

"He wanted some company." Faye shrugs. "You can't blame him, really." She points across the room at the refrigerator. "You should get out the cream, in case someone takes it."

Obediently, Clary crosses to the fridge and tugs it open, the sucking sound of the seal echoing loudly in the kitchen. She stares into the refrigerator and sees the almond milk there—Annie's almond milk. It's only ever her who drinks it, and most of the time they throw out the full carton when one of them thinks to check the expiration date and finds it long past. Clary blinks back tears and closes the fridge, forgetting what she opened it for.

She thinks of Annie's request. They had been standing in this same kitchen the first time Annie brought it up. Faye had left them to do the dishes. "Don't ask me to do that," she'd said to her cousin. "It's not fair." She wonders if Annie is staying away to force her hand. If it were that simple, would she just go ahead and tell Travis? If it meant Annie would come back? It would be just like Annie to orchestrate it so that Clary would do the one thing in the world she didn't want to do.

But, despite her flair for the dramatic, even Annie wouldn't push it this far.

"Clary?" Faye reminds her. "The cream?" Behind her, she hears Faye turn on the tap and fill the coffeepot all the way. These are, Clary thinks, the sounds of crisis.

She opens the refrigerator a second time, pulls out the half-and-half, and places it beside the sugar bowl. In response, the coffee machine makes a hiss and burble noise as it begins to force water through the grounds. She smells the coffee as it hits the pot, wishes it were morning and she was smelling coffee where coffee belongs. Beside her, Faye clatters around in the cabinets, pulls out far too many mugs.

"Expecting a crowd?" Clary quips. She reaches for the extra mugs, to put them away, to keep busy. She leaves just the four out.

Faye comes behind her, takes two mugs back out, and sets them down emphatically. "I know what I'm doing," she says.

Clary narrows her eyes at the extra mugs, feels her heart pick up speed, as if it already knows the answer to the question she has not yet posed. "Who else is coming over here, Mother?" she asks. She hears the catch in her own voice.

In answer to her question, she hears a knock at the front door, hears Tracy hop up to answer it as if she lives there. "You invited *him* over here?" Clary turns to her mother. "When did you have time?"

Faye looks away from her, sweeps invisible crumbs from the counter, and nods. "He called earlier because he couldn't get Annie on the phone, either. I told him what was going on, and he offered to come over."

She hears his voice in the next room, as familiar as if they'd just spoken yesterday. But she hasn't spoken to Travis Dove for years. Another voice, a feminine one, echoes his. Clary lowers her voice to something more like a hiss. "His wife, too?"

Faye snaps her head up. "Well, of course. What's he supposed to do—leave her behind?" Faye's voice is a whisper but with an edge, that mother voice that can still remind Clary which of them is the parent and which is the child.

She looks down at herself. She is wearing sweats and an old T-shirt that she probably owned back when they dated. Her only consolation is that she is at least wearing a bra. She hears Travis Dove laugh, and it is sandpaper on her frayed nerves. What could he be laughing about at a time like this? She wants to glance at her reflection in the microwave, but her mother will see her do it and know exactly what's going through her mind. As if what Travis Dove does or doesn't think of her makes any difference at all now. Still, she runs a hand through her hair, sweeps fingers under both eyes to wipe away the mascara, undoubtedly smeared from sleeping.

She could die right then and there. She could die, and Travis Dove would have no more chances to save her soul. She thinks about their last conversation, the things he said that rendered her speechless in a time she'd intended to say some things of her own. She'd been silent ever since. She hears Annie's words in her mind: *You need to tell him what happened.* But Annie isn't here to push her on this and, for a guilty moment, Clary is glad. Everything that happened between Travis and her—what ruined them—is Annie's fault anyway.

Annie was the one, after all, who invited him to that church camp in the first place. It had taken her a long time to forgive Annie and her do-gooding ways for effectively ruining their relationship by inviting God into it. To be fair, Clary was supposed to go, too, but she got sick and, for reasons she will never understand except that it was destiny, Travis still went. "You'll just be home in bed all weekend, and the church already gave me the camp scholarship, so . . . I think I will."

Travis's parents had been fighting a lot at that point, and she knew he was looking for a place to escape. So she forgave him for leaving her. But she never expected him to come home an entirely different person. He even looked different when he got back: softer, with the reckless, restless energy that used to emanate from him magically, mysteriously gone.

He told her all about the peace he had found and how she could have it, too. But he didn't understand that she didn't want peace. She wanted disruption; she wanted uncertainty. She liked it; she craved it. At least, back then she did. She wonders, as she has a thousand times since, how her life might've been different if she hadn't gotten sick that fateful weekend.

"Might as well get it over with," Faye says quietly but loudly enough for Clary to hear. She gives her the slightest push, but it's enough to propel her forward.

She wishes Annie were here. But if Annie were here, Travis certainly wouldn't be—not in the middle of the night. He would be home in bed with his lovely wife. As things should be, as she was prepared for them to be. As bad as she'd feared seeing him would be, this is worse. *Where are you, Annie?* she thinks. *Why are you letting this happen?*

The Doves' heads turn in unison when Faye and Clary enter the room; Travis and his wife both fix their eyes on Faye, as if Clary is not there at all. "Faye," Travis says, and takes a step toward them before he registers Clary's presence, too. He blinks just once, then pivots back to Faye, reaching to cover his hands with hers. His eyes are filled with concern, and Clary, knowing him better than anyone, sees that the concern is genuine.

His wife closes the gap between him and her, tucks her hand into the crook of his elbow proprietarily. Clary can't blame her; she has to have heard the stories about the two of them, of their epic rebel romance, their passionate first love. Of course she would feel compelled to draw the boundary lines in clear sight of her rival. With one movement, Travis's wife is saying loud and clear, *He's mine now.*

Travis's wife probably expects that Clary is still pining for him. Clary herself had wondered if perhaps seeing him would stir up old feelings. She expected to feel some emotion when it happened, some sense of loss or regret or pain. Perhaps it's because she is distracted by Annie's disappearance, or perhaps it is because enough time has passed that whatever she once felt has had time to wither away. Or maybe it is because the Travis standing before her now isn't even remotely the boy she knew then.

But looking at him standing in her living room, Clary knows this: she does not want Travis. She just wants to get through this weekend as unscathed as possible, preferably without spilling the secret she's protected for the last eight years. She wonders, if Annie were here right now, would she bring it up in front of everyone? Would she announce it herself? Or would she see that they are all okay and that well enough really is better left alone?

"I'm so sorry about Annie," Travis's wife says, her voice high and sweet. She is too sweet for Travis, too good. Clary can see that from here, in two seconds. "We've been praying nonstop since we heard."

"Yes," Travis agrees, remembering his role. Somehow, as absurd as it is, Travis Dove is there to be their spiritual leader. She wants to laugh but is stopped by his next words: "In fact, let's all pray together." His eyes are wide and expectant as he raises his hands, presumably for someone to grab.

Faye looks startled by this demand. She glances at Clary so fast it's likely no one else sees it. Faye knows this is a bad idea. Clary praying at all is a long shot, but Clary praying with Travis leading the prayer is way worse.

"Well," Faye says, "I just made coffee, so what say we have that first?" Clary is so grateful to her mother she vows then and there to do the dishes for a week. Without griping.

Everyone murmurs their approval of this idea, and suddenly they are up, moving toward the kitchen to pour coffee. Travis claps his arm around Scott, begins to say pastorly words, words of comfort and hope, Clary supposes. She cannot hear; she has edged toward the perimeter of the room, in hopes of making a clean getaway. She will slip outside, hide with the doves until Travis is gone. She read that doves are so pure, they're the one form Satan can't change himself into. When she thinks about it that way, she is safer out there with them.

She waits until the others are all in the kitchen before she begins backstepping out of the room. She hears the low murmur of voices, the sounds of silver hitting china, thinks of that lone mug that will be left on the counter once they've all served themselves. Oh well, she didn't want coffee anyway. She didn't want any of this.

MAY 30

Bridesmaids' Luncheon Day

Two Days until the Wedding

Faye

Faye wakes up entirely too early and, for a moment, reality doesn't register. For a moment, her mind is deliciously blank. But then the events of yesterday come to her in a rush—realizing Annie was missing, searching for her, pouring coffee for guests in the wee hours of the morning. She'd thought the coffee would leave her unable to sleep, but exhaustion set in and, for a few hours at least, she succumbed to it. She sits up and grabs for her phone, hoping for news, ideally from Annie herself. But there are no texts or missed calls. Nothing has changed while she slept. When Annie comes back, Faye is going to let her have it. For once, she's going to tell her exactly how she feels. This time, Annie has gone too far, stayed gone too long. She doesn't care what compelled her to leave; she has no right to make them all worry.

In typical Annie fashion, she will have no real idea of the trouble she has caused. And, once she speaks her mind, Faye will forgive her for this like she did when Annie forked Pastor Melton's lawn on a dare (which Faye suspects is the real reason Annie asked Travis to perform her wedding ceremony, not Travis's celebrity pastor status like Clary says—Annie couldn't care less about such things) or when Annie started a rumor that Faye had lied about going to cosmetology school and was really self-taught. It took her weeks to convince her customers that the license hanging on the wall was real and not created on a home computer, as Annie had claimed.

Annie had tried to look penitent as Faye railed about what the rumor had done to her business, but the entire time, she'd been biting back a smile. Sometimes that girl reminds her of Lydia so much it's eerie. If she closes her eyes, Faye can still picture a young Lydia, kicking her feet as she sat outside the principal's office of their middle school. She'd been part of a group of kids who set off stink bombs in unison in every hall of the school, filling the building with such an overpowering stench that some kids had gotten nauseous and had to go home early. Lydia had taken the punishment without ever giving up who the other kids involved were.

Faye smiles at the memory. Faye had been one of the other kids who had been part of the prank. She'd enjoyed punishment-free days while Lydia did work duty at the school, the church, and, when she was done with that, at home. Once when Faye had tried to help her, Lydia had said, "No, they'll figure it out," and shooed her away, her eyes insistent as she pled with Faye to go about her business and leave her to the task. "You'll make it up to me later," she had said.

"I'd say I've more than made up for it," Faye says now to no one.

She heads out to the kitchen to start another pot of coffee and finds Tracy and Scott both asleep on the couches in her den. She stops walking and shakes her head as she remembers, delirious from exhaustion and worry, telling Tracy and Scott they could just stay there if they wanted to wait for news of Annie. She retrieved extra blankets and pillows, assured them it was no trouble at all. What was she thinking? Now she will have to go to the grocery store.

With a sigh, she goes to dress and brush her hair. She doesn't bother with makeup. She doesn't leave a note for Clary or her guests. She'll likely be back before anyone wakes. They are nearly out of cream after the late-night coffee, and there is barely any food in the house to boot. With her house being the de facto gathering spot for the wedding-party-turned-search-party, she feels the pressure of playing hostess. If she goes to the store early enough, she can dash in and out without running into anyone she knows. At least, so she hopes.

But that hope is dashed within the first five minutes of entering the Food Lion. She spots Millicent Craft at the very same time Millicent spots her, which means it is too late to duck into the next aisle to hide. Millicent is her customer and is supposed to be a guest at Annie's wedding in two days. Which means that, if this town's gossip mill is in full working order, she's already heard that Annie is missing.

Millicent's expression tells her that the gossip mill is not only working, it just might be in overdrive. She envelops Faye in a hug, smashing her against her bountiful breasts and rocking her back and forth for a moment. "Has there been any word at all?" she asks.

Faye closes her eyes, slowly shaking her head.

Millicent begins shaking her head in time with Faye's, her mouth in a grim line. "We are just praying and praying," Millicent says.

"Well, we're mighty grateful for the prayers," Faye says. Faye likes Millicent well enough; she just doesn't want to talk to anyone about Annie.

"How are you holding up?" Millicent asks as she studies Faye's makeup-less face. "You look exhausted."

This, Faye knows, is the nice southern way of saying that someone looks awful. Faye starts to give the obligatory, reassuring response that she is holding up fine, but Millicent doesn't wait for an answer. "I don't know why in the world you're here today. You know anyone would've been glad to come get whatever you need."

An idea dawns on Millicent just then; Faye sees it happen, watches her eyes grow bigger and brighter as the thought strikes her. "I'm going to go home right now and start a meal sign-up. I know how to do it on the computer." She holds her finger up in the air for no apparent reason, her eyes darting from side to side. "I'll let the ladies' circle know and the girls in my garden club, just for starters." She reaches for the buggy that Faye had plucked out of the line of buggies at the front of the store. "You just put this away now," she orders.

But Faye grips the buggy tighter before she can wrest it away from her. "I actually need a few things right away," she says. Then adds, "But of course we'd appreciate the meals." She forces herself to smile, tells herself this is a kind thing Millicent is doing, even if Faye prefers to take care of herself, to be the one doing instead of the one being done for. "One less thing to worry about, right?" she says brightly.

Millicent reaches for her and smashes her into another, briefer hug. "That's right," she says. "You've got enough to worry about." She shakes her head again, the sad look returning to her face, the momentary thrill of do-gooding gone. "I just can't believe Annie has gone missing."

Faye has already grown to hate that word, *missing*, the snakelike quality of it, the way people's tongues get stuck on the *S*'s. It makes her unfairly angry at Millicent for saying it just like that, a hiss instead of a word. Something in Faye rises up in retort. "Well, don't you worry," she says, feigning a sweetness she doesn't feel. "We're gonna find our girl."

Millicent looks shocked, and Faye can tell that she has already decided this isn't going to end well. She is already anticipating tragedy, tasting it on her tongue like the ham that comes with funerals. As Millicent struggles for something positive to say in response, Faye uses the pause to push her buggy forward, away from Millicent and her meals and prayers. She doesn't want them. She wants to be putting on a bridesmaids' luncheon in a few hours. She wants to give her niece a lovely wedding, one Lydia would've wanted her daughter to have. For a moment, she hates her sister for not being here for this, hates that she can't just be Annie's concerned aunt who lives in another town.

A child's cry distracts her from her thoughts, and she looks up to see a boy being grabbed roughly by a bedraggled woman who could only be his mother. Faye recognizes the look on the woman's face, can guess what they're doing here this early. No milk for cereal. No bread for toast. But that is not what the woman is yelling at the boy about.

"I told you not to bring that shit in here!"

As she shakes her son, he loses his grip on a sketchbook and pencil he is carrying. The sketchbook falls open on the floor to reveal drawings of birds. One of the pages tears away from the spiral coil, and the pencil rolls in Faye's direction, stopping at her feet. She picks it up and impulsively starts to return it. The boy's dark eyes meet hers. He shakes his head, a barely perceptible *no*.

Behind the woman, two other smaller boys clutch each other, looking both concerned and relieved. They are glad it is not them their mother is angry at this time. Faye remembers the exhaustion and stress of motherhood that could lead to a complete and total loss of perspective. She wants to tell the woman to let it go, that whatever has angered her in this moment won't last, that someday she will think back on moments like these and feel such intense sorrow and regret. It's not worth it, Faye wants to say to her. But this woman's issues are none of her business. She has issues of her own. She puts the pencil down on the ground for the boy to collect himself and heads to the dairy case. She needs to buy coffee creamer for all the company who will be coming. She should get the largest size they have.

Kenny

They sleep in in the morning, spooned together just the way he likes. He wakes before her and pulls her closer, feeling her remold her body to his. He sniffs her, inhaling her scent, thinking how much he likes it on his sheets. This, he tells himself—like he always does—is good enough. This is happiness. His cell phone rings—his mother, he can tell from the ringtone—but he does not move to answer it, lest he wake his sleeping beauty. She likes it when he calls her that, likes it when they fall asleep in each other's arms.

Lying there watching her sleep, he decides that he is going to ask her to marry him as soon as possible. Perhaps even while they are on their trip to Charleston. They could find a little jewelry store somewhere, pop in, and pick out a ring. It will be spur-of-the-moment, romantic. He will propose right there in that park by the water, the one with the beautiful fountain. He will make a speech about the future and how he can't see himself spending it with anyone else but her.

But of course that is not true.

Because when he thinks about standing beside a body of water with a woman, he thinks of Annie and how they used to drive to Falls Park, their own park by the water, pretending that they were getting out of Ludlow when they actually weren't going far enough to qualify. They would take a picnic and eat on a blanket, then lie on their backs by the river, full and warm, and talk for hours. He told Annie everything; he's never talked to anyone the way he talked to her. And she told him things, too, things she never told anyone else. He saw the real Annie, the flawed one, the struggling one. With him, she didn't have to be perfect or pleasing. She didn't have to act grateful for Faye's care or pretend she and Clary were close just to make everyone think she was appropriately thankful. With him, she could say anything. And she did. She wished aloud for her mother, imagined what her life would've been like if she'd lived. With him, she stopped giving the right answers and gave the honest ones.

Together, they dreamed of escaping Ludlow forever, moving somewhere new where no one knew them, where they could be anything—or anyone—at all. On Tuesday night they'd gone for one last walk—that's how she'd put it—and he'd thrown caution to the wind. He'd pled with her to leave with him, to finally be brave enough to try being the people they'd dreamed of being, to take a leap of faith with him into another life, to leave it all behind.

She'd stopped walking and looked at him like he was speaking another language. In that horrible silent moment, he'd wanted to take back everything he'd just said. But it was out there now: his daring, irretrievable request.

He'd waited as she blinked at him, searching for the right words. Knowing Annie, she'd been searching for the kindest ones, the way to let him down easy. "I can't do that," she'd said finally. "Kenny. You know that."

Her words had been gentle, softly spoken. But they weren't gentle or soft. In four words, she had felled him. He'd risked it all by asking, and she'd stood by and watched him topple. Even now, it made him both angry and sad at the same time, rage and heartbreak all tied up together in a tangled knot.

Sometimes he wonders if the Annie he knows is just one more facet of her, a side she showed him and no one else but only a side, not the total picture. Sometimes he feels like Annie has always been whoever she thought people needed her to be, morphing into a different iteration of herself depending on who she was standing in front of, sloughing off one identity for the next with a callous ease that, looking back, should've frightened him. As much as he'd wanted to believe he knew the real Annie, he isn't sure there is one. In the end, she'd made him feel like everyone else.

In a flash, he was that boy again—the outsider, the newcomer. He was small and fearful back then, an easy target. People in Ludlow didn't trust people who hadn't been there all their lives. They looked at him as trouble simply because he'd been born in a different zip code and was being raised by a single mom. So the parents looked the other way as their kids tormented him. And they blamed him first whenever anything went wrong. As a child, Annie had been the one to rescue him from bullies. Now she was the bully. He could forgive everyone else because that was all he'd come to expect from them. But Annie? Annie had been a different story. Annie's betrayal had stung in a way that no other had.

His phone rings again, and his mother's face appears on the screen again, a photo his girlfriend snapped of him and his mother having lunch after church one day. In the photo, his mother is grinning ear to ear, but Kenny is barely smiling.

With the phone in his hand, he slips out of bed and heads into the kitchen. By the time he gets there, the phone has stopped ringing, so he fills the kettle with water and puts it on the burner for tea. He doesn't drink coffee like most people do. He prefers tea. His girlfriend does, too, or she does now. At first, she used to complain that he didn't have any coffee, but eventually she came around to his way of thinking. Now they sit at the kitchen table in the mornings and sip tea, like people in England do.

He and Annie used to talk about living in England. Back then, he'd believed with his whole heart that they would someday. He'd been certain she would come around to his way of thinking about the two of them just like his girlfriend had come around to tea instead of coffee. Annie would come to understand that they were meant to be. They would live in London, have children who called her "Mummy" and played in the garden instead of the yard.

He calls his mother back and listens as she launches into the latest town gossip while he waits for the water to boil. Did he hear that Annie Taft is missing? Didn't he know her from school? Everyone thinks she's up and run off with someone else.

It is all he can do to finish the conversation without saying something to give himself away, to make his mom suspicious. As far as she knows, Annie is an old classmate and nothing more. Her run of morning gossip should be nothing more than idle chitchat and not life-altering news. Annie is missing. People are worried. Rumors are flying. It won't take long, he knows, for people to figure out that he is at the heart of Annie's disappearance. It won't take long for the talk to turn to him. Fingers will point at him, and Annie won't be there to intervene this time.

He thinks of his daring request on his last walk with Annie, how people might not understand their friendship if they found out about it, especially now that she's gone missing. He should come forward, he thinks. He should offer his help, tell what he knows. But that could turn out badly for him. And Annie was going to leave him anyway. Isn't that what the past few weeks have been about? One long, inevitable goodbye? What will making himself a target change about that? He was always going to lose her one way or another. Annie's disappearance is sad, but it was always going to be sad. As he listens to his mother drone on and on, he decides to keep quiet, to speak only if spoken to.

His mother outlines her personal theories about Annie's disappearance, as well as the theories of some of her cronies, as he remembers what happened after Annie turned him down. A residual fear creeps back into his throat, making it hard to swallow. He listens until the kettle begins to whistle, until the shrill sound drowns out his mother's words and, in the next room, wakes his sleeping girlfriend from her dreams.

Clary

It was Faye who decided that the two of them would go to the country club in person to explain that there would be no bridesmaids' luncheon. Clary knows that Faye is hoping they will make allowances for this last-minute cancelation, cluck their tongues and say, *Well, of course you won't be charged a penny at a time like this.* Clary doesn't think this will be the case, but she goes along with Faye because it is easier than trying to talk sense into her. Faye isn't in the mood to listen to sense.

She walks in just behind Faye, spying as she does two employees dismantling the table configurations for the bridesmaids' luncheon as if they already know that it is not to be. Faye and Clary pause to watch as the two women tug on either end of a long table, breaking it in two. On the table closest to the door there are, as promised, the two boxes of decorations intended for this occasion. Faye had made her deliver them to Hunt Run Country Club last week on her way to drive Miss Minnie. She'd driven there with her teeth gritted, internally cussing both Faye and Annie. Either one of them should've been running the errand, but they were too busy. Get Clary! She'll do it!

Clary can see, peeking out of the top of the boxes, the mason jars that were supposed to be filled with wildflowers, in keeping with the farmer's market theme that Annie came up with. They were all supposed to wear floral sundresses, and the food was going to be locally sourced and fresh. Annie's eyes had shone as she talked about it.

Clary thought it was all a little silly, but she could see what Annie was going for. It would've been lovely, of course. And all the other bridesmaids would think it was adorable. Because it was. Just like everything Annie did. If cuteness were a trait that could be inherited, Annie got their family's allotment.

Clary recalls accompanying Annie and Faye to the appointment with the wedding photographer.

"What *tone* do you want for your photos?" the photographer, earnest and intent, had asked.

Tone? Faye had mouthed at Clary, and made a face.

Making sure Annie and the photographer weren't looking, Clary had rolled her eyes in response and Faye had smiled. In that moment, they'd been mother and daughter, of a pair, as it should be. Annie wasn't part of them; she was different.

Which was why she wasn't confused at all by the photographer's question. "Oh, I know some people go for romantic or moody or whatever. But I'm none of those things." She'd thought about it for a second and shrugged. "I'm cute," she'd said, and wrinkled her button nose as if to prove it. "I've heard it all my life. So I say let's go with that."

"Yes," Clary had said, sounding serious when really she was getting a dig in. "Let's definitely play up your cute factor."

The next time no one was looking, Annie had flipped her the bird, then gave a grin that lit up her face and was—it had to be said—adorable. They'd both cracked up laughing because what else could you do except love each other anyway, somehow?

Clary feels tears prick her eyes, scans the room as if she expects Annie to magically appear, to wink at her and say, *Gotcha! You didn't think I was actually missing, did you?*

I wish this was nothing more than an elaborate—and sadistic—practical joke, Clary thinks. *I'd want to kill her for it, but I'd be so happy to see her I wouldn't actually kill her.*

She goes to one of the boxes, reaches to pick it up and haul it away, but stops when she spies the bridesmaids' gifts inside, stemless champagne flutes etched with each girl's initial. And labels Annie had printed for the bottles of champagne she was supposed to be bringing today that say, I'LL ONLY BE A HAPPY BRIDE IF I HAVE MY GIRLS BY MY SIDE.

She supposes it would've been Faye and her in a corner this morning, slapping the damn labels on the bottles, another thankless task in a stream of thankless tasks in the name of "Annie's wedding." She thinks of Tracy and Faye and herself. Not to mention the other girls in the wedding party, high school and college and work friends of Annie's. They are all ready to be by Annie's side just like those labels say. But Annie isn't there. Clary wants to pull her hair out, to scream loudly, anything to relieve the pressure building steadily inside her with each minute that passes without Annie.

Faye puts her hand on Clary's back, and the touch softens her some, helps her remember why they are there. Faye marches forward, asks to speak to someone in charge, and one of the girls takes one look at Faye and scurries out the rear door of the room, off to fetch her supervisor. This conversation is above her pay grade. When Clary tries to look the other girl in the eye, she drops her gaze to the floor, and Clary knows everyone has already heard that Annie is missing and there will be no bridesmaids' luncheon as planned.

After a quick conversation with the supervisor, Faye turns to Clary. "We should just take these things home and store them," she says. She is holding her eyes wide open as she says it, the way she does when she is forcing herself to be optimistic. Clary has seen those same eyes before, when the chocolate in their hidden Easter eggs had melted on an unseasonably hot Easter Sunday, striping their pastel dresses with unsightly brown stains. She's seen them when she left for Charlotte after graduation—but not to attend college. She's seen them when Pastor Melton rang the doorbell, holding a fistful of plastic forks and wondering if Annie knew anything about them. Clary knows that when her mother is wearing that expression, she'd be better off to go along with whatever she says. So she turns to the boxes with a barely repressed sigh.

"What are we going to do with this stuff?" she asks aloud, not expecting an answer.

Put it away for your wedding, she imagines Annie saying with a wink.

And then Clary would say, *As if I would ever do something this tacky. I mean, really, Annie, mason jars as centerpieces? You're so basic.*

Then Annie would cock her head, study Clary's hair, and ask something stupid like, *Do you even know what color your hair actually is anymore?*

Then Faye would shake her head, give a weary laugh, and say, *You girls.* And in their bickering, all would be right with the world, because this is how they are. This is who they are. Annie is supposed to be there, being a pain in Clary's ass. Without her, Clary doesn't know who she is. She has been Annie Taft's cousin, played that all-important role, for the better part of her life. And she is still playing it, harder than ever, but this time without Annie.

She reaches to pick up the box of mason jars instead of the box with those champagne labels. Beside her, Faye bristles, and she can feel it as if she is in Faye's skin and is bristling herself. She looks across the room, in the direction of the doorway where Faye is looking. A young woman who looks vaguely familiar has entered the room but stops short upon seeing them. The young woman is carrying a camera and, when she sees them, she pulls it into her chest, like a mother might pull a child about to be harmed.

Faye strides across the room, and Clary, curious, follows her. She has realized who the young woman is. Laurel Haines. Her boss's wayward daughter, returned home. Though Glynnis had mentioned her being back more than once, this is the first time Clary has seen her. She knew Laurel in high school, of course—everyone did; she was Laurel

Haines, after all—but she was definitely not friends with her. She and Laurel were not the same kind of people then, and Clary guesses they probably aren't now, either.

"You might as well put that away," Faye snaps at Laurel, and Clary knows this is not Faye's first time to see the girl since she returned. Clary knows that she is working for the *Ludlow Ledger*—a favor Tad Collins paid Glynnis on account of their families being friends for so long. This delighted Clary to no end to hear. She remembers Laurel's graduation speech about her dream of traveling the world as an investigative reporter. Guess that didn't work out so well. Clary thinks that, okay, maybe they do have that in common—life not ending up the way they thought it would in high school. She almost feels sorry for Laurel, walking directly into Faye's line of sight on a day like today. "This is no place for you today," Faye adds.

"With all due respect," Laurel responds, "Annie's wedding was news in this town. Now, with her disappearing, it's even bigger news." She swallows and grips the camera tighter, as if Faye might snatch it from her hand. "It's my job to report the story." Her voice wavers, and she looks over at the country club employees, who are openly watching the exchange.

"I think you should leave," Faye says. "Be respectful of what we have to do here."

"I'm just doing my job," she repeats, and her voice sounds the tiniest bit whiny.

"Like I give a rat's ass about your job," Faye says, and sniffs like she smells something bad. "All I care about right now is finding my niece. But first I have to—" Faye's voice breaks, and Clary puts her hand on her mother's shoulder to bolster her. *Don't fall apart now, here, Mama,* she thinks.

Faye looks at Clary, gathers the strength Clary is offering, and looks at the reporter. "First I have to collect the decorations for a bridesmaids' luncheon that isn't going to happen. You want something to report, report that."

Faye turns and walks back toward the boxes, leaving Clary to stare down the reporter long enough for her to lose her nerve and bolt from the room still gripping that camera. Clary stands and waits to feel good for winning, for besting Laurel Haines, a feat she would've relished in high school. But all she feels is bad, and all she wants to do is set things right, if only she knew how.

Laurel

Laurel pauses outside the small ballroom that was to have been the site of Annie's bridal luncheon. She debates going back in, standing her ground. She shouldn't have let Faye run her out like that. It's like Damon said, how is she ever going to be the kind of investigative reporter she wants to be if a small-town hairdresser can scare her off? But she doubts Damon has ever been stared down by Faye Wilkins.

She hears the ugly voice inside her head—the one that sounds like a really mean version of her mother: *This is why you couldn't cut it in Minneapolis. This is why you'll never cut it anywhere. You might as well let your mother find you a husband, join this country club, and learn to play tennis.* She looks back over her shoulder, watches through the small pane of glass as Faye and Clary heft boxes of champagne flutes and mason jars and exit the rear door. She would've liked to get a photo of that. A picture is worth a thousand words, after all.

"I'm sure you'll tell me you're just following the story of the missing bride," she hears a familiar voice say behind her left shoulder, "but it looks like you're just using that as an excuse to be nosy." He's got a lazy, confident drawl, the kind of voice that women respond to. And he knows it.

She turns to face Damon. "What are you doing here?" she asks, sounding caught. Which, she supposes, she is.

He grins, points down at his tacky shoes with the cleats growing out of the bottoms. "I play here with my dad every Thursday. Seven thirty a.m. tee time." He holds out his arms as if he owns the place, which he might. "Been doing it for half my life."

Damon moves closer to her, past what would be considered a professional distance. He grins again, and she smells liquor on his breath, suddenly aware that golfing is not the only thing he and his dad have been doing this morning. She glances from side to side to see if anyone else sees them. She can't let anyone in this club see her and Damon looking even the least bit cozy, or Glynnis will hear and get the wrong idea.

"You looking for someone to rescue you?" he asks, his tone joking, but still she is uncomfortable being here, with him, like this.

"N-no," she stammers.

"Why don't you like me?" he asks, and she could swear he has somehow moved closer, but maybe it's just his words that press up against her.

"I—I do," she says, and she can tell by his smirk that he thinks she is lying, but he goes along with it, nodding a few times as he fixes her with his clear green gaze until she has to look away again.

"Well, I better get going." He hitches his thumb in a direction to the left of them. "Dad's waiting."

She nods mutely, expecting him to mosey off. But he continues to stand in front of her. "I'm glad you like me, Ace," he says, using a nickname he gave her the first week she worked there. "Laurel Haines, Ace Reporter," he called her, reminding her too much of that annoying kid he used to be.

He leans forward and, with a surprising quickness, plants a kiss, light and warm, on her cheek. She looks up at him, but he is already walking away. She watches his back for a moment before reaching up to cover the spot on her cheek where his lips landed. She reminds herself that he has been drinking. The kiss was probably a joke—one that she doesn't appreciate, much like when they were kids. She watches as he turns a corner, and the sound of his cleats clacking across the marble floor fades away. She prepares to leave, and as she does, she spots a sign opposite where they stood—a sign that she could not see but he'd been staring at the whole time. She rolls her eyes as she reads it:

PLEASE REMOVE GOLF SHOES WHEN INSIDE THE CLUBHOUSE.

Kenny

They are nearly done packing when there is a knock at the door. His girlfriend raises her eyebrows at him. "Expecting someone?" she asks.

He freezes, a pair of boxers in his hands. He shakes his head, raises his eyebrows to match her quizzical expression. He is going for a nonchalant look, but he's not sure he's pulling it off, his heart knocking hard inside his chest. He doesn't like unexpected guests on his doorstep on the best days, but he really doesn't like it today. The knock sounds again, louder this time. In a way, he's been waiting for this moment since his mother called. He's made his decision: he will admit nothing.

"Want me to get it?" she asks. She is surprised by the visit but not deterred by it. She is thinking that they will get rid of whoever it is and proceed with their trip. But something tells him it is not going to be that simple. He casts about for a good explanation for the knock—a salesman (if salesmen are ever good explanations), a child looking for a lost dog, a neighbor asking to borrow a cup of sugar.

"I'll get it," he says, hoping for the best. He wants to open the door to find a small person on his threshold with buckteeth and freckles, asking if he's seen Spot.

But when he opens the door, there is no time to look down, because he is eye to eye with a man in uniform. A cop who asks if he knows Annie Taft and if he has seen her or has any knowledge of her whereabouts.

His girlfriend sidles up to him, her eyes widening when she sees the two uniformed police officers there. "Is something wrong?" she asks. He wants to tell her to go back inside the house, wants to keep her from hearing what the officers are saying. He doesn't want the inevitable questions about Annie that she will pepper him with after the policemen are gone.

"It's . . . nothing," he says. "They're just . . . looking for someone."

"Ma'am," the other officer says, turning his gaze from Kenny to her. "Do you know Annie Taft?"

The girlfriend looks confused. "Annie Taft?" she repeats. "*Nnnnn.* No." But when she says it, she sounds unsure. Though Kenny knows she is just unsure about what is going on, it makes her sound guilty, like she's lying.

"She doesn't know her," he says to them. There is impatience in his voice.

"But you do, Mr.—" The cop glances down at a little notebook he is carrying. "Spacey?" He looks up.

Kenny nods, acknowledging his last name. He's always hated it; it just gave the kids at school more fodder. "I knew her from school."

She was the only one who was nice to me when I first moved here, he thinks but does not say. In a flash, he sees Annie in seventh grade. Annie, who was smart and pretty and popular. Annie, who had a tragic story that he'd already heard before she ever spoke to him. He does not know how he knew her story; he really didn't have any friends who would've shared it with him. It was as if, in Ludlow, the story of Annie's tragedy floated in the air like a child's balloon, bobbing along the streets of both town and country, eventually making its rounds to every house. Annie, who became the best friend he ever had and the great love of his life, was as much a part of the atmosphere in this town as oxygen.

He looks at his girlfriend. "I knew her a long time ago," he explains to her, as if the cops aren't even there. "We were kids. She . . ." He sees Annie, with a mouth full of metal that would shape her smile into the head-turner it became. But he liked her smile before all that. "She stood up for me when I was new in town and some kids took to picking on me. They were her friends, and once she told them to lay off, they did. She did a nice thing for me back then. That's all."

He turns back to the officers and realizes he is still holding the boxer shorts. He is afraid this makes him look even more suspicious. He suppresses a grimace, considers tossing the underwear over his shoulder just to get rid of them. If he walks inside to set them down, that might seem like an invitation to the cops to follow him. He's heard you don't have to let cops in unless they have a warrant, so he has no intention of throwing open his door, of saying, *Come on in, fellas.* Cops are like vampires; they have to be invited in, but once you invite them in, they have the power.

"And you haven't spoken with her recently or heard from her?" the cop presses.

He grips the boxer shorts tighter. "No," he says. Later, they will learn that he has lied. But he cannot tell the truth in front of his girl-friend. It is a Pandora's box of questions that he cannot afford to open. He thinks of her decision to work from home this morning instead of getting an early start to Charleston. He thinks of this and regrets agreeing to it.

The cops trade looks. The one standing in front of him peers over his shoulder into the apartment, wanting, he knows, to get inside. He wonders what evidence against him they could gather. Annie's DNA is most assuredly there, in every room. For now, he is the only one besides Annie who knows this. And he intends to keep it that way if at all possible.

The other cop, the one to his left, hands him a card. "Well, if you think of anything that could help us find her, please call this number," he says. They step backward, as if they're going to leave, and he feels himself relax. Bullet dodged.

Then the one in front of him pauses, adds, "We might have some more questions for you, Mr. Spacey. So don't go far."

"But—" His girlfriend starts to argue, to tell the police they are about to leave town. He puts the hand holding the business card on her shoulder to quiet her.

"Sure thing," he says, and gives them what he hopes is a reassuring smile. He knows what this is. He is now a person of interest in Annie's disappearance. But he does not let the smile falter; he leaves it on his face until they are in their cars, all the while thinking of how like Annie this is: to get in the way of any chance at happiness he might find apart from her.

◆ ◆ ◆

His girlfriend is pacing back and forth, wearing a path in the already threadbare carpet. Kenny watches her, since there is nothing else to look at. This apartment isn't much of a home, which he never gave a great deal of thought to until his girlfriend started spending more time here. Her roommate is a librarian and likes the place quiet, for reading. She was displeased every time he was there, with his big, heavy steps, his tendency to absentmindedly hum. So, though they never really talked about it, his girlfriend gradually moved in with him. He supposes that has left her apartment very quiet, just the way the roommate likes it.

"And you haven't seen this Annie person in . . . how long?" his girlfriend says. She does not stop pacing as she says it. Kenny doesn't think she even expects an answer. He has answered this same question already, more than once. She stops pacing, which gets his attention. He looks up to find her watching him warily.

"Why won't you answer me?" she asks, her words accusing.

"Because I already have," he says. "A bunch of times. I wish you would believe me."

"But you never told me about her!" She raises her voice, lifts her hands out to her sides in a display of exasperation. "I thought we told each other everything!" she cries, and he winces at the shrillness of her voice.

"She's just someone from high school. From when I was a kid." He rolls his eyes. "She's not in my life anymore." He is pleased with himself for the way he has phrased his words because they are all true. He likes feeling—being—clever.

"Then why were the police here asking you about her?" This is also a question she has asked more than once. The smile he felt that was starting to form is gone before it can make it to his face.

"I told you. She's missing. They're looking for her. Someone probably remembered that we used to be friends, so they questioned me. They're desperate to find her, that's all."

He stands up, deciding that this inquisition is over. "Let's go to Hops Haven, grab a beer, get out of the apartment."

She glances over at their half-packed suitcases. "We were supposed to be on a trip right now." She pouts.

"I know. And I'm sorry. But you heard them. They want me to stay in town."

She squints. "But you don't have to. You're not under arrest or anything. They have no right to tell you you can't travel."

He thinks about this. He would actually love to get the hell out of this town. He thinks about how much he and Annie used to dream of exactly that. And now she is keeping him from being able to do so. "I can't," he says. He sighs and shakes his head. "If I do, it'll make it look like I'm running, like I have something to hide. And I don't."

She crosses her arms, cocks her head at him. "You really don't?" she asks.

There are freckles on her arms. He counted them once: twenty-eight on her right forearm and thirty-six on her left. "You're asymmetrical," he'd said, and she had giggled and scooted closer to him, and he'd known that she was his chance.

"I really don't," he says. And this time he is outright lying. But she doesn't know that. He holds out his hand. She takes it. He pulls her to him and whispers into her hair that he is sorry. He doesn't say for what, and she doesn't ask.

Faye

From across the room, she spies Tracy entering the house, her eyes wide as she takes in the crowd that has gathered. The police are there again, ostensibly to brief Faye on the search and the visit they paid to Kenny Spacey. But they have done that, and now they are mostly loitering. Travis and his wife have also showed up, and Scott seems to have taken up residence. Her usually empty house feels quite full. She is hosting the world's most morbid party.

Faye is glad she made the early-morning run to the grocery store, even if she did have to encounter Millicent while she was there. There is plenty of coffee with cream, which the younger officers have drunk so much of she doesn't know how they aren't coming out of their own skin from all the caffeine. She has set out cookies, too, and made some chicken salad sandwiches, but those are going mostly uneaten. She glances at the food, wonders at what point she should wrap it up and put it away. She does not know the rule for food going bad, but it can't be good for chicken to sit out that long. She wonders how she can think of something so basic at a time like this.

She is heading to the kitchen when Hal comes over, picks up a chicken salad sandwich, and shoves half of it in his mouth. With his mouth full, he says, "I always did like good homemade chicken salad, Faye. Where'd you find the time?"

She doesn't tell him that she bought it in the deli at the Food Lion. She just says, "Oh well, you know, I just threw something together. Besides, I hear your wife's chicken salad is the best in town. I'm sure mine can't compare." She picks up a dishcloth and rings it out, hard, her back to him. He was just a beat cop when Lydia died, a beat cop who dreamed of being right where he is now. And Lydia's case helped him get there. This is something they both know but do not say to each other, now or ever.

When she'd walked into the police station, it'd been Hal who was holding three-year-old Annie, wrapped in a blanket that looked too scratchy to Faye, but they couldn't get it away from the traumatized little girl. They also couldn't get Annie away from Hal. The child had clung to him like he was her long-lost daddy.

Annie's daddy was a bad decision named Larry Taft who'd lured Lydia down to Ludlow just before he got himself killed in a motorcycle accident and left her there with a baby. Faye had begged Lydia to come home to Virginia, but Lydia was too proud to admit her mistake and return home with her tail between her legs. Faye thinks now about what the Bible says about pride, how it goes before a fall. It sure was true in Lydia's case. Her pride had been her downfall—if she'd just packed up Annie and come home, she'd be alive now. At least, Faye likes to think so. She daydreams sometimes about a life where Lydia made different decisions and all their lives turned out different. No, not just different. Better.

For instance, Faye wouldn't be in this kitchen making small talk with a sheriff she's known too long and for the wrong reasons. She wishes he would take his men and leave, but instead, finished with his sandwich, he reaches for a cookie, holds it up. "Good," he says, and she thinks he's being too friendly and happy. She is close to telling him so when Tracy walks over.

"I thought when I saw all the cop cars here that they'd found her," she says to Faye, ignoring Hal's presence. "I thought I'd walk in, and she'd be sitting in the middle of everything, telling the story of what happened."

Faye puts her arm around Annie's best friend, gives her a little squeeze. She knows that roller coaster, the highest height followed by the deepest depth. It's enough to keep your stomach permanently in your throat. She remembers this all from when Lydia died, is surprised how effortlessly it has come back to her. It is just as hard the second time.

Hal swallows his cookie and says, "We're working on it, honey. Greenville cops, too. We'll find her." He winks at Tracy.

Faye is sure he means to be reassuring, but she thinks he just looks like a creepy old man. But she will not say that in front of Tracy, who excuses herself to go and sit beside Scott. Those two sure are chummy. She wonders if it is premature to have a little talk with Tracy about the way it looks for her to be quite so close with Annie's fiancé. Maybe she's being a fuddy-duddy, but she doesn't think it's fitting. She is about to ask Hal what he thinks, but before she can, he announces that they'd best get going. He puts his hand on her shoulder, and it is big and warm and comforting. She has to stop herself from moving toward him.

"Thank you," she says instead, all business.

She thinks about the text she received earlier asking if she could meet, if she could get away. He is breaking the rules, and she knows why. Annie being gone has changed everything, brought back a long-ago time that neither of them ever forgot and always shared. She thinks about this as she watches Hal leave with his men, taking his big, strong hands with him. She thinks of responding to the text, figuring out a way she can get away, go and seek comfort for her own self, decorum be damned. Later she will respond; she will make a plan. Later she just might seek comfort in the arms of the one person who she most wants to provide it. But for now there is the chicken salad to put up and someone else at the door bearing food.

Clary

As they round the bend, Miss Minnie gets to the end of her story, just as she always does. It is not just the story itself that is familiar; there are the points in the road that correspond to the story. She cannot drive this road without pairing them in her mind, even when Miss Minnie is not in her car. She knows this will be true long after Miss Minnie is gone, after the dementia has finally caused her brain to stop telling her to eat, her heart to beat, her lungs to take in and expel air. Miss Minnie will be gone, but her story will live on.

The story itself is quite simple, a snippet of an ordinary day carried out many years ago when life was, Clary imagines, happier. When her husband was alive and her children still at home. When she was the mistress of her domain and drove herself along this familiar road instead of depending on someone else to do it for her. The story is about a day that she and her husband left the sporting goods store they owned and decided to take a drive for no particular reason at all.

He just said, "Let's go for a drive, Sugar," Miss Minnie always begins.

Clary likes that part, thinks it would be nice to have a man call her "Sugar."

"And I said, 'Well, okay.' So we got in the car, and we took a drive with the radio on real low. And we talked about things, the kind of things that don't really matter in the end but you talk about anyway. Because at the time they seem like they need sayin'. When we were finished with our drive, we went to Neil's baseball game. We sat outside with the sun on our shoulders and watched our son throw the ball so fast it would make your head spin. He was quite a baseball player, don'tcha know."

At this part, Clary always says the same thing: "I didn't know that." Because now she has become part of Minnie's story, too.

Clary thinks about this while they drive, how we become part of each other's stories, sometimes because we want to and sometimes because we don't but have to anyway. Whether we have a main role or a bit part; we are onstage in each other's lives. She thinks about Annie and their role in each other's stories, how they were meant to be bit parts—the cousin you saw only once a year, maybe twice—but ended up in leading roles. In high school English, they'd learned that there are two kinds of characters: protagonists and antagonists. Clary thinks that she and Annie are both to each other. She thinks of that last conversation they had, how each of them saw the other as the antagonist that day. Clary recalls how angry she was with Annie. Now she wishes she could take her angry words back, could stay on the phone instead of hanging up.

Annie was pushing Clary to tell Travis about what happened after he left. Clary never intends to tell Travis what happened after he left. She never intended to tell anyone, but Annie, in her Annie way, found out. Sometimes she catches Annie looking at her, and she knows that Annie is thinking about the day she came to Charlotte to visit Clary. The visit was a total surprise—for both of them, it turned out.

They pull up to the house, interrupting Clary's wandering thoughts. Minnie turns to her as she always does, just as Clary is shifting the car into park. "Family is the most important thing," Minnie says, her filmy eyes imploring Clary to agree with her. So Clary does. She nods vigorously and, as she does, tears fill her eyes. This time Minnie does something she never does. She reaches out to pat Clary lovingly on the shoulder.

"It'll be all right, dear," Minnie says. Then she reaches for the door handle and, while Clary collects herself, Minnie gets her own self out of the car. Clary is too caught up in the moment to think about this show of strength from Minnie. The old woman hasn't opened her own door in months.

She jumps from the car and runs over to her charge, who is already making her way toward the little sidewalk that leads to her house. "Miss Minnie!" she exclaims. "You got out of the car by yourself!" She wonders if this is a turning point, if Miss Minnie is somehow getting better. Something good in the midst of all this bad. This is all Clary has ever wanted to do—with her doves, with Miss Minnie, even with what happened after Travis left—make other people's lives better.

She is glad she came today. When she'd showed up to take Minnie out, Glynnis had met her at the door. "Oh, I already told Mama you weren't coming today," she said, glancing over her shoulder as if Minnie might catch her. "You'd asked off for the wedding starting today, and I figured, with everything going on, you'd just stay home."

Clary had held up both her hands. "I can't just sit at home and wait. I need to stay busy. Mama's at home with a bunch of cops hanging out in our house. I don't exactly want to be there."

Glynnis had looked over her shoulder again, then nodded. "I can understand that." She frowned, seemed worried. "I told Mama about Annie, and she got rightly upset. I probably shouldn't have said anything. I didn't know she'd get so upset! I just got her calmed down. I don't know if I should get her all riled up again. I think she even remembered Annie driving her." Glynnis thought about this. "Or something."

"Keeping to her routine might do her good," Clary had offered. Glynnis had rolled her eyes around in her head as she thought that one over.

"Good point," she finally said. And before Clary knew it, Miss Minnie had been in her car just like it was any other day.

But it isn't any other day, and now their drive is over. She walks Miss Minnie into the house, settles her in her chair, turns the TV over to the History channel, and sets about preparing her dinner. She makes Minnie's favorite, Kraft macaroni and cheese. It is comfort food, and Miss Minnie seems like she could use the comfort. They all could. Once Minnie is settled in, Clary says the same thing she always does.

"Glynnis will be by later to get you tucked in. You have a good night, okay?" But Minnie, absorbed in a show about World War II, doesn't respond. That, too, is just like any other day.

◆　◆　◆

Clary pulls up in front of her house to find a few police cars still there and a car that has claimed what seems a permanent spot. A snazzy SUV with Florida license plates that looks nothing like the sedate sedan a pastor should be driving. The vehicle has a car seat in the back. She walks quickly past, scolding herself for even glancing inside it. She does not need to see the evidence of Travis's life now, his happy family life. She goes inside.

Tracy and Scott are there, sitting beside each other on the couch, talking intently. They seem to be spending all their time together. She wonders if that is right or wrong, then supposes that, at this point, it doesn't matter. There are no rules for this type of thing. There are times in life when there simply aren't, and it is up to us to write our own. This is what Clary did in Charlotte all those years ago. She wrote her own rules. She notes—but does not look directly at—Travis and his wife, standing in the dining area between the kitchen and the living area. There is food all over the table—platters brought by both good-intentioned and downright nosy people as soon as the news about Annie got out.

Clary's stomach rumbles at the sight of the food, and she feels guilty for her hunger. She should not be eating when Annie is missing. She hopes that, wherever she is, Annie is eating, keeping up her strength. An unwelcome thought pushes its way into the front of her mind: Annie kidnapped by a psycho, like in that movie *The Silence of the Lambs*. Annie at the bottom of a hole, food being lowered in a basket. Annie scared and cold and alone.

But this is Ludlow, South Carolina. Things like that don't happen here. There are no psychopaths. Of course, would she hear if there was a psycho roaming around? Is this the kind of thing decent people discuss in everyday conversation? Clary doesn't think so.

"You're worried about your cousin," a voice says, which is a reasonable guess. She looks to her left and, standing beside her, with a plate of ham biscuits and deviled eggs in her hand, is Travis's wife, Deandra. It doesn't sound like a pastor's wife's name. Deandra Dove. It sounds like a porn star's. How can anyone take her seriously with that name? Clary has watched her in Travis's church videos online, joining Travis onstage for some announcement or another and, once, for a sermon on marriage. Clary had run from the computer, her hand over her mouth. She'd made it to the toilet before she threw up.

"Secrets make you sick," Annie had said in that last conversation. Annie can be so self-righteous. Clary knows Annie doesn't have any secrets, so it's easy for her to be sanctimonious about people who do.

"Yes." Clary forces a polite response to Travis's wife. "Very worried."

With her free hand, Deandra Dove reaches out to pat her shoulder, the same shoulder that Minnie patted earlier. "We are all praying. So hard," she says. "For Annie and for your family." Deandra's eyes float over in Travis's direction, then back to Clary. "Especially Travis," she says.

Clary offers a weak thank-you in response, her voice thick in her throat. She does not want to be prayed for by Travis Dove's wife or by Travis. She does not want to be patted by Travis Dove's wife. She wishes Travis Dove *and* his wife would get in their SUV with the car seat in the back and drive back southward where they belong. But Travis is in his element, circling the room in pastor mode. She even saw him stop and pray with one of the cops, his baritone voice growing louder so that everyone in the room lowered their own voices and ducked, if not bowed, their heads.

Clary wanted to go over and shake him, scream, *Who are you?*

She recalls Travis at age sixteen, hanging over an overpass with a can of spray paint, painting their names across the side of the bridge as she shrieked at him to be careful. When he turned to look back at her, there was zeal on his face, the exhilaration of risk, of danger, as visible as the neon spray paint he'd used to proclaim his love for her to everyone who drove under that bridge the next morning. Later that day, Hal York had hauled him down to the station. "You dummies shouldn't have used your real names," Hal had scolded.

Travis, once her wild, fun instigator, has become an appropriate, measured responder. Instead of stirring up trouble, now he's helping people through it. She guesses this is to be admired, but there is something in her that can only hate it.

Deandra Dove sticks out her hand. "I'm Deandra, by the way," she says. "Travis's wife," she adds, as if Clary needs that explanation.

She wants to say, *I'm Clary. Travis's ex.* But instead she merely grips the woman's hand in what passes for a handshake. Clary is the first to let go, thinking as she does, *This is the hand that touches Travis now.* She resists the urge to wipe her palm on her shorts and instead points to the plate of food. "Any good?" she asks, just to be polite, to prove that, no matter what Travis or anyone else has told Deandra, Clary has class. Hell, she was in a country club just this morning.

"Yes," she says, and emits a little giggle as she rests her hand on her stomach. "I've just been feeling so bad I had to make myself eat something. They call it morning sickness, but it's not just mornings for me."

"You're—you're—" Clary swallows around her tongue, grown thick in her mouth. "Pregnant?" She thinks of the car seat in the back of the SUV. They already have a baby. "Again?" she asks.

Deandra smiles like the pregnant cat that ate the sympathy food at a missing bride's family's house while her husband's pitiful ex looked on. "Well, we didn't intend on having them so close together, but it just . . . happened."

That little-girl giggle punctuates her words again. She sounds silly, like a person who can't be trusted with adult things. *Why are you here?* Clary wants to ask this woman child. *Why are you in my home while my cousin is missing?* She looks across the room, hoping to make eye contact with her mother, to make an excuse to excuse herself, but all she sees is Travis, warily watching them both. *Don't worry, honey,* she thinks, *I will not taint her. I will not tell her what you used to be like.*

"Well," Clary says, "congratulations." She shifts her purse on her shoulder, making it look like it has suddenly grown heavy, like she must go put it away right this very minute. "I better go set this down and get something to eat myself." Before Deandra can respond, she starts to walk away, then remembers her manners and turns back. "Nice to meet you," she adds.

Deandra nods and gives her a smile, the same smile she uses onstage with Travis. Clary looks up to see if Travis is still watching them, if he still looks worried. She hopes that he sees that smile on his wife's face and knows that she hasn't done what he expected her to do. Their eyes meet, and she sees him tilt his chin down slightly, the barest acknowledgment. Above his head, a bright light suddenly shines, and for the briefest moment, she thinks that perhaps Travis's transformation is complete, that he has actually begun to emit light like a celestial being.

But before the thought can even fully form, she realizes it is not Travis who is shining; it is something shining through the window behind him, something from the front yard. She moves forward to investigate the source of the light, her gaze fixed just past him. She sees him turn to find out what she is looking at. And so, together, they are the first ones to spot the television reporter on the lawn, the large lights erected for a live broadcast: BRIDE MISSING: NEWS AT ELEVEN.

Laurel

When her phone rings, it is a welcome distraction. For a moment, she thinks that maybe it is Damon, calling to say he is sorry about this morning. But it's not Damon. It is Scott, the groom, asking her to come to Faye's, because he'd like to give her a statement.

"I've had some other news people get in contact with me," he says, then exhales loudly into the phone, weary of all this. "But Damon Collins says I should give you an exclusive."

An exclusive. The words make her heart pick up speed. Of course she goes.

When she arrives, Scott is nowhere to be seen. She stands just inside the doorway, feeling like she's snuck into a party she wasn't invited to, until Tracy bustles over and pulls her to a corner. "Just hang out for a bit," Tracy says, looking very pleased to be in the know. "He does want to talk to you."

Laurel nods obediently, all the while wondering why Tracy is Scott's spokesperson now. She wonders if he has really said this or if Tracy is making it up.

Tracy points toward a hall off the main room where they are standing and rolls her eyes. "The cops have him sequestered back there, asking a million questions. Again. I told him it might be time to think about getting a lawyer." She glances backward, as if willing the closed door to open and Scott to emerge.

Still watching the door, Tracy adds, "I mean, if he's a suspect, he shouldn't be talking to them without an attorney. Everyone knows that. I'm trying to help him think through all this, help him . . . navigate these uncharted waters." She shrugs and makes eye contact with Laurel again. "He didn't have anything to do with Annie's disappearance, of course," she adds with certainty.

She gives Laurel a pinched smile and moves away, leaving Laurel to stand alone awkwardly, wondering how Tracy is so sure Scott didn't have anything to do with it. It doesn't seem that anyone knows anything for certain in this case. Laurel can see that Tracy feels superior to her because she is in the know, deigning to allow Laurel into the situation, the purveyor of valuable information. Tracy, who would barely speak in high school, always nipping at Annie's heels, obviously grateful to be designated Annie's best friend. Now she seems just as grateful to be designated Scott's confidante. Laurel wouldn't be surprised if Tracy was nursing a little crush on Annie's fiancé.

She watches Tracy make small talk with a stranger and waits for something to happen. Either Scott will emerge from the bedroom so they can finally talk, or Faye will throw Laurel out. She probably would've already if not for the arrival of one of her best customers, there to offer her support. Laurel has seen Faye's eyes dart over to her several times, a worried look on her face. It is, she fears, only a matter of time before Faye breaks away from her conversation and heads her way with that set in her jaw that Laurel has come to recognize—the one that means Faye is not happy and is about to do something about it. She saw it this morning at the country club. Was it just this morning? It already seems like days ago.

Laurel taps a nearby cop on the shoulder in the middle of his bite of ham biscuit. He begins to chew faster, giving her a look in the meantime that says, *Yeah?*

"Do you by chance know where the restroom is?" she asks, desperate to find a place to hide out while she waits on Scott, if for no other reason than to stay out of Faye's sight.

The cop swallows and shrugs, gives her a grin. "I have no idea," he says.

"Okay," she responds, feeling every bit as stupid as he must think she is. She starts to walk away, but his voice stops her.

"Hey, aren't you Laurel Haines? We went to high school together. I didn't know you were back in town." He grins and leans against the wall, settling in for a catch-up.

"I'm sorry," she says. "I need to find the restroom." She scoots away quickly, before he can see the two spots of color that have risen on her cheeks. The last thing she wants to do is stand in Faye's living room and reminisce about high school. She tries the first door she comes to, anxious to slip away.

The door reveals what must be Clary's bedroom. Feeling guilty for breaching her privacy, she quickly shuts the door. But not before she registers that Clary's room is a juxtaposition of old and new, of past and present. Laurel's room at her parents' home is much the same: a ratty stuffed bunny sits beside an over-the-counter sleep aid, makeup brushes hunker in a clay pot formed by ten-year-old hands. The girl she was coexists with the woman she has become.

She moves on before Clary spies her loitering outside her bedroom and yells at her for snooping. Clary was always a wild child, unpredictable and unafraid. Though Laurel has seen her only briefly since she's been back, she knows that Clary now cares for Laurel's grandmother in the afternoons. That she raises doves and releases them at weddings and funerals. Far from the wild, bohemian life Laurel would've expected. Clary does not seem to be the same person she was back then. But, then again, none of them is.

The second door she tries is the right one. She slips inside the bathroom and closes the door, standing in the quiet darkness with a sigh of relief before she flips on the light. She sees a purple toothbrush in a little holder, a pump bottle of face cleanser beside it, a smudge of toothpaste on the counter that she resists the urge to wipe away.

She looks up at her face in the mirror, trying to imagine Annie standing in this very same spot. This was her bathroom, too, for her whole life and another few days at least. A young Annie got ready for dates and rehearsed breakup speeches and practiced kissing in this mirror. Laurel puckers her lips, and as she does, the annoying image of Damon leaning so close to her at the country club enters her brain. She shakes her head, and the image disappears.

She stands there for a few minutes longer, then flushes the toilet to make her trip seem plausible, just in case anyone is listening. She waits until the toilet has completely stopped running to buy more time before leaving the safe haven of the bathroom. Only when the pipes stop running does she hear the ruckus outside.

She flings open the bathroom door and steps out into the hallway. From her vantage point, she can see that everyone in the living area has sort of clumped together, all their eyes looking in the same direction, all their mouths agape, even the cops'. Something is happening. She hears someone yelling, but from a distance, and realizes the front door to the house must be open and the person yelling is outside.

It is nearly full dark, yet there is light shining through the big window at the front of the house, light that reflects on surprised faces. She sees Scott and Tracy, standing together. She sees Travis Dove and his wife, too. She moves toward the light and the shouting, slipping into a thin spot between one of the church ladies who brought food and the customer of Faye's. She silently watches as Faye gesticulates and screams at a television crew gathered on her lawn. She points at the street and then at the camera, and, though they can't hear every word, Laurel gets the gist: Faye wants them to leave.

Behind her, Clary tries helplessly to stop her mother, to pull her back inside. Then Sheriff York drives up, and they all watch as he gets out of his car and ambles calmly over to where the conflict is occurring.

He puts his hand on Faye's shoulder and gently tugs her away, speaking to her in a low voice. When he stops speaking, Clary guides her mom back toward the house. As the two of them draw closer, the cluster of people in the living room breaks up, as if they weren't watching with mouths agape seconds earlier. People turn their heads as Clary and Faye enter, and the hum of conversation resumes as if nothing has happened at all.

Laurel is deciding that this would be a good time to leave when Scott catches her eye and motions for her to come over to where he is standing. Tracy, Laurel notices, has already worked her way back to his side. A headline forms in her head, *Bridesmaid Stands by Groom's Side as Hunt for Bride Continues.* But of course she will not write that. Tracy and Scott are doing nothing wrong as far as she can see. Still, she can't help but wonder how Tracy is so confident that Scott isn't involved in Annie's disappearance. Anything is possible.

Scott starts talking as soon as Laurel gets close enough to hear him. "Sorry, I was . . . detained when you got here. The cops are asking a ton of questions about this guy Annie knew in high school, if I knew him and all that." He shrugs. "I mean I knew about him but I didn't know him."

"Yeah, I heard something about that," Laurel lies.

"I sort of feel bad," Tracy pipes up, her face intent. She looks from Scott to Laurel, clearly enjoying being part of things. "I'm the one who told the cops about him. They just asked about her friends, and once I saw Annie ignore a call and I saw his name on the screen. You know how you can see someone's name on the screen when they call?"

Tracy looks to Laurel for affirmation, so Laurel nods.

"And I said to Annie, I said, 'You can get that.' And she said, 'Oh, it's gotta be a wrong number.' But it was his name with a picture. And I remember the picture was of the British flag. But, like, Annie had to have done that on her phone—added his name to her contacts with that British flag so it would come up on the screen like that." Tracy pauses.

"At least, I think it was a British flag? The one with the cross and the *X* and the red, white, and blue. You know the one I'm talking about, right?" This time she looks to Scott for affirmation. Scott's nod at her is tense, and Laurel notices a muscle working in his jaw.

Tracy doesn't seem to notice. She just continues, "Anyway, I've been racking my brain trying to think of anyone who might know anything. So I told Sheriff York about it just as soon as I remembered. But I didn't know they'd home in on him like that. I hadn't thought about Kenny in years. Do you remember him, Laurel?"

Laurel realizes high school is going to keep coming up, and there is nothing she can do to stop it. "No," Laurel says. "I don't believe I do."

Tracy looks around, then lowers her voice as if someone associated with Kenny might hear them. "He was real odd. Kind of kept to himself? A nerd, I guess you'd say." Tracy narrows her eyes at Laurel. "I'm fairly sure you'd know him if you saw him."

Laurel has tried to forget everyone from high school—from the star quarterback down to the lady who served up slices of pizza in the cafeteria. "If you say so," she says. "I'm sure I would."

This answer does not satisfy Tracy. "Thing was, he was kind of cute. But weird, so it was like he couldn't be fully cute. Like maybe if he grew out of his weirdness, he'd turn hot. I do remember Annie was always nice to him. But she never said they kept in touch." Tracy is puzzling this out in front of them, giving Kenny Whatever His Name Is far more thought than she ever has before. Without thinking that she's standing beside Annie's fiancé—or maybe because she's standing beside Annie's fiancé—she says, "Maybe that's what happened?" she asks.

"Maybe what's what happened?" Laurel asks.

"Maybe they stayed friends, and Kenny turned hot. And . . ." She wrinkles her nose, as if this theory smells bad. "That still doesn't explain that British flag, though. I don't remember him having an English accent. That I'd remember. I *love* English accents."

Laurel glances outside, at the reporters who have moved off Faye's lawn and are now resettling in a common area across the street. They've found the same story she has. But she is here first. She is being given access those people outside would kill for. It's all about being in the right place at the right time. Damon asked Scott for a favor, threw her a bone because of his connection to Scott. So she is here only because of Damon, and she sort of hates that. But she also appreciates it. Because, as Professor Sharp used to say, it doesn't matter how you get there. It just matters that you're there. And today she is.

She fishes around in her purse and pulls out her notepad and pen. Outside, the station from Greenville is clamoring for a story and being rejected. They're just the first outlet to show up. There will be other stations coming soon, no doubt. But this is her story. Hers. The blood is electric in her veins, whooshing quickly through her whole body as it lights her up inside. She has to fight to keep from smiling. There is a woman missing, after all; there is a tragedy happening inside this room.

Scott speaks up, interrupting Tracy's diatribe on the mysterious Kenny. "I guess I should give my statement now," he says. He glances over at Tracy as if to say, *Are you sure I should do this?*

Tracy nods.

"We"—he glances at Tracy again, and she gives another nod, the look on her face both maternal and devoted—"decided to give it until six tonight for Annie to show up before I made the call. But with tomorrow being the rehearsal and still no sign of her, we think it might be best to call off the wedding." He swallows. "For now."

Laurel writes four words on her notepad in all caps: THE WEDDING IS OFF.

Tracy jumps in. "If Annie returns tomorrow, she will most likely not be up for the rehearsal and rehearsal dinner. If she left of her own free will, then there's the question of why she wasn't here. That will be a conversation she and Scott will need to have. And if she didn't leave

of her own free will, well . . . she won't be up to getting married now."
Tracy's mouth turns down, and for a horrifying moment, Laurel is afraid
she's going to start bawling. But she composes herself.

Scott speaks again. "I thought you could go ahead and write a
story about the decision, then people would know why I'm calling it
off without my having to repeat myself again and again," he says. His
eyes stray to the reporters across the street. "I meant it just for the town.
For our friends and family. Damon thought it would be a good idea to,
you know, control the story that gets out. I guess I didn't know they'd
show up here. Now."

His voice sounds less strong by the minute, like someone has kicked
him in the chest and he's having trouble taking a deep breath. Laurel
knows that the police are looking at him, but like Tracy, she doesn't
think Scott Hanson did anything to Annie Taft. She thinks he is a
victim, too, that his intended life has been stolen right out from under
his nose.

"I will," she says. She swallows. "And I'm sorry. About the wedding." This story, she understands anew, is far from over. It is only going
to get bigger. Her story in tomorrow's paper will most likely get picked
up, go viral. More news outlets will show up, looking for an angle,
some insight. But she has the insight. She has the exclusive that Scott
has called off the wedding.

"I'll go get to work on the story right away," she says to Scott and
Tracy. "So it'll make the morning paper."

Scott nods grimly. "Thank you," he says.

"Yes, thank you," Tracy echoes.

Laurel shrugs. "Just doing my job," she says. She exits the house
and walks quickly past the news van and its crew, busy as bees in a hive,
buzzing over a story unfolding.

Faye

She lies on her back and stares at the ceiling, listening to the sounds of her house at night, tuning her ears toward any sounds that don't belong but hearing none.

Would Annie return in the night, just show up under cover of darkness? Would she offer an explanation or withhold it? Faye knows it wouldn't matter. She would just wrap that girl in her arms and be glad.

A wave of what can be described only as physical pain assaults her as memories play out in her mind. Annie at eight years old shyly handing her a permission form to go on a field trip. When Faye checked the box for guardian instead of parent, Annie piped up, "Why'd you check that box, Aunt Faye?"

"Because I'm not your mama," Faye had answered, then handed the paper back to the child and hurried off to the next task.

As a single working mom, she was always so busy, so short with both the girls. Now she thinks about the little-girl version of Annie, standing there holding that paper, puzzling over the word *guardian*, probably too afraid to ask any more questions. And Annie never did. She must've figured out on her own what *guardian* meant. Faye wants to go back in time, to slow down long enough to look into Annie's eyes and explain it all to her, to be a guardian in the truest sense of the word.

Having Annie was a luxury she never fully appreciated. Having Annie was a gift her sister was denied. She should've treated her as such.

Why does it take loss to make you realize what you had? This is one of the great injustices of life. It was the same with losing Lydia. She never knew how much her sister meant to her until she died. Lydia used to call her after she got Annie down for the night and beg her to come visit. "I'm so lonely, Faye. You've got to come keep me company. I feel like I might die of loneliness."

Sometimes Faye has thought of this—wondering if Lydia's loneliness caused her to let the wrong person into her life. She wonders if, in its own way, loneliness did kill her sister. And she kicks herself for not just telling T. J. Wilkins where to stick it and coming to Ludlow to rescue her sister. They were both lonely, back then, each isolated by their individual circumstances, both too proud to tell the other what was really happening in their lives. What if Lydia had confessed that she was, as the rumor went, seeing a married man? What if Faye had told Lydia that she was afraid of her husband? Perhaps the two could've rescued each other.

She tries to think about something else, her mind shifting to Tracy and Scott sleeping on her couches for a second night. They're out there right now, maybe whispering in the dark, maybe cuddling together on one couch doing God knows what under the blankets that Faye has provided. What would Annie think if she walked back in and saw her best friend and her fiancé all cozied up? It's tacky, and they should see that without having to be told. Some people just have no sense.

Faye wonders if she should be allowing this, but she also doesn't know how she can stop it. They're grown-ass adults who can conduct themselves any way they see fit. The two of them have been thick as thieves, sitting together for meals, huddling in corners talking, acting as if each is the other's long-lost best friend. She meant to ask Clary what she thought about it, but things got so crazy that she forgot. The truth is, in the grand scheme of things, Faye doesn't really care. All she really cares about is finding Annie. The cops have told her that the likelihood of that is growing smaller with each passing hour, but she can't listen to such negative talk. She has made a promise to herself: she will find Annie. She has to.

The last time she felt this intent was when she vowed to find Lydia's killer. It had driven her nearly crazy, the desire to identify and punish whoever it was who had put his hands around her sister's throat and choked the life out of her. Annie had told her story about Cordell Lewis, but Faye was hesitant to take a little child's word for it. Night after night, she wrestled over what to do. Annie seemed so certain that Uncle Cord had done it. Yet Faye didn't want to point the finger at an innocent man unless she was sure.

The police seemed to take their cues from her, and this was not a position she relished being in. She could feel the town's desire to solve Lydia's murder mounting with each passing day. She'd gotten so desperate she'd gone to see a psychic, a woman who lived in the North Carolina mountains and had contacted her promising a revelation she'd been given. Faye had gone there on impulse and in desperation, which, in hindsight, was not the best combination.

Clary and Annie napped on the drive, then watched cartoons in the woman's living room while she and Faye sat on the front porch of her very normal, very modest house that overlooked a ring of mountains. There were no crystals or talismans or tarot cards. There was no incense or candles burning. The psychic was just an average-looking middle-aged woman with a pensive look and a dachshund. She could've been a teacher or a florist. She could've been anyone at all.

It had been a chilly day, the weather turning colder the longer they sat there. Faye had hung on the woman's every word, desperate for insight, ignoring the chill. The woman had known things without Faye having to tell her. Things she could've gotten from the paper, sure, but some things that weren't reported. She'd known that Lydia was a single mother, that she'd potentially been involved with several men at the time of her death (that was the rumor, but Faye never did believe it), and that she loved the outdoors. She'd known that Lydia died outside;

she'd said that Annie was cold after Lydia died, that she'd wandered out of the tent, away from her still, silent mother, and that the police had wrapped her in a blanket when they found her.

When she'd looked at Faye and said, "Trust the child," the air had shifted, blowing in a new direction, raising the hairs on the back of Faye's neck.

The woman charged her $200 for the revelation. Faye wrote a check for the last of her money and wondered how she would buy groceries. Later, Hal gave her money, told her she was stupid for paying some psychic who claimed to know something.

"You can't fall for that," he'd said. "She could've gotten every single thing she told you right out of the papers."

But Faye had fallen for it. She'd fallen for it so much, she'd believed the woman wholeheartedly. She'd pushed to prosecute based on Annie's word. She'd trusted the child like the woman had said to do. Once she'd given her assent, small-town justice had taken over. And it had cost a man twenty-three years of his life. She wonders again if that man decided to seek retribution on the child Faye had trusted all those years ago. The police say he has an alibi for when Annie went missing, but something niggles at her. The timing is just too close: his release and Annie's wedding. If it were her, in jail for all those years for a crime she didn't commit, she would want someone to pay.

She rolls over in her bed with an audible sigh, punching her pillow into a better position for her head, filled with all its busy, sleep-stealing thoughts. She stares up at the ceiling, wishing Lydia were here, that she could tell Lydia all that is happening and ask her what she should do. But Lydia isn't here, and neither is Annie. And Faye has never felt so alone.

MAY 31

Rehearsal Day

One Day until the Wedding

Ludlow Ledger

Missing Bride's Fiancé Calls off Wedding
By Laurel Haines, staff reporter

Scott Hanson, fiancé of missing bride Annie Taft, has decided to call off their wedding, which was to take place this Saturday at First Baptist Ludlow. Scott Hanson said of the decision, "I hate to use the word *cancel*. I'm saying *postpone*. But I just don't see another way. I gave myself a deadline that, if she wasn't back by six p.m. on Thursday, I would have to do something. We've reached a point that, even if she returns tomorrow, she's not going to be up to going ahead with the original plans."

Scott Hanson is a twenty-eight-year-old medical sales representative who met Annie Taft in Greenville through mutual friends. After a year of dating, they began discussing marriage. Scott proposed on a weekend trip to Savannah, Georgia, one of their favorite places. "It was so romantic," says Tracy Douglas, one of Annie's oldest friends who was to be a bridesmaid in the wedding. "Annie was thrilled. She couldn't wait to marry Scott."

Family and friends are holding out hope that Annie will fulfill her dream of saying, "I do," to the man she loves, and that they will celebrate her safe return very soon. A candlelight prayer vigil will take place this evening at First Baptist Ludlow at the time her wedding rehearsal would've been held. Anyone who would like to gather to pray for Annie Taft's safe return is invited to come at six o'clock.

Laurel

"Nice job," Damon says. He is standing over her desk, holding up today's paper. Her story is the lead, and probably the only story anyone will read. Already, hits on the paper's site have quadrupled as people hungry for information on the lovely missing bride have searched it out. Twenty-six hundred people and counting have shared the story on Facebook, and the number grows each time Laurel checks, which is often. It is breaking news, and she is the one who broke it. Okay, it was given to her—she didn't have to go uncover it—but no one has to know that.

Damon starts prattling on about sending her to cover the prayer vigil, adding his thoughts about angles and sidebar stories she might want to pursue. She stops listening. This is her story, and she will cover it her way. She sees it all in front of her: who she will talk to, what she will write, how she will angle it. It is as clear to her as if it is already done. Some people see lines on a page and can turn them into a physical building. Some people see a blank canvas and can turn it into a masterpiece. Some people see a mangled human body and can make it whole again. Her? She sees a story and knows exactly the way it should be told. This is her gift, the one thing in life she knows for sure she has been given.

The news, Laurel learned when her classmate got sick, can change everything. She would hold her number two yellow pencil with the eraser nearly gone and wonder what she could write with it, whose life she could change with words. She believed in the power of that pencil with her whole heart. She'd almost forgotten that until Annie's story came along.

Numbed by reporting on yet another garden club or ladies' circle meeting, more coverage of the minutes of the Chamber of Commerce, or "breaking news" about the sinkhole on Main Street in downtown Ludlow, she'd lost sight of there being anything truly worthy to write about. She'd been angry the day Damon handed her the assignment to interview Faye. She was tired of silly, no-count stories that served only as filler, despondent of ever being able to write something that mattered. Laurel has learned something already in the few days since then: you never know when a story will turn.

She realizes Damon is looking at her, waiting, it seems, for the answer to a question she didn't hear him ask. She nods. "Sure," she says, hearing the uncertainty in her voice. She wonders if he hears it as well.

"Okay, good. It's a plan," he says, and claps his hands together once, loudly, clearly pleased with her answer.

"What . . . time?" she asks, casting about for a clue as to what she has just agreed to.

"Well, the vigil is at six, so we better get there early, don't you think?" He nods, agreeing with himself. "I can get some shots of the church, the people walking in, who knows what else."

Shots? Did she just agree to let Damon be her photographer on this story? Damon isn't a photographer. At least, not that she's ever been aware of. Sure, he has a collection of cameras on the shelves in his office. But she always thought they were there for decoration, leftover from the days when it was his father's office.

"We can ride together?" he asks, and his voice is so hopeful and excited that she cannot say no. She has never been in Damon's car. She knows what kind it is: a BMW X1, bought for his college graduation. She imagines it smells like his cologne inside. His cologne mixed with the lingering smell of new car. She can't imagine riding in Damon's car, sharing such a small, private space.

"Sure," Laurel says again, telling herself that this will be fine. Damon can be there with her as her photographer. They can be there to cover the story, writer and photographer, business people doing business, plain and simple. They can ride together; they can be professionals. There is no harm in this; it will not change a thing.

◆ ◆ ◆

At the church, they watch as the faithful gather to pray, their faces somber and penitent, as if they themselves had something to do with Annie's disappearance. Of course, it's possible that one of them could have. Scott has been questioned at length. And based on the gossip she's hearing, that Kenny guy from high school is of particular interest.

She watches as Travis Dove takes his place behind the pulpit to say a few words. But his few words turn into many as he recounts what Annie means to them all. He speaks of Annie's vivacious personality, her sunshiny smile, her ability to make everyone in the room feel special and seen. He tells the story of how one invitation from Annie became the catalyst for his decision to become a pastor. Laurel did not know this. All she remembers about Travis is that he used to skulk around with Clary, looking edgy and dangerous. She glances over at Clary to gauge her reaction. But Clary is stone-faced as she watches him speak, her face emotionless. She either truly feels nothing or she's a very good actress.

When Travis is done speaking, he relinquishes the pulpit to Faye, who puts her face too close to the microphone to speak, causing feedback to startle everyone, a whoosh of unease moving through the room. Faye apologizes, moves her head back a few inches, and tries again. She thanks everyone for coming, agrees with what Travis has said, and then urges people to keep praying. "We can't give up on our girl," she finishes, her voice thick with unspent tears.

Up next, Scott, who doesn't look capable of murder. Of course, if capability were a deciding factor, half the people in prison wouldn't be there. You don't have to be capable of murdering someone all the time. You just have to be capable for the one moment it takes to lash out, to do something you can't take back.

Scott tells everyone how much he loves Annie, how hard the decision was to call off the wedding, and how he hopes they will get their chance to gather here in this church for the wedding "real soon." When he is done speaking, he flashes them a million-dollar smile, and Laurel thinks how lovely Annie and Scott's children would've been. She immediately feels bad for thinking in the past tense. But the longer this goes on, the more pessimistic she's becoming. She looks around at the pinched faces of the people gathered here—some familiar and some strange—and can tell she's not the only one who is losing hope.

Travis Dove takes the pulpit again, his face filled with a strange mix of sympathy and smugness as he scans the crowd with his hooded dark eyes. He has done this before; he is used to leading people through dark times. He knows he can do this and do it right. This is what he was born for, like Laurel was born for the news. It strikes her then, how they are both there to do their jobs, to carry on even as things are falling apart. This is what their respective callings require. She is filled with it, driven by it. And so is Travis Dove.

Beside her, Damon frames that look on Travis Dove's face with the camera lens, and she knows that he has seen it, too. She looks over at Damon, and he looks back at her, gives her the tiniest hint of a smile. In spite of the seriousness of the scene, Damon is joyous. Laurel realizes that the joy is coming from the camera in his hands. She looks away, pretends to scribble something important in the small notebook she brought along. But it is merely a prop. Later, she will write the story by simply replaying what she has seen, like someone watching a movie.

Travis has just begun to pray for Annie's safe and speedy return when the rear door of the church swings wide and a group of cops enter, with Hal York in the lead. A ripple of fear runs through the crowd as people register what is going on. Why would the police interrupt the vigil if not for an urgent reason? Travis stops praying and leaves the pulpit to meet the officers in the aisle, like a bouncer assessing the credentials of the people trying to get into the club. The men confer, and then Travis nods, gestures to Faye, and steps back so they can walk over to her. The sheriff is the first one to reach her, and everyone hears her start to cry as he puts his hand on her shoulder and begins to speak into her ear.

Kenny

As that pastor, Travis, the one who used to date Annie's cousin, drones on and on during the vigil, he catches people looking at him, then quickly looking away. Word has obviously gotten out that the police paid him a visit, that he was asked not to leave town. He knows this is only the beginning, that there will be more suspicion to come. He has lied more than once, and his mother always warned him that his lies would find him out.

He should not be here at the vigil. It was a bad idea to come. But he wanted to be where people who also love Annie are. And he didn't want to be alone with his thoughts anymore. Because they were bad thoughts, the kind of thoughts that can make someone go crazy if they think them too long. So when his mother asked if he would drive her to the vigil (apparently it was the place to be in Ludlow, South Carolina, on this fine summer evening), he said yes, not thinking about the looks he would get, not thinking about the questions his mom would ask about where his girlfriend is.

He lies to his mom, tells her his girlfriend is away on business, when really she has gone away to think about things. That's how she put it. He does not know if she will be back. No matter how much he tried to downplay who Annie was to him, she somehow sensed that there was more he was not telling her. He guesses it showed on his face. She says she feels she can no longer trust him; she will never understand why he kept Annie from her. He told her he cannot give her a good reason, and that is the truth. The only reason he might offer is that Annie is his; she is not something he can share with anyone. But that would not sound right if he said it out loud.

So he remained silent while she ranted until eventually she ran out of things to say. She took her packed bag that was intended for their trip, put it in her car, and drove away. It occurred to him that he should be concerned for her, driving when she was so upset, but he just stood and stared at the door she'd slammed behind her, the same door the cops came to just a few hours before. He stood there until his legs began to ache and he had to sit down, a white noise whooshing in his head.

Now, sitting in the church as policemen enter, he feels like someone has turned a spotlight right on him. He feels people glancing his way, just for a moment, before their eyes dart away. They are gauging whether or not he has done something to Annie, whether he knows where she is. He can feel it as surely as someone feels warm sunshine or wet raindrops. He can sense their judgment, and he is used to this.

This is what it means for him to live here. He can claim he stayed for his mother, but the truth is he stayed for Annie. And he will remain here. Because he knows she will always come back. Back to the place where her mother died. Back to her home. It is smart to stay where she can always find him.

The only way he would ever leave is with her. He has been waiting for that moment his whole life, it seems—the one where Annie realizes she belongs with him. Everything else—his job, his mother, his girlfriend—has been filler. He closes his eyes, conjures up Annie's face. He has only ever lived for her. He knows how pathetic this is; he knows what people would think if they knew the depths of his devotion. But he cannot stop himself. Annie is the one. But now Annie is gone. And one of the policemen is walking toward him.

Clary

On the way into the church, Glynnis had stopped her, pulling her into a hug and rocking her back and forth like a child, her floral perfume enveloping them both like a cloud descending. "You poor thing," Glynnis intoned as they swayed together. "You poor, poor thing."

Behind Glynnis, her daughter, Laurel, had looked on, her eyes wide. Clary gave Laurel a small smile to let her know it was okay for Glynnis to be accosting her that way. Even if Glynnis's overwhelming perfume was likely going to give Clary a headache.

Glynnis had let go and turned to see the look on Laurel's face. "What?" she asked her daughter. "She's practically family. Our families go way back." She looked back at Clary. "I even knew your aunt Lydia, God rest her soul. She worked with me at our family's sporting goods store for a time."

"You? Worked?" Laurel had said, and though they have both left their teenage years behind and are now supposed to be adults, Clary couldn't help but chuckle as she walked away. Laurel sounded like a teenager talking to her mom. Clary knows at times she sounds that way with Faye as well. Her mother just has a way of bringing out the belligerent teen in her. She supposes that's the way it is with mothers and daughters.

She thinks of her own daughter, feels the pain of loss as she still does from time to time. She wonders if her daughter would think she was ridiculous or overbearing or bossy or fun. If she had kept her, if she had been the one to raise her. Clary takes her seat, avoiding eye contact with Travis, and spends the rest of the vigil trying to focus on her missing cousin. But her thoughts stubbornly return to her daughter, missing from her life. It is only when the back door of the church opens and Hal York and some of his men walk in that she sits up and pays attention.

She can tell from the look on Travis's face that he doesn't appreciate this interruption, busting in on his moment. She saw how he angled himself when he was praying so that Damon Collins could get a good shot of him up there, doing his thing. She sees how much he loves the spotlight, how in spite of this tragedy he is finding a way to shine.

This is what he would do if she told him. This is what she was trying to tell Annie in their last phone call. She'd tried to tell Annie about the day she almost told him about the baby, about what he'd said and why she'd changed her mind. But Annie just wouldn't listen. So they'd both gotten angry. And they'd said awful things. And now Clary can't take back what happened.

Clary watches as one of the policemen turns in her direction. Her heart pounds, but the officer walks right past her, stopping at the next row in front of that boy who used to hang around Annie all through school with a worshipful look on his face, the one Clary always said was weird. And Annie would say back, "Who're you calling weird?" and point to her newest piercing or her shocking choice of hair color.

The policeman makes a motion for the boy, who is now a man, to stand up and come with him, and the man, without a moment's pause, does. His face is impassive, as if he has gone to a place deep inside himself. Clary recalls his face when it was younger, wearing the same faraway expression as he stood in front of some nameless, faceless bully. She recalls Annie standing up to whoever it was, and then she hears Annie say his name as she pulls him away: "Kenny." That's his name, Clary remembers. Kenny Spacey. He was in love with Annie. But Annie was going to marry someone else. Now he's being led away by a cop. And Annie is missing.

Faye

She follows Hal out to his truck, composing herself as she walks. If he thinks she's falling apart, there's no way he will say yes. She needs to look like she can handle seeing Annie's car.

"I want to go with you," she says.

Scott, standing beside Hal, shifts his stance and looks down. She cannot tell if it is because he is uncomfortable with the situation at hand or uncomfortable around her specifically. It occurs to her that he hasn't spoken directly to her since that conversation they had back when they first realized Annie was really and truly missing. He has kept Tracy around him at all times, let Tracy do all the talking for him. She wonders if perhaps this is on purpose, if he is using Tracy as some sort of shield. But against what?

"That all right with you?" Hal asks Scott, who is basically being forced to go and open Annie's car. Since he has a key, it'll be easier and less damaging to any evidence to use the key to gain access. She knows all this, not from her years of being a cop's wife but from her years of being a cop's best friend.

Scott shrugs, and Faye wants to yell at Hal, *Why does he get a say?* but she maintains her composure, forces herself to smile as Hal opens the passenger door and motions for them both to get in. Scott shakes his head, points at Tracy, standing beside her nondescript sedan. "I've got a ride," Scott says.

"Then you'll need to follow me," Hal says. He steps out of the way to let Scott walk over to Tracy, then indicates that Faye should get in the passenger side of his truck. They ride away together, like it's the most natural thing in the world. Neither of them speaks as he drives to the spot where the car was found.

She makes up a scenario as they drive, the best possible outcome: Annie had a one-car accident while driving home, ran off the road, was confused and delirious, and wandered off. They will find her asleep in the woods somewhere near where her car was found. She will be taken to a hospital, have a recovery period, but be fine in the end. Faye tries to hang on to this hope, to ignore the voice of reality that asserts its dissent even as the optimistic side of her brain is trying to find a scrap of hope. These two sides of her always seem to be at war: reality versus possibility. She wishes that, just once, possibility would win.

They turn onto a dirt road that hardly warrants the name. It is really more of a path. The caravan of vehicles bounces along the ruts as they go deeper and deeper into the trees. Annie would never pull off the road out here willingly—no sensible woman would. But maybe she was meeting someone? Maybe Annie had a secret life no one knew about? A secret lover? A clandestine meeting, a spur-of-the-moment decision to run away? That would be better than involuntarily disappearing, right? But that is not like Annie. At least, Faye doesn't think it is.

The cars all come to a stop, and she sees Annie's SUV. Annie always kept it pristine, but now it is dirty, spotted with bird poop and covered in a fine yellow-brown dust. Scott gets out of Tracy's car at the same time that Hal gets out of his truck, as if they have synchronized their movements.

"Stay here," Hal commands, then walks away. Together, the two men approach the Honda CR-V, white with tan interior, with childproof locks and a sunroof and satellite radio and a remote trunk lock, keeping a safe distance from it. Other cops guard the perimeter with serious faces, protecting potential evidence inside from being compromised. She watches the scene and recalls when Annie came home with the car, whooping and hollering for Faye to come see "her baby."

At one point she teased Annie, "I don't know which you love more, Scott or that car."

"Shhh, don't tell him," Annie had teased back.

As Hal confers with Scott, Faye wonders if the cops will find any clues inside, if the car will bring them closer to finding Annie. The other officers join them, and they all turn toward the vehicle. She watches as Scott holds up the key fob and ceremoniously presses it.

"It's a family car," Annie had said the first time she drove it home and proudly showed it off. She called it her "Mom Mobile."

Faye expects that they will tell Scott to leave now that he did what they brought him here to do. But then she sees Hal talking to him, gesturing toward the rear of the car. She sees Scott look down at the key fob, still in his hand, and she knows what they are asking him to do now. She sees his pinched expression. She guesses they don't really need Scott any further—that this is just some cop trick to break Scott down. Hal must not have entirely dismissed him as a possible suspect.

She and Tracy must both figure out what's happening at the same time, because at that moment Tracy gets out of the car and runs to Scott's side. Faye finds herself sliding out of the truck as well. If Tracy can be there, then she can, too. As usual, Tracy speaks up on Scott's behalf. "I don't think it's a good idea for you to ask him to open that trunk," the girl says. She points at the car, her finger jabbing the humid air. "You have no idea what's in there."

"Well, we think Scott here might," Hal retorts. Scott looks afraid, and for a moment Faye wonders if he's afraid of being caught or afraid of what's in the trunk. She squints at the rear of the car, but with the tinted windows it's impossible to see what's inside. Around her, the cops maintain their safe distance, waiting, she knows, for the moment they can descend on that car.

Tracy turns to Scott. "You don't have to do this. And I don't think you should without a lawyer present—"

"Aw, come on," Hal interrupts, losing his cool. "We ain't got time for that. Do you want to find your friend or not?"

Tracy, indignant, gestures to the scene, to the abandoned car in the middle of the woods, to the muddy creek filled with stagnant water nearby, to the ring of stalwart officers. "This," she says, "is a crime scene. Who's to say that you're not going to use his presence here now as some sort of indication that he was present here before?" Faye thinks Tracy sounds like she's watched one too many true-crime shows.

Hal looks at Faye, realizing, seemingly for the first time, that she's there, too. She sees him start to tell her to get back in the truck but then decide against it. "Look," Hal says wearily. "I need that trunk open." He points at the rear of the car. "Because I need to see if Annie Taft is inside it. Possibly still alive. Possibly hearing all this, wishing you'd shut your damn mouth and let us get on with it." He turns back to Scott. "Hit the button, son," he says, turning his back on all of them and moving toward the car.

"Wait!" Tracy calls out.

They all turn around with a huff, out of patience with her now. Tracy holds up her phone, fiddles with it, then turns it around and begins to take a video of the scene.

"Okay, go ahead now," she calls out.

Faye has to admit, she would've never thought the girl had it in her. She can't wait to tell Annie about this just as soon as she sees her. They will laugh and laugh.

They all watch as the trunk hatch sails into the air, revealing its contents. They move in unison toward it, Scott included.

"No!" Tracy calls out to him to stay clear of the trunk.

Scott steps back and gives Faye a stricken look. The first officer to get there calls out, "Clear!"

Faye exhales the breath she was holding, relieved that her niece is not in that trunk. But at the very same time, the thought occurs to her: If she's not there, then where is she?

Clary

She goes back to the house, again, to wait for news, again. Though Faye has not come home since Hal walked her out of the church, this is what Clary has pieced together: Kenny Spacey has been taken in for questioning based on evidence of recent contact with Annie that he didn't share when the police first questioned him. And Annie's missing car was found in a wooded ravine near the park where Annie's mother was murdered.

A text pings on her phone: her mother. With Hal at the site where her car was found. She's not here.

Clary puts the phone back in her pocket, swallows the hope of a miracle—of Annie being somehow found alive. In the morning volunteers from the community are gathering to walk the wooded area where her car was found, to search for her. But until daylight, there is nothing they can do but wait. The police are searching Annie's car.

Clary gets up, passes through the house, out the back door, toward the dove shed. The four walls have been moving closer and closer with each passing hour. It is full dark now, and she wonders if they have brought lights out to where Annie's car is or if they've stopped searching it for now. She doesn't want them to stop, not until they find Annie and this is all over. She hears a voice a few feet away and realizes it is Travis, standing near the dove shed, talking on the phone, trying to get some privacy. The doves' cooing masks the sound of her creeping closer.

She knows she should step back inside, but she can't help but listen, picking up what's going on from his one-sided conversation. He is talking to Deandra. Clary understands from what he is saying that she is flying back to Florida, to their son, who they left with her mother. She is at the airport now. He says he loves her, tells her to keep praying for Annie, and hangs up.

Clary hurries back to the house and flattens herself against the wall, thinking that perhaps in the darkness he won't see her when he passes by. Her mother is not there, Scott and Tracy (of course she went with him) haven't returned from going to open the car for the police, and Travis's wife, she has just learned, isn't here. The officers who were there earlier have left. Somehow, in the crush of constant company, they have ended up alone.

She feels her mouth go dry as he stops in front of her. He turns to face her, and there is a flash of memory, the barest flicker, but it is so real it is as if it is happening here and now. She imagines his mouth against her neck, saying to her, "This place is boring; let's go find some trouble." She's always thought of that boy—the one in her memory—as a kind of ghost. And now he has materialized in front of her. The last time they were alone was when he told her he was going to become a pastor. He'd been called, he'd said. Then he'd leveled her with six words. "But you're not pastor's wife material." In that moment, the words in her mouth had died on her tongue, and to this day she's never spoken them. But Annie wants her to now.

She tries to think of something to say, something that will explain her presence there, outside, where he was talking privately on the phone. But before she can speak, he says, "I sent Deandra home." He shrugs, closes his eyes. From the floodlight on the back of the house, she can see him as clear as day.

He continues, "There's not going to be a wedding, so there was no sense in her staying. Our little boy is cutting some teeth, fussing a lot. He needs his mother. I thought about going home, but . . . I feel like

I'm needed here." He looks at her, and she wonders, does he think she needs him? Is he talking about her—or all of them?

"Did you hear about the car?" he asks. "That there's no sign of her?"

She nods, thinking of what Annie wanted her to tell him. The truth. The truth is always the right answer. Faye used to say that. But the truth is too far away now. And he is so scarily close. She wants to get away from him. She wants to turn around and run, but she is frozen against that wall. She wishes Annie were here. But if Annie were here, Annie would tell. She would open her mouth and tell about that time she surprised her in Charlotte after graduation. She would tell him what she saw. Which is why they had that fight. Because Clary can't afford for Annie to tell.

Travis speaks, interrupting her thoughts. "I prayed so hard."

"We all prayed," she says.

"I know, I know," he says. "We all did. I just thought—"

She hears it but doesn't believe what she has heard. "You just thought what?" She laughs, because it is just the confirmation she was looking for. If only Annie were there to witness it. *I was right!* she thinks.

"You thought that your prayers were *special*? That God hears you better? That if *you* prayed, He would have to do as you ask?"

Travis looks at her, stunned at being challenged, and she sees anger uncurl inside him, an anger that matches her own. She sees him again as the kid he was, remembers the angry boy who would ball up his fist and swing at anyone who threatened or teased him before he even thought about it, back before God got ahold of him. She sees now that the angry young man is still in there. She has just gotten a full glimpse of him, the boy who was once all hers. He is still in there. And she both hates and loves this knowledge.

She wishes that she could replace this man with that boy, in all his wildness, all his passion. Because it did not scare her; it thrilled her. She feels all his anger rise to the surface, anger at being called out, and she realizes that he has forgotten what it is to be challenged. His sheepish wife, his subservient staff, his stalwart followers—they do not challenge or question him. They make things happen for him. She knows what he has become. And she has protected their daughter from that.

Annie wanted her to tell him about that child's existence, the one she went to Charlotte to have, the one she kept secret and lied about. The child who is now living in a happy home, with two loving parents who waited years for her. She gets a letter every quarter updating her on their daughter's life—her friends, her favorites, her school. She also gets a picture of a beautiful little girl with dark hooded eyes and a wide, daring grin. Those letters are the highlight of Clary's life. She will not let him take that away from her. He took his love away a long time ago, but he left her with this one thing she could still do right. And she'd done the rightest thing she knew to do.

"I can't believe what you've become," she says.

He moves closer, leans his full weight onto the wall she is still flattened against. She feels his closeness, smells his skin. Though he is so different, he still smells like she remembers. He looks at her, and she sees his confusion, his brokenness, giving her a glimpse of himself she doubts he lets anyone else see, ever.

"I can't, either," he says. Then he walks away. She watches his back until he moves out from under the spotlight and disappears into the darkness.

Faye

When they leave the site where Annie's car was found, Faye tells Hal she wants to go to the salon rather than home.

"I'll pay bills or tidy up. I don't want to go back home. I just can't sit there anymore," she says.

"I understand," he says, and turns them back into town instead of away from it. She is glad they are in his truck and not in an obvious patrol car. Though everyone knows the sheriff's truck. It's not like they are incognito. They never have been, and that is the trouble.

As he drives, Hal keeps his eyes on the windshield, and she watches his profile. It has softened through the years; his eyes droop slightly at the edges now; his chin isn't nearly as taut. She's sure if someone were to stare at her, they would note similar changes. They have both grown older. She'd like to say they've also grown up. They've made good decisions ever since that one bad one when he took her to fetch her things from her ex, T. J. She'd been afraid, and he'd offered to go with her, to protect her, as a friend. They both knew it was more than that, but they'd lied to themselves and each other.

They began because she needed someone to hold her: she was staying in a town she'd never intended to live in, her marriage was ending, and she had no one save the two little girls clinging to her. But she didn't want to be clung to; she wanted to be held. Somehow he knew that just by looking at her. It was just the one time, on the way back from Virginia. They'd gotten two hotel rooms, but one of the two was never slept in. Since then, they've done everything they can not to hurt anybody. But look where it's gotten them.

He parks the truck and starts to open his door. She reaches out to stop him, out of habit. Each of them is careful to remind each other of the danger zones. Being alone at night is one of them. "I'll be fine by myself," she says, and opens her door. "You should go on home to your wife."

The dome light goes on, and in the starkness, she sees the lines beside his eyes, the creases beside his mouth. But none of that matters. This, she imagines, is what a lifelong marriage would be like. You look at the older version, but all you see is the person you fell in love with. Only without the guilt for feeling that way. She knows he sees her the same way because when he describes her, it is always as if she's the same young woman who came blowing into the police station all those years ago. He sees the earlier model, not the current one. It is a trick of love, she thinks. The best trick of all.

"I'm going to walk you in," he says. "With everything going on, I'm not going to let you go into a dark place alone."

She nods once and climbs out of the car. Together, they walk across the parking lot. She notices the shadows as she does, the places someone intending harm could hide. People say Ludlow is a safe town, but none of them is the sister of a girl who was murdered here. She is grateful for Hal's insistence on walking her in, his steady, formidable presence beside her as she unlocks the door. She fumbles with the keys, and he sees her hands are shaking. She feels his large hand cover hers.

"Give them to me," he says.

As he works the lock and opens the door, she asks a question that's been on her mind since he explained to her what was going on: they'd found Annie's car in a ravine near where Lydia died; they've brought in a friend of hers from high school who was, apparently, the last person to ever talk to her. "Do you think that kid did it?" she ventures.

"It's likely," he says.

"But why?" she asks. She feels tentative this time. The same things are happening with Annie that happened with Lydia—the last person known to be with her is the first person suspected. In Lydia's case, they never looked any further. Faye thinks of Cordell Lewis sitting in prison all those years, begging someone to believe him. And now someone finally has. And yet, history seems to be repeating itself: here we go again.

"He didn't tell us about seeing her the night she disappeared. We've got the proof on her phone, which was in her car. They were in communication that night; to what extent and what all transpired is what we're trying to figure out. We believe he's the one who drove her car and left it out there. We think—" He stops talking, and she feels her heart pick up speed in the space of the words he does not say.

She swallows. "You think what?"

He shifts on his feet and looks away. "We don't really know," he says.

"Don't lie to me!" she says, her own voice shrill in her ears. "Don't you dare start lying to me now!"

He steps toward her with his calm, concerned face, the same one he wore last night when he was reasoning with her about the reporters in her yard. "It's sensitive information is all. Not anything I want to share right yet."

She crosses her arms and raises her eyebrows as she stares at him, waiting.

He shifts under her gaze, opens his mouth, thinks better of it, closes it again. "Don't give me that look," he grouses. "You know I'll tell you just as soon as I can, Faye."

He reaches for her, pulls her to him, as much to stop her from staring as to make contact. She knows he isn't being sexual and, because of that, she allows him to do it. Because she trusts his intent, she lets herself believe that her intent is pure, too. She denies the flickers inside her that come with his touch, denies the deep need she has to be held by no one but him right now. She glances toward the front windows, to make sure the blinds are closed, before she allows herself to bury her face in his chest. They stand silent and still for a few minutes. She listens to the intimate sound of his heart beating inside his chest, the rhythm of his breathing.

The kiss happens before either of them can think better of it. By the time she does, things are already moving too fast to stop. Or, at least, that is what she will tell herself later. *Things just moved too fast. I couldn't stop it. It was fate.* Without letting her mind think about what's happening—all the rules they're breaking—she leads him to the spa chair, the one she told everyone she installed so she could expand her business and start offering facials. It wasn't a complete lie. She did start offering facials.

But mostly it was for this moment, in the hopes that one day this moment would come. How many times had she spied that spa chair in its place there at the back of the shop, looking innocuous, when she alone knew its real destiny? She'd ordered it because when the spa chair was reclined all the way back, it was wide enough and comfortable enough to make a decent makeshift bed for two people who had nowhere else to go.

Headlights swing into the parking lot, and they both freeze in the midst of undressing. She knows he is as scared of getting caught as she is, especially now with the investigation, with their lives intersecting all over again. The waters are muddier than ever. But the car is just turning around in the parking lot. When the shop goes dark again, Faye says it aloud for the first time, practicing it on him, her safe place, not caring if it breaks the mood, knowing that it won't.

"I think she's dead," she says, and her voice is clear and firm in the empty store.

His response is immediate. "Don't say that."

"What else could it be?" she challenges, moving as far away from him as she can get in that spa chair. "It's what you wouldn't say before."

She crosses her hands over her chest, aware of their mutual nakedness, aware that he is not hers to be naked with, that this is a theft of its own sort, as surely as the ones he investigates. And yet, at this point, she is helpless to abandon her crime.

It has been that way since Lydia's death. They grew close in the ensuing investigation; it was inevitable. Another cop—one who wasn't married—asked her out right in front of him, and she said yes, because she was lonely and because she'd just filed legal separation papers from her husband back in Virginia, a man she'd been afraid of, a man she'd unwittingly been able to escape from thanks to a single late-night phone call.

The next time Hal was alone with her, he'd asked her not to go out with that guy. She'd gotten angry. Asked, "Why in the hell not?" He'd wrapped his arms around her and held her close as his answer, and she'd understood why he didn't want her to see someone else. She'd thought she was the only one with these misplaced feelings. But that turned out not to be true.

But other than that one time in a roadside hotel somewhere between South Carolina and Virginia, they'd never crossed the line again. They told themselves it was just because of Lydia's case, that they would most likely drift apart once they weren't spending so much time together. But their feelings didn't end when the bars slammed shut behind Cordell Lewis. She'd raised her kids, and he'd raised his with his wife, Brenda. She'd even done Brenda's hair for years, learning that Brenda is a woman who is far more obsessed with her three daughters than she is with her husband.

Sometimes Faye tells herself that this is why Hal needs her, why he comes to her to talk, to troubleshoot, to gripe. Faye understands that he needs someone who will listen to him without bringing up his children. And she is that person. She'd supported his decision to run for sheriff; he'd encouraged her to buy the shop from her boss. They'd been friends; they'd observed the rules they'd made up on that long car ride home the morning after. They'd done a damn good job at denying themselves, if you asked her. And no one was ever the wiser.

But now, with Annie missing, she feels exposed, a beam shining on a lifetime of loving another woman's husband, of the lies she's told, all her sins catching up with her in one furious moment. She sees the way Travis Dove looks at her, as if he has special insight into the blackness of her heart. She fights the urge to confess it all to the boy pastor, even though he is not a priest, and she's never been inside a Catholic church. She's heard that confession is good for the soul. But the one person she truly should confess to has gone missing.

She's spent so much time telling this one story—the one about her being a saint who sacrificed everything to step in and rescue poor orphaned Annie—that she's started to believe it herself. She has believed it so much she's let Annie believe it, too. She's let Annie believe that Faye saved her, when it was the other way around. She wants the chance to tell Annie that, to tell the truth. She wants one more chance to set things right, but she fears now she will not get it. She begins to cry, at first a sniffle that quickly builds into a sob. Hal pulls her close, so close that they are aligned cheek to cheek, chest to chest, limb to limb. For once, there is nothing between them.

◆ ◆ ◆

His ringing phone awakens them both. Faye sits up with a jolt, fearing an angry Brenda is on the other end. His wife never says an accusing word about their relationship, never even hints at the possibility of his unfaithfulness. She trusts him implicitly, which makes Faye feel awful inside, especially when the woman is standing right in front of her face. Brenda York, former beauty queen, used to intimidate Faye. Respected and well liked around town, her reputation preceded her. At first, Faye couldn't imagine what Hal saw in her when Brenda had it all. But over time Faye realized that, while Brenda was sweet as pie, she wasn't very exciting. And Hal needed some excitement.

She listens to the conversation from Hal's end, determines it is not his wife looking for him but something about the case. Something serious. He ends the call and looks at her, his brow furrowed, and she knows that it's about Annie.

Please don't say she's dead, she thinks, even though just a few hours ago, she'd practiced saying it out loud to him.

"What?" she asks, and she can hear the panic in her voice. The shop is dark, but she can make out the familiar shapes: the row of hair dryers; the sinks where women rest slender necks on cold, hard porcelain; the three mirrors and chairs where she and two other stylists stand just about all day long. This is the place where beauty happens, she thinks. Mirror, mirror on the wall, who's the fairest of them all?

"There's trouble over at Cordell's," he says. "A group of men showed up there, looking for Annie. They're convinced he's got her. His sister called the police because they won't leave. They're mostly just drunks and probably harmless, but I better get over there." He looks at Faye, making sure she understands what he's saying. She nods, the last vestiges of sleep vanishing with her understanding.

"You don't think he really does, do you?" she asks. It's a hopeful statement, but her voice comes out weak and uncertain. She clears her throat.

Hal shakes his head, his mouth a grim line. "Of course not. We did question him. He's got the best alibi around—his lawyer was with him during the time she went missing. And his sister, too." He pauses. "I wish he did." He presses his mouth to her cheek without any emotion behind it. He is already out the door in his mind, racing toward the unfolding scene at Cordell Lewis's house. She understands this about him. She would've made a good cop's wife. Too bad Brenda York held prior claim.

"Also," he continues, "the Spacey kid?" He lifts his eyebrows to make sure she's tracking with him.

She nods.

"I probably shouldn't tell you this, but they've checked the cell towers. It looks like Annie was at or near his residence the night she went missing. That's why they took him in tonight at the vigil." He pauses. "I figured you were dying to ask."

"And I figured you'd tell me when you could."

Faye feels her heart rate pick up speed thinking of Annie's lie about spending the night at Tracy's. Faye has racked her brain to recall Kenny Spacey. All she can come up with is a fuzzy memory of a fifteen-year-old boy skulking around, his eyes only on Annie. Tall and thin, an inch of pale skin poking out of pants he'd outgrown. She recalls thinking the boy resembled a praying mantis with his large eyes set in his small face.

"You know that boy's in love with you, don't you?" she'd asked Annie.

"Oh, Aunt Faye," Annie would always respond, then wave her hand in the air like Kenny wasn't worth talking about.

"He gives me the creeps," Faye'd said. But she'd said it only once. Maybe she should've said it more.

Hal starts to get up and winces. They fell asleep tangled up in this stupid chair. They're too old to be doing such things. They are not the younger versions of themselves. Never has she been more aware of that than in the midst of all this. She fears that in the years to come, they will not so much outgrow each other, or grow apart, but that they will just grow old, with less energy to pursue a friendship that can never be anything more. Just keeping up with regular, everyday life is hard enough.

And yet, she cannot imagine her life without him in it. She has wrestled with their unconventional arrangement long enough to come to terms with it. She loves him and knows he loves her, too. He loves her in ways he cannot love his wife, though she knows he loves his wife as well. She wishes she were his wife, that it could be that simple. But it has never been simple with them, from the moment she walked into that station and found him there holding her niece. Back then, Annie had been the one unwilling to let him go, and now it's her.

She, too, makes that first move to stand and pays for it. She moans as she reaches for her clothing. They do not watch each other put on their clothes, an unspoken agreement not to witness each other changing back into who they were before he walked her inside the salon. She has grown so adept at treating him just like anyone else, at cramming all her feelings into bite-size bits of time. This, she thinks, is no way to live. But she doesn't have time to think about that now.

Hal looks at the chair for a moment, an amused expression on his face.

She rolls her eyes. "Don't go getting all impressed with yourself. This doesn't change a thing," she says to him, even though of course it is a lie. After decades of erecting boundaries, one night has torn them down.

"I was just thinking how glad I am that you've got this chair in here. It came in handy tonight."

She blushes and gives him a demure look.

"What?" he goads, a playful grin giving away how pleased he is with himself.

She shrugs. "It's possible I've thought of it before. That the chair would be good for, well, you know, if the situation ever . . . presented itself."

He raises his eyebrows as his grin grows wider. "You did, huh?"

She cocks her head and gives him the smallest of smiles, all she will allow herself under the circumstances. "Maybe," she says.

"I promise I won't let it go to my head," he says.

"Liar," she retorts.

And then, just as soon as the moment comes, it's gone. They remember who they are, where they are, and what's happening. In unison, they silently sink back down into the chair and lean into each other, their breathing synchronizing as they collect themselves. It happened, but it is not all that happened. It's not even close to the most important thing.

She is the one to turn the conversation back around. "You'd better get a move on."

Hal leans forward and nods. He has a bald spot on the back of his head, the tiniest spot—barely noticeable unless you really look. She has seen it spread to the size of a half dollar in the time she has known him, a slow, gradual loss that he seems unaware of. She wonders if the hole will grow any larger, if she will be around to see it, or if one day she will run into him in the grocery store. He will be picking up extra buns for hamburgers; she will be buying a microwave meal for one. They will chat, keeping everything light and on the surface in case people are watching, like they've grown adept at doing. Then he will walk away, and she will turn to get one last look. She will notice it then. She will see that the spot has grown as big as a man's clenched fist.

He kisses the top of her head, already lost to her, already mentally in his car and headed toward the situation at hand. She doesn't mind this. She has grown used to it. He rises, and she hears vertebrae crack in protest as he does.

"I'll call you later," he says.

She nods, but before he can walk away, she grabs his hand to stop him. He turns, surprise on his face. She does not usually stop him from leaving. This, too, has been their unspoken agreement: they are free to go at any time, free to live their other lives. Though, it occurs to her, she doesn't have as much of an "other life" as he does. He has his wife and his daughters, one of whom just had her first child. He is a grandfather now. (He shows her pictures of the little boy almost every time she sees him; she pretends to be interested.)

Faye, on the other hand, has a life that seems to dwindle a little more each year. Her family shrinks instead of grows. She does not have a significant other, a life partner, or whatever it is they're calling it these days. She has no one to love but Hal. And this doesn't seem right. Her life, in this assessment, falls far short of how she'd like to describe it. She can feel something shift in the air, something that feels dark and threatening. She does not think he can feel it, though, and she doesn't tell him.

All she says is, "Don't give up on her." She doesn't bother to hide the desperation in her voice. She cannot hide things from him anyway. He knows her too well. He doesn't answer her; he only walks away, and she watches him go. In the dark room, she cannot see the bald spot on the back of his head, but she knows it is there.

Kenny

A cop comes into the interview room and awakens him from a fitful sleep, his head resting on his folded arms on the table, like he used to do in school. He is dreaming of Annie walking with him by the river, her hand resting in the crook of his elbow, her head on his shoulder. He wakes in a panic and, disoriented, looks to his left, at the spot where his girlfriend would be sleeping if he were at home in his bed. But of course he's not, and even if he were, his girlfriend wouldn't be there. He really should train himself to sleep right smack in the middle of the bed, he thinks as the cop takes a seat in front of him and pushes a Coke in his direction. Maybe he will grow accustomed to her absence faster that way. His mind will come to terms with the fact that she's gone.

She'd sent him a text after she took her bag and left, saying that she's still deciding what to do, that she needs more time. But he knows this is a kindness. She is letting him down gently. She will keep needing more time and more time, until eventually they both just give up. She will move on, but he isn't sure he will. She is the first girl other than Annie who he has truly cared about. She made him believe there could be life after Annie. He'd grown hopeful during his time with her, optimistic, which is not his nature. What is it they say about being a fool for love? Yes, love has made him foolish. More than once.

There is no life after Annie. He has known this all along, he supposes. He has known it from that first conversation he ever had with her, back in middle school, when the pretty girl stood up for the weird boy, and a friendship was formed. He was lost to her in that moment, terminally lost, in a way that ruined him. But he doesn't want to think about that now. It is all too sad to think about. Now he has to say whatever is necessary to get the hell out of here.

The cop cracks open his own can of Coke, the noise loud in the tiny enclosed room. Kenny forces himself to take a nice, controlled sip of the can in front of him, willing himself to stay calm, to *appear* calm. But he hates cops. He has ever since he was in tenth grade and got framed for shoplifting by some guys who pretended to be his friends, invited him to the mall in Greenville, then made it look like he'd stolen things when it was them who did it. "Hey, hold this bag," they'd said, and, gullibly, he'd taken the bag from their hands so that when the cops arrived, it was him holding the stolen goods, not them.

The cops had believed those guys, of course, because they'd come from good homes; they'd had rich fathers. What did they need to steal for? Kenny's own father was gone, his mom was poor, and he was stupid enough to think that they'd liked him, that he'd finally had some real friends. The next day at school, they'd started calling him a thief, and they would've kept on calling him that for the rest of high school had Annie not intervened. Annie was always saving his ass. But Annie isn't here now.

Another cop comes in and sits beside the guy who handed him the Coke. This one wastes no time in getting to the point. "Mr. Spacey, we've got a few questions for you." His mute partner just sits beside him, the silent, supportive type.

He squints at the two of them, Tweedledee and Tweedledum. "Are you arresting me for something?" he asks.

The chatty one answers with a smirk. "Should we be arresting you for something?"

"No," he responds. "But you've kept me in here for hours, and I haven't gotten my phone call," he says. He looks at his watch. It is the middle of the night. He'd been hustled out of the church service hours earlier. "And I can't very well rouse my attorney at this hour." He is bluffing. He doesn't have an attorney, doesn't even have the faintest idea who to call. He should've called and set something up, just for safety's sake, after the first time the cops came by. He is kicking himself now that he didn't. He keeps up with his bluff. "I won't answer any questions without my attorney present."

He knows how this works: if you refuse to answer questions, you look guilty. If you hire an attorney, you look guilty. Yet people who voluntarily and freely talk to police often regret it later. The officer, momentarily beaten, stands. "Then we'll let you work on getting in touch with your attorney. Once he gets here—"

"Or *she*," Kenny interjects, just to be an ass.

The guy rolls his eyes, amends himself. "Once he or *she* gets here, the four of us will sit down and have ourselves a nice little chat." Kenny has never heard the word *chat* sound so menacing.

The cops leave the room—they are in plain clothes, so he thinks they must be detectives. As the door closes behind them, Kenny fears asking for an attorney, instead of freely answering questions, has just made him look guiltier. But he can guess what they've found, what they will ask him about. And he knows that his answers will not satisfy them. He knows that once they start asking questions, he will likely not leave this station, unless it is to be transported to the courthouse or prison. He has lived in this town long enough to know the way things work. When people see him, they automatically smell smoke. It stings their noses, fills their heads. What these cops have discovered is enough to give off the spark they've been waiting for since the day he arrived in this town.

Faye

She arrives home to find Travis sitting motionless on her couch, clutching his phone as he stares straight ahead. There is no sign of Clary or Tracy or Scott. She doesn't want to ask Travis about Clary. And she got a message from Tracy saying she and Scott were going to a bar for a much-needed drink after the police made him open Annie's car. But if they'd just had one drink, they would be back by now. *Lord knows what those two are up to.* Faye is not comfortable with it, especially if it's going on in her house. But what right does she have to say anything after what she and Hal just did? She should ask Travis where that reference is in the Bible about people without sin casting the first stone. She would bet he knows right where it is, chapter and verse.

But this is what she knows—tragedy brings out the best and the worst in people. The state of suspended reality that comes with a time of tragedy can make people believe that nothing they do right now counts. There is a freedom that comes with that feeling, a pass to do anything you want, damn the consequences. So she will keep her mouth shut about Tracy and Scott, if for no other reason than she hates hypocrites and doesn't intend to start being one tonight.

Travis, blessedly, doesn't ask where she's been or what she's been doing out at this hour. He simply nods and looks back at the phone in his hand. She doesn't understand why he is here, why he doesn't just go to his hotel or even home. She wonders how long he intends to stay, why he's staying at all.

He isn't their pastor; he owes them nothing. He came up here to officiate a wedding, and the wedding is off. He should go back to his megachurch, his loving wife, his adoring fans. And yet he's sitting in the dark in the wee hours of the morning on her couch, looking pensive and lost. It is the lost look that gives her pause, that keeps her from just heading to her room and her bed like she wants. "You okay?" she asks him.

He looks up from his phone, startled. He blinks a few times. "Wh-what?"

"You look upset. I mean, well, of course you're upset—we all are. I just wanted to make sure there wasn't something I could do to . . . help." She doesn't know what she is saying. She is too tired to make much sense. She regrets opening her mouth at all.

Travis presses his lips together in an almost smile and cocks his head. "You're asking me if there's something you can do for me. When I should be asking you that," he says. She watches as he slips into his pastor persona like someone else would slip on a pair of sunglasses. She wishes she could stop him, tell him he doesn't have to do that for her, remind him that she knew him long before he became the person he is now. But she doesn't.

She senses the past is territory Travis doesn't venture into at all if he can help it. She can't blame him. His past isn't exactly compatible with his present. She recalls finding him on her doorstep passed-out drunk one time, vomit on his shirt and her daughter's name on his lips. She recalls the numerous times she was called to the school or to the police station to retrieve Clary, caught doing something crazy with Travis, the two of them intent on rattling the cage of youth every chance they got.

Faye hasn't thought about that Clary—her wild child—in so long. She's become used to the current version, the one who came back from Charlotte, where she went to nurse her wounds after Travis ended things. She'd wanted to escape the reminders of Travis at every turn in

Ludlow, so she'd gone to the closest big city, found a job and a place to live. Though she'd missed her, Faye had understood. Clary had come back from Charlotte different. Faye had attributed it to her growing up, maturing. But she wonders now if perhaps it was something else. She'd been so relieved to have Clary back she hadn't pushed her on anything, afraid that if she did, Clary would leave again. But now she wonders if maybe she should've pushed harder.

"I guess it's weird, being back here," she says to Travis, because she can't think of anything else to say.

"Yeah, I don't get back often enough. So much going on with the church and stuff. And with my parents gone, there's just never really a reason."

"I was sorry to hear about both of them."

"Yeah," he says. "After my mom died, Dad lost the will to live. You hear about that happening, but I'd never seen it for myself. It was like he just faded away." Travis looks wistful for a moment. "I guess I never realized how much he loved her till then. I just remember all the fights." He shrugs. "So it was nice, even though it was hard, to know that he really didn't want to live without her." Travis smiles proudly. "He died six months to the day after she did. And I'm happy to say I know where they both are now. They both got saved the year before." He nods. "Of all the things I've accomplished since I left here, I'm proudest of that."

"I heard they gave up drinking," she says.

"Yeah. Sometimes I wonder if that's not what killed them. Their bodies had gotten so used to the alcohol they didn't know how to operate without it." He looks at her. "Do you think that's possible?"

She gives him a small, sad smile. "I think anything's possible."

He smiles back, this time with his whole face, and she can see what draws people to him, what makes his followers want to buy what he's selling. "That's what the Bible says."

"Well, I hope it's possible that I'll get some sleep tonight," she says, and gives a little laugh to lighten the mood.

"Good night, Faye," Travis says. "I sure do appreciate the hospitality. If you ever get down to Florida, maybe I can return the favor."

"Sure thing," she says, giving him a little wave as she retreats to her room. She removes her shoes and crawls into bed without even taking off her clothes. She tucks the pillow under her head just so, pulls the covers to her chin, and closes her eyes, listening to the complete silence. She thinks of Hal leaving in a hurry, off to save Cordell Lewis from an angry mob. She wonders if he's thinking of her or if he's already put their tryst out of his mind. Hal is good at compartmentalizing. She closes her eyes again, trying not to think about Hal or Cordell Lewis or her lost niece, who sits at the center of all this.

She lost Annie once when she was little—just the one time, which she thinks is a pretty good track record. Throughout Annie's childhood, she felt Lydia there, watching her, judging her performance, rating her motherhood efforts. Lydia, the not-so-angelic angel on her shoulder, saying things like, "You sure that candy is a good idea? You don't want her to get a cavity, do you?" Or, "How could you forget to sign that paper? Now she's not going to be able to go on that field trip!" Or, "You lost my child? I trusted you with her, and you lost her?"

Things like that. Lydia, her annoying sister in life, could be just as annoying in death, if you got right down to it.

In her own defense, she'd turned her back for only a second. (Isn't that what they all say?) They'd been at the fair. Clary had tugged on her to go one way, and Annie had tugged on her to go the other. Clary wanted the carousel, and Annie wanted the Tilt-A-Whirl, the pair of them always pulling her in different directions, nearly splitting her in two in the process.

She'd turned to scold Clary (she always scolded Clary first, always more comfortable faulting her own child instead of her niece, making Annie the perpetual guest in her own home), and she'd dropped Annie's hand when she did. Clary had argued (Clary always argued), and after she had finished with Clary, she'd turned back to speak to Annie. But Annie was gone.

She can still recall what it felt like to look at the empty space beside her, then look past that space—to the right and to the left—to see swarms of people. To scream Annie's name as people gave her quizzical looks, to grasp Clary's hand so tightly that Clary cried out in pain. But she paid Clary no mind; she just called Annie's name louder, scanning the crowd. So many faces and none of them Annie's. All the while, she could feel Lydia on her shoulder, shaking her head in disappointment. Though Annie was missing for maybe three minutes (they found her— where else?—over by the Tilt-A-Whirl, where she'd wanted to go), it was the longest, most terrifying three minutes of her life.

And that is what it feels like all over again. Except three minutes has turned into three days, and she cannot shake the panic, or the fear, or the sense of failure. She has let her sister down, her poor dead sister who never got to live her life. The one thing she could do for her was to take care of her daughter. And she has failed at it.

She sighs, thinking that perhaps she should ask Travis to pray with her. Maybe that would calm her nerves. But she doesn't want to pray with Travis. She doesn't want to pray with anyone. She just wants to keep moving, keep busy, keep her mind off things as much as possible. Because thinking of Annie's disappearance is making her think of lots of other things, too—things she's spent the last twenty-three years telling herself to forget about.

She got to Ludlow and wrote herself a new story, one she could control, one that had a happy ending, even though it began in tragedy. She and the girls became a family, a phoenix rising from the ashes. They became synonymous with hope and triumph in the town, and that is just what she wanted. Though in those first few weeks, she kept telling herself she'd go back to Virginia, return to her marriage, do what was expected of her by the people back home. But when she looked at Annie, she couldn't imagine taking her away from all she knew. She couldn't imagine plunking the child down in a home that was growing increasingly volatile with a man who was growing increasingly dangerous.

This is the part she has told no one except Hal. When people tell her how good and kind she was to uproot her life to help Annie, she just smiles and says it was nothing. She lets people believe she was this altruistic, giving soul who put Annie above all else. She never told anyone that the same night she'd gotten the phone call, her husband had punched her in the stomach—he was always careful to hit her in places where bruises didn't show—so hard that she'd blacked out for a moment and woken up in a heap on the floor.

She doesn't remember now why he'd punched her. It could've been for no reason at all. It could've been because he had a bad day at work, and she didn't smile at him right when he walked in the door. She's never told anyone that, as she fell asleep that night, she'd been thinking of ways to kill him and get away with it. And she'd been serious about it.

Then the phone had rung on the bedside table, its ring piercing the silence, splitting her life in two: before and after. Her husband had fumbled for the phone, answered it with a gruff "Yeah?" Then sat straight up when the person on the other end identified themselves as a cop. That person—she knows now—was Hal York, a young beat cop desperate to find someone who'd come get this kid who'd attached herself to him like Velcro.

Her husband allowed her to go see to Annie—but with the expectation that she would bring Annie home once things were sorted. That's what she'd told him when she left: she would take Clary, go get Annie and Lydia's body, and bring them both back—Lydia to be buried and Annie to be raised. She hadn't even known that she was leaving him when she threw clothes in a bag, lifted a sleeping Clary into her booster seat, got into her ancient Honda Accord, and drove through the night to reach her traumatized niece. This was a mercy mission. It had taken years to admit to herself that the object of that mission was really herself.

And yet, when people started telling her how amazing she was, she'd soaked it up; she'd practically preened under their adoring gazes. In Ludlow, she became someone new, someone different. She wasn't T. J. Wilkins's wife; she wasn't her father's daughter. She was anyone she wanted to be. In Ludlow, she began to understand why Lydia hadn't returned after her husband died in that motorcycle accident. Lydia, she knew now, had reinvented herself. And so had Faye. The longer she stayed, the more she settled in, the more she saw the good that came with the tragedy of her sister's murder. It was just like people said—there was a silver lining: Lydia's death had given Faye a chance at a whole new life, apart from who she'd been, a ticket out of a marriage and a life she'd been miserable in.

She flourished there, as if Ludlow's soil were richer, more conducive for her growth than her hometown had been. She wasn't just a mediocre hairstylist in a two-bit salon, a girl who went to cosmetology school because her parents weren't rich enough to send her to college. In Ludlow, she became a business owner of one of the most popular salons in town. She'd joined the Chamber of Commerce for crying out loud. She was somebody—and not just somebody, an altruistic angel somebody. An extraordinary person.

As Annie grew up, she heard this from just about everyone. And Faye stood by and let that become her truth—hers and Annie's. She was someone who sacrificed for a child, who gave up everything to relocate and care for her so she didn't go through more trauma. Annie was beholden to Faye for what she'd done, to hear people tell it. The girl accepted this truth, Faye absorbed it, and it became who they were. It informed their dynamic. And here is what she knows: the more you think something, the more it becomes truth in your life—whether it's actually true or not.

You should be grateful, she'd said to Annie—in both words and actions—the child's whole life.

She pushes back the covers and rises from the bed, which is no refuge after all. Her thoughts follow her there as well as anywhere. She cannot escape them, and she cannot get away from the fear that she will never have a chance to set things right with Annie. She swings her feet to the ground and rests them there for a moment as sadness swoops down on her, like a hawk swoops down on a field mouse, overtaking her. She feels a heaviness fill her body. She will never get the chance to confess how wrong she has been to let Annie believe anything except that Faye benefited from their arrangement every bit as much as Annie did. Possibly even more.

Laurel

It is very late, and she and Damon are in the *Ledger*'s office working on the story about Annie's vigil, and all that happened there, when she hears the alert on the police scanner: Sheriff York has been summoned to Cordell Lewis's house. An angry mob is there, demanding he produce Annie, convinced he has taken her. There's a new angle to this ever-unfolding story, and no matter the hour, she must follow it. She grabs her purse and goes toward the door without a word to Damon, assuming he heard the scanner, too, that he knows exactly what she's doing. But she has assumed wrong, and Damon comes running after her.

"Hey! Hey!" he calls, his voice anxious.

She freezes as he catches up to her just before she reaches the door. They are so close she can see the faint traces of lines beside his eyes. They are the beginnings of what will be full-blown wrinkles one day. But right now, they are just the barest hints of a maturity that is coming. She can see in his eyes that he is tired. She still doesn't understand why he stayed to work with her. She's told him more than once that he doesn't have to. But he wanted to add his pictures to her story.

"I'm sorry I said that about us making a good team. I hope you didn't . . . read anything into it," he says, referring to something he said moments before she heard the scanner. He moves so that he is now standing in front of the door, blocking her exit, concern on his face. *He thinks,* she realizes, *I'm leaving because of what he said.*

"N-no," she answers. He is her boss. Her younger, spoiled, unde-serving, annoying boss. She hasn't read anything into the evening. They are working together. It's business. "I figured you just wanted to be in on this part of the process." She gives him her most sincere smile.

He nods. "When I was a kid, I loved taking photos. I used to say I wanted to be a photojournalist, tell an entire story with just one photo. A picture's worth a thousand words and all that. I said I wanted to travel all over the world. Ya know?" He shakes his head. "I forget who I'm talking to—you're the one who invented the dream."

"Invented the dream?" she asks.

He blanches, tries to recover, but fails. Caught, he sputters. "I-I mean, you're the one who was always talking about seeing the world, about being a journalist. You were the one who made it sound so excit-ing. I guess it rubbed off on me."

She gives him an amused expression. "Really? I never knew you cared two flips about what I said."

He nods. "Yeah. Of course. I thought you were the coolest, with all your big plans."

"Huh," she says. "And here I thought you were just an annoying pest."

"Ouch," he says.

She crosses her arms. "Do I need to catalog the various ways you tortured me? You were awful."

He holds his arms up like a man surrendering. "I had a huge crush on you, and I was immature. Didn't your mother ever tell you that's how boys act when they like you?"

She feels the conversation going sideways and hurries to rein it back in even as her mind processes what she just heard. Damon? Had a crush on her? When they were kids? This is news.

"Well, good thing we're not kids anymore," she quips, hoping it'll work. They look at each other, and a memory plays in her head from when they were fourteen and thirteen. They were at a party at the country club, in a group of kids all sitting around. There was a boy sitting beside Damon who Laurel thought was cute. She was hanging around Damon to be near him, hoping he would talk to her. A server brought out a tray of ice cream to the group of kids asking, "Who wants chocolate?" When Laurel raised her hand, Damon said, "Laurel, put your arm down," waving his hand in front of his nose as if she had BO. Everyone laughed as Laurel, red-faced, quickly lowered her arm and fled for the bathroom.

"Yeah," Damon says now, his voice gone softer. "Good thing." They look at each other again, and she decides to forgive him for being a little shit back then. But that is as far as she will go.

"And here we are," she says. "Look at us—both in the newspaper business."

He shakes his head. "Yeah. The newspaper business." He rolls his eyes. "I'm hardly a photojournalist."

"Well, I'm hardly an award-winning writer."

"Aren't we a pair?" he says. And they both give a half-hearted laugh. But then Damon's smile fades, and he starts talking again.

"When I was a senior at Clemson, my dad showed up one day and took me to lunch. I'd just won a photojournalism contest, and I thought he was there to congratulate me, to tell me he was proud. Instead he was there to set me straight." He deepens his voice in what she assumes is his impression of his father. "'Your mother and I both feel that you should come back to Ludlow after graduation and help out with the family business. I'll let you run the paper, but that's as far as this photography interest of yours can go. You're our only son, and I won't have you traipsing around the world like some nomad.'"

Damon is silent for a moment, and when he speaks again, it is in his normal voice. "I didn't fight him on it." He looks around the office as if he's surprised he's there. "I'm not sure why I didn't. But I didn't. I used my camera collection as decorations for my office and did exactly what he wanted."

He laughs, injecting a little levity to dispel his vulnerability. "Now I just try to keep the advertisers happy and make sure people still subscribe to our little paper." He rolls his eyes, and she gives a laugh to match his, to help them both out of this awkward moment. He claps her on the back. "'Course with your coverage of this story, I haven't had to worry about that recently."

His clap is a bit too forceful, but she isn't going to admit that to him. No sense showing weakness just because he has. She ignores the stinging sensation and forces a smile. She's had enough vulnerability for one night. Time to get back to business. "I'm going to go see what's going on at Cordell Lewis's house," she says.

"Cordell Lewis?" he asks. He must've been so focused on working that he hadn't heard the scanner. Her mother always says that men can't do two things at once, and this is proof.

"Yeah," she says. "Apparently there's an angry mob there demanding Annie."

"An angry *drunk* mob if I know this town," he says.

"Either way, it's a story."

She watches as Damon strolls back over to her desk where they were working and types for a moment, then looks up. "Okay," he says, "the story is filed. Let's go."

"Let's?" she asks, not saying the word *together* but thinking it.

He nods eagerly, grabs his phone, and grins at her. "Yeah, we'd better get going." He strides back over to her. "I'll even drive."

She makes a motion for him to follow her out the door, trusting that he will follow. And he does.

◆ ◆ ◆

By the time they arrive at the Lewis home, the sheriff is there, and the crowd has scattered. Hal York stands in the front yard, an imposing silhouette looking down at a couple of characters. Framed in the doorway, under his porch light, Cordell Lewis watches. The expression on his face is somewhere between fear and shame. Laurel wonders if he can ever hope to have a normal life in this town. She wonders if he is truly innocent in the disappearance of Annie Taft. The timing, anyone can admit, is suspect. Even if he didn't directly do it, she wonders if he could've arranged for someone else to do it.

They watch as the sheriff ushers the men into the back of his car, then briefly speaks to Cordell Lewis before leaving. Laurel cannot hear what he says, of course, but she can't help but wonder if he is apologizing on behalf of the town. She hopes so. Cordell Lewis goes inside, closes the door behind him. Sheriff York gets into his car and drives away. Laurel and Damon sit in silence for a moment before she speaks up. She is bone tired, but she's not ready to go home yet. There is something in her that does not want this night to end. Maybe it's the excitement of all that has happened; maybe it's that she and Damon are actually getting along. Whatever it is, she wants to stretch it out just a little longer.

"Wanna go see what's happening at Faye Wilkins's house?" she asks.

He gives her an inquisitive look. "Faye Wilkins? Why?"

She gives him a knowing smile. "Because something is always going on at her house."

He glances at the clock on the dashboard at the same moment that he turns the key in the ignition. "Faye Wilkins's house, huh?"

She nods.

"You're in luck," he says. "I just happen to know the way."

The clock reads 1:48 a.m. when they turn in to the cul-de-sac where Faye's house is located, the headlights sweeping across two figures embracing in the driveway. As they drive past, Laurel peers through the dark glass to get a better view. She makes a noise that is somewhere between a squeal and a shriek when she sees who it is. "Pull away! Pull away!" she says, and Damon guns the engine in a hasty retreat. Laurel looks back to see the two figures, separate now, scurrying up the sidewalk, heads tucked in shame, as they try to escape inside the house.

Damon drives for a bit, then pulls over and kills the engine. He looks over at her. "Was that . . . ?" he asks, his eyes wide.

She starts to laugh. She doesn't realize she is going to until the laughter bubbles out of her, a hysterical force that has been building inside her over these last few days, destined to emerge at an unspecified time in an undetermined way. It could've been a cry or a scream, but instead it is laughter. She covers her mouth to try to stop. She knows this is inappropriate. Not to mention unprofessional. Damon is the one who's supposed to be acting this way. Not her.

"I'm sorry," she says. "It's not funny." She closes her eyes to center herself. This is a missing person investigation. She is covering this story. Two people making out in a driveway is not a laughing matter, especially when those two people are the best friend and fiancé of the bride. But then the image of the two of them turning around in shock, their eyes round like cartoon characters, reenters her mind, and she starts laughing all over again.

Damon gives her a quick, sympathetic smile. He almost looks like he pities her. She is about to say something about how he of all people should not be judging *her* when their eyes meet, and his effort to keep a straight face fails. He starts to laugh, too. At first it's just a chuckle, followed by another chuckle, but he quickly lapses into an outburst of uncontrollable laughter. Every time they try to get it together, one of them looks at the other, and they collapse into hysterics again. It dawns on her, as they laugh, that she's not sure they even know what they're laughing at anymore. They're just laughing. By the time they collect themselves, her sides are hurting and her jaw muscles ache.

They are silent and still for a moment. When she looks over at him, Damon playfully shields his eyes. "Don't you dare try to get me going again," he says. He exhales. "Man, I haven't laughed like that in a long time." He scrunches up his shoulders and makes a mock-serious face. "Always working, being so busy and responsible. Being an adult."

"Yeah," she agrees, and rolls her eyes. She thinks about it for a moment. "It wasn't even that funny." She pictures their shocked faces one more time, the matching surprised looks frozen in place as the headlights exposed them. "Well," she amends, "it was funny. But not that funny."

He looks toward the roof of the car, thinking. "Eh, it was pretty funny. They were busted, and they knew it." He shakes his head. "Plus I think that we both needed to laugh. Things have been pretty . . . intense lately."

He looks at her, and something in her face makes him amend his statement. "I mean, with the case and all. The missing bride and the competing outlets wanting the story. You know, intense with that."

He stops talking and swallows, and even though it's fairly dark in the car, her vision has adjusted enough to see his eyes imploring her for reassurance that he hasn't crossed some line. A thousand thoughts swirl in her mind, mostly that she wishes she could just be out of this car and inside already, away from this moment in this dark car with the guy who used to be a pest but is now her boss but tonight has felt more like a friend.

She finds herself thinking about the small space between them, how easy it would be to lean forward and cross it. If one of them just moved even a few inches, the other could move, too, and then it would be them kissing like the couple they saw moments ago. It would be them acting on something that wouldn't happen in the light of day. It would be something wonderful and awful, wrong and right at the same time. It would be—

Headlights go past them, illuminating both their faces. She feels as though the thoughts she has been entertaining have been exposed and is suddenly self-conscious. She makes herself speak, and with the sound of her voice, her silly fantasy disappears, back to the recesses of her mind where it belongs. As the car goes past, she realizes it is the sheriff in his truck.

"Wow, this is a busy place tonight," she says, gesturing to the vehicle.

"Maybe something's going on," Damon says.

"Do you think . . . ," she begins, but she doesn't finish the thought, doesn't say, *They've found her*. She hates thinking it, can't bring herself to utter it. She's been constructing the happy ending in her mind every day since the moment she realized Annie was truly missing. She's prepared to write that story, the one that fits. Annie deserves a happy ending. Laurel can't imagine accepting anything less.

She is coming to understand a truth about journalism: no matter how much her mind wants to rush ahead to the resolution, she must wait for the rest of the story to emerge. To start writing the end before you know the middle will lead only to bitter disappointment. She has no control over any part of the story because, though she may be reporting it, she isn't the one writing it.

JUNE 1

Wedding Day

Laurel

She pauses at the edge of the area where the searchers have gathered. They are anxious to receive instructions and fan out to look for Annie. Laurel only half listens to what the sheriff is saying as she surveys the crowd. She is still bleary-eyed from her late night with Damon, but she couldn't miss covering this story. He has said he will catch up with her here after he's had a shower. She does not wait on him, though. There is work to be done. She knows the other news outlets will be here, too, and she is using her hometown advantage to coax some quotes out of Ludlow citizens. She's already off to a good start, getting input from Annie's childhood Sunday school teacher, an old friend from her Girl Scouts troop, and the boy who took Annie to the high school prom.

From the looks of things, the whole town has shown up for the search party. In spite of the reason for the gathering, the scene has the feel of an outdoor festival. Local restaurants have sent over doughnuts, biscuits, and coffee for the searchers. The police circulate within the crowd, watching, surmising, and conferring with one another, moving and pausing, moving and pausing. They are, she knows, keeping a lookout for anyone who seems suspicious. If Kenny Spacey isn't guilty, then there is a possibility that the person involved with Annie's disappearance could be here. Just across from her, Laurel can see several search and rescue dogs. Their handlers cinch their leashes tighter, to keep control.

She has heard they've already done some searching with the dogs and come up empty. But this is a very large, very wooded area, and Annie could be anywhere or nowhere. They are hoping that, with the extra man power, untrained though these people are, they can cover more ground. The sheriff has cautioned that just because Annie's car was found in the area doesn't mean she will be. And yet, there is anticipation in the air. The dogs tilt their snouts up and sniff, as if they can smell the anticipation, too.

A woman standing nearby catches Laurel's eye and gives her a tight smile, polite but tense. Laurel takes the overture as the opening she needs and walks over to the woman. "Hello," she says, giving her warmest, most reassuring smile. She extends her hand. "I'm Laurel Haines, and I'm a reporter with the *Ludlow Ledger*. I'd love to get a quote from you about the search. And, maybe, about Annie Taft. Do you know her?"

The woman's politeness turns to wariness. Instead of meeting Laurel's gaze, she scans the perimeter as if she's searching for the nearest exit. Not finding a way out, she stutters a response. "Oh—oh, I j-just . . ." She throws her hands up. "I just came because I felt bad for her, you know, and for the family." She lowers her hands and her voice. "I mean, they're supposed to be having a wedding today."

She pulls a miserable face, then rearranges her features to look merely sorrowful. "I don't know them or anything. I mean, I did go to Faye's shop to get my hair cut a few years ago, but that's as far as it goes." She shrugs. "I just wanted to do what I could to help."

She looks at Laurel, and her eyebrows go from two arches to one straight line of concern. "You didn't write anything down," she says. "Is that not what you wanted?" She looks like a student concerned about her test grade.

Laurel stifles a smile and taps her forehead with her index finger. "I'll remember it," she tells the woman.

For a moment, the woman forgets the seriousness of the situation and gives Laurel a relieved laugh. "Well, I'm glad you will, 'cause I have no idea what I just said."

Laurel pulls out her notepad, holds up her pen with an official stance. "Tell me your name so I'll be sure to get it right."

"Oh, well, I don't know if I want my name in the paper . . ." Her voice trails off as she looks around at her fellow townspeople. "I mean, it's not like I have any connection to the bride."

Laurel also surveys the crowd. The atmosphere has become more frenzied as more people have arrived. Some have brought their older children, who are happily stuffing their mouths with the doughnuts that have gone uneaten and are now glassy-eyed and hyper from the sugar. One of the search dogs rises up on his hind legs and paws at the air like a rearing stallion. *There are so many men here,* she thinks. And any one of them could be the man who took Annie. The sheriff grips the pistol on his hip and looks tense. At that moment, his eyes meet hers across the crowd of people, and he gives her a nod of recognition.

"I really should go," the woman says apologetically. Laurel can see her consider something. She holds up a finger. "You know who you should talk to . . ." She stops speaking as she scans the crowd again. She points surreptitiously and lowers her voice. "See that lady right over there?" She indicates a woman standing by the coffee table, holding an empty cup as she waits for her turn. Laurel could use a cup of coffee herself.

"Yes," Laurel says. "Who is she?"

"Her name is Sue Quinn. She was Annie's mother's best friend." She lowers her voice, which makes it hard for Laurel to hear her with all the noise. "You know about her mother, right?"

Laurel nods.

Nearby, a frazzled-looking mother runs through the crowd calling a boy's name. "Daniel!" the beleaguered woman hollers, her eyes darting to the right and left as she takes in the crowd, as if she is surprised to find them all there. Laurel watches for a moment as the woman runs over to Sheriff York, grips his arm, her face pleading. Something's up over there, she thinks. But she is not here to find a new story. Annie's story is national news. This is just another kid who wandered off. She turns back to her interview subject.

The woman hasn't even noticed that Laurel's attention momentarily strayed. She is too busy shaking her head at the misfortune that hangs over Annie Taft. "So sad," she says. "And now this." She sighs and looks heavenward.

Laurel needs to wrap up this particular interview. The search parties will soon head into the woods, and then her interview subjects will be harder to find. The woman looks back at Laurel, remembering herself. She raises her eyebrows. "Sue always maintained that they sent the wrong man to prison. She said the police were protecting someone, but no one would listen to her. She just gave up and shut up after a while. But I know she's happy about Cordell Lewis's release. The wheels of justice turned slowly, but they turned." She smiles and points at Laurel's notebook. "You can write that down if you want."

Obediently, Laurel does. When she looks up again, the woman has walked away, slipping beside a man who puts his arm around her protectively. She gives Laurel a little wave as if to say, *We're done talking now.* Laurel never got her name. But she did get another name: Sue Quinn. She'd read about Lydia's best friend in her research about the murder, tried to locate her to interview when she wrote the initial story about Cordell Lewis's release. But she'd had the name Susan Reed, not Sue Quinn. She must've gotten married, changed her name, tried to move on—move past—what happened to her best friend.

Laurel walks quickly, grateful that the coffee line is long. She slides in behind Sue Quinn and gives her the same disarming smile she gave the other woman. It worked before; maybe it will work now. But Sue only presses her lips into a thin line, giving her an obliging smile before she turns her back on Laurel.

Laurel waits a few seconds. Then says, "A great turnout today." She hopes that Sue Quinn will respond. But she doesn't. She tries again. "I wonder if they expected this many people."

Sue turns and scans Laurel's face with a dismissive glance. She shrugs in response to Laurel's question and turns her back again. Laurel musters up her courage and taps Sue on the shoulder. "Excuse me," she says, her voice hesitant. "You're not . . . Sue Quinn, are you?"

Sue looks over her shoulder and squints at Laurel. "I don't believe I know you, honey," she says.

"I tried to find you," Laurel says. It is not what she intended to say, but it's what comes out. Sue's eyes widen in confusion. She takes a step away. But now that it's out there, Laurel goes with it. She fumbles for an explanation. "I—I—wrote the article about Cordell Lewis's release a few days ago?" She extends her hand, gambling on the fact that Sue's good southern upbringing will oblige her to respond in kind. She's bet correctly. Sue grips her hand briefly, then lets go. "I'm Laurel Haines, a reporter for the *Ludlow Ledger*."

Sue Quinn nods, seemingly unfazed by the news that the woman she's speaking with is a reporter. "I know your people," Sue explains. "We go way back." Laurel wonders if perhaps she should've pressed her mother for more about what she remembers from when Lydia was murdered. But Glynnis claimed not to know anything at all.

Now Sue Quinn is standing in front of her. Laurel goes for broke, fudging on the next part. "In my research, I saw something that said you believed that Cordell Lewis wasn't guilty. I would've liked to get your feelings about his release," she says. She acts as if the story is over, no longer news, so it's just girls chatting after the fact.

Sue Quinn eyes her as if she is not sure if she can believe her. And Laurel sees in that moment that so much time has gone by and so much has changed that Sue simply doesn't care anymore.

"None of that matters anymore," Sue says. "Cordell might finally be free. But Annie is missing."

"Yes," Laurel finds herself agreeing.

It is Sue's turn in line, and she thrusts her cup under a nearly empty urn. Laurel helps her tip the urn forward to get the last of the coffee out. Sue thanks her and starts to walk away.

"Could I get a quote from you now?" Laurel takes a chance before Sue can disappear into the crowd. She hears the note of hope in her voice, how childish she sounds. But in the moment, she thinks, it doesn't matter. It is childish hope that has brought them all there. Innocent optimism that happy endings are still possible has drawn them all to these woods. They will holler Annie's name over and over, their voices startling animals and echoing off trees, hoping against hope that one of them will get a response.

Sue turns back. "A quote?" she asks, her eyebrows forming two matching arches over each eye. She is a beautiful woman. Laurel bets she was something else twenty-three years ago. She and Lydia were probably quite a pair, turning heads wherever they went. In her mind, she can picture them, pushing baby Annie in a stroller, pretending they don't see the men's glances as they talk and laugh, their heads inclined toward each other. The only thing that could distract the two of them, Laurel imagines, was Annie.

"About Annie," she says. "About the search."

Sue lowers her coffee cup. The steam does a little dance as it lifts toward the sky and dissipates into the air. Laurel waits, knowing not to rush her. But then a whistle blows, rushing them both. They turn in unison to the source of the whistle. The K-9 officer is waving that it's time to get into groups, to fan out, to look for Annie. Sue looks over her shoulder at Laurel.

Sue turns the coffee she waited so long for upside down, and the dark liquid spills over into the ground in a black stream. "Tell them that we came out for Annie today because we love her. Tragedy doesn't just happen to a person. It happens to a community. I think that's what you see today." She takes aim, chucks the cup into a nearby trash can, and gives Laurel a last look. "After Lydia died, we needed Annie to carry on. We needed to hope in her. And she became everything we needed her to be. We owe her this." She widens her eyes as if to say, *Do you understand?*

Laurel finds herself nodding even though she hasn't really been asked a question. She watches as Sue walks away. This time she does not call after her, does not ask for any clarification. With every day that passes, she understands this story a little more.

Clary

She watches as Travis leads the prayer for the search parties before they go their separate ways. He holds his hands up and out, palms facing down, as he invokes a blessing over all those searching, praying for safety, praying for vision, praying for a miracle. She has grown accustomed to his praying by now. It doesn't even seem odd anymore. This is who he is now. And she is who she is. Travis was right all those years ago: she is not pastor's wife material. They are two different people. They were, even then. She just didn't know it yet.

In some ways, it's as if they never knew each other at all. And, as fearful as she was of seeing him again, she is strangely at peace with it now. She wonders, if Annie had been here, pushing and urging, if things would've been different. For the barest moment, she is glad Annie has been gone; it has let her off the hook, allowed her to hang on to her precious secret. She is immediately seized by guilt at this thought.

"I'm sorry, Annie," she whispers.

Travis ends his prayer, and the crowd says, "Amen." Released, the volunteers all charge out in different directions. They are not giggling or chatting. They are somber and resolute. Which is, Clary thinks, the way it should be.

Hal York had asked the family to come and be visible, but he stressed that no one expected them to search. Clary, however, wants to walk, even for a little bit, so she tails after one of the groups. She wants to be a part of what is happening. She feels as though something is going to happen today. It is, after all, Annie's wedding day. Something *should* happen today.

Someone falls into step beside her, and she looks over to find Travis there. He sees her surprised expression and gives her a small, weak smile in return. "Mind if I walk with you?" he asks.

She shrugs. "Guess not."

They walk along in silence, both hanging back from the group of searchers. It is clear neither of them will walk very far. Soon one or the other will make an excuse to turn back. And yet they keep walking, going deeper and deeper into Eden Hill State Park, neither of them speaking yet neither of them making a move to leave. It is like when they used to see who could hold a lighter up to their skin the longest. Who would flinch, who would pull away.

They round a bend, and she sees the clearing, which stops her in her tracks. She has never approached it from this direction, so she is surprised they're upon it so fast. Travis looks to see what has caused this reaction, and she sees recognition dawn on him as he slowly places where they are. He turns to look at her. "Is this . . . ?"

She nods, her eyes round. Of course she knew that they were near it. She and Faye had even mused this morning about the connection between Annie's car being found near the place where her mother was murdered. Perhaps, the police theorized, Annie had gone there and fallen, or become ill, or been attacked by someone. People still went there from time to time, to see the place where the murder happened or on a dare to spend the night there. Town lore says the place is haunted. But it isn't haunted. Clary thinks that people, rather than places, are more likely to be haunted.

Travis stands quietly beside her, his eyes scanning the small area as if something—or someone—might be lurking in the woods. But she is not afraid. In her mind, she can clearly picture Lydia and little Annie, sitting outside their tent all those years ago. Clary envisions it as though she were watching a movie: it's a cool night, so Lydia keeps a blanket wrapped around their shoulders. Annie points up at the stars with a tiny finger as Lydia teaches her to make a wish. Annie wishes for a puppy. Lydia is about to make her own wish when they hear a twig break under someone's foot. The two of them look in the direction of the sound, their matching blue eyes wide as the figure comes toward them. Clary wishes she could see who it is. Is it someone Lydia invited? Or a stranger?

A thought occurs to her: maybe if she tells Travis, if she does what Annie wanted, Annie will return to them. She decides it is worth a try.

"Travis," she hears herself say, the saliva in her mouth congealing even as she tries to swallow it.

He looks back at her, and she sees that familiar fight-or-flight look he used to get whenever he felt threatened. "Yeah?" The word comes out strangled. *He knows,* she thinks. *He knows what I'm about to say.* She almost asks him if that's true, but instead she decides just to get it over with. She will say it; she will let the chips fall where they may, and when they return she will hear that Annie has been found. She's hurt maybe, but she's at the hospital. She will be okay. The fantasy forces Clary to keep talking.

"What if I told you there's something I need to tell you about, um, after we, um. Well, after you left." Smooth, she thinks.

He cocks his head at her. Gives her a small smile that she recognizes instantly. It was his get-out-of-trouble smile, the one he used to defuse situations he didn't want to be in. He holds her gaze for a beat, then says, "I'd say that was a very long time ago."

"Yes," she agrees.

"I'd say neither of us needs to go back there. Do we?"

"Annie seemed to think so," she says quietly. She looks down at the ground, gathers her courage to say the next thing. The thing that will make Annie come back. As she does, she recalls what she said to Annie on the phone that last time.

"If I tell him, you know what he'll do. He'll find her. He will prevail upon her parents to let him have a part in her life. And they will go along with it because they are good people. He'll make them believe they're helping people. In a few months, or years, or whatever, he'll convince them to get onstage with him and introduce her to the world. He will turn this into some heartwarming story—maybe even write a book about it. You know what he does. He will make her his story. But she's not his story. She's her own story."

Clary looks up to find Travis watching her warily. The get-out-of-trouble smile is gone, and all that's left on his face is fear. Real fear. She waits for him to say, *Okay, go ahead.*

But instead, he tugs on her elbow. "Come on," he says. "Let's keep moving."

Stunned by his response, she almost goes along, falls into step beside him as if what just almost happened didn't happen at all. As if now that the moment has passed, they can go on with their lives. But something stops her. It is not that she wants to stay there in that place where her aunt was murdered and her cousin was orphaned—she doesn't. It's that she does not want to do what Travis expects. She does not want to go one step farther with him. In that moment, the one desire is simply stronger than the other.

"No," she says. "You go. I'll stay."

"Come on, Clary," he says. "I can't leave you here, of all places, at a time like this."

She digs her heels into the ground a little, staking her place. "I'll be fine," she says, and as she says it, she feels strangely happy. "You can go."

This time, it is her choice to stay behind. Just like it was her choice to have the baby without telling Travis. Annie says it was selfish of her. But she doesn't understand what Clary knew then and now. Burdened by his religion, he would've done "the right thing." He would've come back to Ludlow, married her, raised their little girl. He would've taken a job, shelved his calling, and ended up a bitter drunk like his father. He wouldn't go on to become a famous preacher. He wouldn't have more than a million Instagram followers.

Sometimes when Annie accepts the credit Travis gives her for where he is today, Clary wants to correct them both. But of course she doesn't. Because she knows she did what she did as much for herself as for Travis. She lied and said she didn't know the baby's father's identity. Then she'd gone off to Charlotte to handle things herself.

She'd taken every step possible to keep the pregnancy a secret. She'd lied to her mother and cousin, saying that, following the breakup, she just needed to get out of town for a bit. She'd lied about a job offer, when the "job" she'd found was to grow a baby for a couple who couldn't have one of their own. When she spoke to Annie or Faye, she'd made up stories about coworkers who didn't exist, repeated things she'd seen out in public as if they had happened to her. She'd made excuses not to visit during the later months, when she couldn't hide the pregnancy anymore. She'd lived with the adoptive parents, seen their lives firsthand, growing more and more certain as she did that she'd made the exact right choice for her daughter. For a few months, she'd been really happy. When Annie showed up for her surprise visit, she'd been angry at Clary's deception. She'd called her a coward, but Clary had never felt braver.

Their daughter's adoptive father loves her adoptive mother. He smiles whenever she walks into the room. That was how Clary chose them. From among the prospective parents she met with, he was the only one who reached over and took his wife's hand. Oh, several of the wives grasped their husband's hands. But this one reached for his wife's, and it was so natural Clary could tell it happened all the time. For a girl who'd just been rejected by the boy she'd loved all of her short life, that one small action said everything she needed to know.

"Seriously, I want to stay here," she says now. "You can go." She smiles at him with the same encouraging smile she gives her doves when she opens the basket at a release, a smile that says what she couldn't confidently say to Travis when she was eighteen years old. But now, she realizes, she can: *It's okay to go. I'm releasing you. You are free to fly.* This time when he walks away, she doesn't watch him fade out of sight. She turns her back to look at something else, something different.

◆　◆　◆

She is walking alone through the park back to her car when her phone rings, startling her. She stops and fishes it out of her back pocket to see who is calling. An unfamiliar number is on the screen. She almost doesn't answer, but with everything going on, she decides she'd better. "Hello?"

"Is this Clary Wilkins?" an unfamiliar voice asks.

"Yes?"

"Do you own a dove banded with the number"—there is a pause and Clary holds her breath—"AVI 3214537?"

Mica. She's memorized that number by now. "Yes," she says, breathless with excitement. She stops walking and looks up to the sky. You let one thing go, and another thing comes. This time the tears don't just fill her eyes; they spill over onto her cheeks. "Did you find him?"

"We think so, ma'am. I'm at Eden Hill State Park. I need to ask you to come there, to the area where the bandstand is, and I can meet you there. Are you familiar with that area?"

"Yes," she manages to answer. "I'm actually headed there now. I'm . . . here for the search." Her stomach begins to churn, exhilaration being replaced by dread. This doesn't feel right.

The man on the other end doesn't seem fazed by this coincidence. It's as if he already knows. "Okay. I'll see you there."

"But I don't have a cage or anything for him. I need—" She starts to argue that she should go home first but then realizes that whoever it was has hung up. She walks faster toward the bandstand area where, just an hour ago, Travis prayed for a miracle.

When she arrives, the park ranger is waiting for her. She immediately recognizes him from high school but can't recall his name. She guesses it doesn't really matter. He waves her over, and she picks up her pace. When he greets her, it is with a familiarity that tells her he remembers her, too. But now is not the time for a reunion.

"Where is he?"

"This way. You good to walk?" he asks.

She nods and falls into step with him, though it is hard to keep pace with his long stride. They walk in silence, and she recalls the town gossip about him as they do: he was a football star who went to college but didn't have what it took to make it at that level. He lost his scholarship. Came home and was a drunk for a while. Then he found his way.

He stops suddenly. "Listen, I want to prepare you. The bird is pretty weak and starved." He turns to her and takes off his hat, holds it in front of his chest. She feels the sick feeling return. "We think it might be on top of an area of interest," he tells her. "But the police can't really investigate further until the bird is removed."

She stops caring about her bird; all she has heard is *area of interest*. Annie's car, she thinks. The search. The wedding that didn't happen today. She'd known something was going to happen today. But not this. She hadn't let herself think of this. Annie cannot be dead. She can't be. She would know, wouldn't she? She would feel her absence. But she hasn't felt a thing.

"It might not be her," she says aloud.

The park ranger, whose name, she recalls, is Chris, looks at her with deeply sympathetic eyes and, in an act of compassion, lies to her.

"We have no idea what it is," he says. "Right now we'd just like you to take the bird."

"Mica," she says.

"Mica?" He is confused. Annie said it was stupid that she named the birds. But things of value have names.

"He has some silver on his feathers," she explains. "The pattern reminded me of mica. You know, the rocks?"

He nods and picks up his pace. She follows suit.

"I used to collect rocks when I was a kid," she tells him.

"Yeah?" he says. "Me too."

They walk down a small hill and into a scene. Cops are everywhere. Crime tape cordons off the area. Chris walks her to the edge of a drop-off, and she peers down at what appears to be nothing but a deep growth of vegetation. There, sitting on top of a tangle of fern fronds and dead leaves and an overgrowth of kudzu vines, is Mica. She could swear that, weak as he is, he preens a bit when he sees her.

She crouches down as close to the edge of the drop-off as she can get. Behind her, the cops all step forward in unison, and someone says, "Be careful, ma'am."

Clary ignores them and extends her finger. "Hey there," she greets her lost dove. "Where have you been, fella? And how in heaven's name did you get all the way over here?"

Chris places a cage beside her, and she hopes Mica will go into it without too much of a fuss. They all wait wordlessly as Mica debates leaving his spot and coming to her. Clary can smell something foul snaking into the air. She notices that the K-9 handlers at the edge of the scene are holding back their dogs. Cadaver dogs. She wants to get out of here, and fast. She takes in the surroundings, trying to puzzle out how and why her bird could've ended up here. But there will be time for grappling with this irony later.

Beside her left foot, she spots something shiny and squints, at first in confusion, then in shock, as she realizes what it is. She starts to reach for it, but a man's voice behind her calls out, "Ma'am, I'm going to have to ask you not to touch anything."

"But—" She turns to another cop, who was at her house just yesterday drinking coffee and helping himself to a chicken salad sandwich. "It's mine." She points at the antique silver barrette that had been their grandmother's. Annie must've borrowed it from her again. This time Clary hadn't even noticed it was missing.

Faye

Hal doesn't come in person to tell her like she'd imagined it happening. He calls her right from the scene. She can hear people talking and dogs barking. It is so loud she can scarcely hear him. "Faye, are you there?" he shouts into the phone.

"I'm here," she says. She went to the search but left as soon as the parties headed out. She couldn't be there.

"Hang on," he says irritably. She hears the creaking sound of his gun holster moving in tandem with his stride as he walks away from the noise. It gets quieter.

Her cheeks are wet with tears she did not realize she was crying. "I was right," she says to him.

There is a pause. "Yes," he says. "We just found her. It looks like she was on a path and just stepped over the edge somehow, probably in the dark. It was raining hard that night—she probably slipped and fell down into some overgrowth below. It concealed her. That's why we couldn't see her. Which is why I'm calling. Clary wouldn't let anyone drive her home, and I want you to be looking out for her."

"Did Clary find her? Did she *see* her?" She can hear her voice rising into a panic.

"No," Hal rushes to assure her. "It was Clary's lost dove. Some kid saw the dove and went and got a wildlife officer. It was some kid who's apparently obsessed with birds, so he knew someone probably owned the dove. It was just sitting there, roosting on a branch that was covering her." He pauses. "Like it was guarding her." He is silent for a moment, and she listens to him exhale and inhale. "Without that dove, I'm not sure we would've found her."

"Okay, thank you," she says, her voice formal and reserved. Already she can feel this changing them. In the way that Lydia's death brought them together, Annie's death is pushing them apart. She lets this sink in, accepting it. Lydia was the beginning. Annie is the end. Even the best stories have to end sometime.

"So you don't think that boy you brought in did anything to her?"

"I think he knows more than he's telling. But I don't think he killed her, no. I think this was an accident."

"So are you going to let him go?" she asks. She does not want any more lives ruined. She wants, somehow, for them to all move on, to move forward. It will take a long, long time and a lot of healing, but Faye wants that to be possible. She thinks Annie would want that, too.

"I'd like to hear the truth from him first, but yes."

"I think he might've really loved her," Faye says. She is only guessing, based on a feeling. Her heart is a tight ball inside her chest, and someone is gripping it with all their might.

"We all did," Hal says, his voice thick with tears. Then he doesn't say anything at all.

"I'll let you get on with it," Faye says. And she doesn't know if she means the investigation or grieving Annie or his life. She supposes it doesn't matter.

Kenny

He has not slept, he has drunk far too many cups of coffee, and he is bleary-eyed. The walls of the small room they've kept him in are closing in. The cops rotate in and out, each trying to rattle him in a new and experimental way. One plays sympathetic. One plays tough. One hits him with the facts they have. He is the most interesting because he reveals what they have against him.

The cop tells him about the call records, the witness who says she saw the two of them together on that last walk. Kenny knows they have good reason for their suspicions; he's been waiting for this moment. He'd thought he would know what to say when the time came. But no words come, so he sits, mute, as the mouthy cop reveals, Kenny guesses, probably more than his supervisors would've wanted. But no one comes in to stop him.

He is debating telling them the whole story when a woman comes in the room and whispers in the cop's ear. Her face is a grim line, and it is as if she transfers her exact expression onto the cop's face when she speaks. He nudges his partner with his elbow; then they both stand and exit the room with no explanation. Kenny can feel that something significant has happened.

The cops leave him in the little room for a very long time. It is two o'clock on what was to have been Annie's wedding day. He paces back and forth, drums out a rhythm on the tabletop, drains the last of his cold coffee, and grimaces at the taste. They have provided him with pen and paper, but he doesn't dare write down what he is thinking, lest it be used against him later. He gets up and peers out of the tiny glass window in the door, tries the knob. Surprisingly, it turns. He is not locked in. He is free.

He steps out into the hall, looks to the right and left, prepared to use the classic and nonnegotiable "I have to go to the bathroom" if someone comes along to ask why he's standing in the hall. But no one comes along.

He walks into the lobby, thinking they will tackle him, but no one follows. The lobby is, in fact, empty. This is odd. When the cops brought him into the station earlier, he'd raised his eyes long enough to see someone at the reception desk, a few cops milling around, several people in the waiting room chairs. But now it is a ghost town. He stands there, feeling stupid for pausing, for giving them more time to figure out he is gone and hunt him down. He does not want to go back into that small, windowless room.

But he can sense something is wrong. So, like a character in a horror movie, his curiosity gets the better of him, driving him to turn around and go in search of where everyone has disappeared to. He turns and heads back in the direction he came from, his ears pricked for the sound of voices, or coffee brewing, or . . . something. But the station is deathly silent. He looks around for a camera that is recording his movements, wonders if somewhere the whole lot of them are gathered around, watching him search, and laughing. He is so used to people pranking him, poking fun at him, using him as the butt of a joke, he half expects it, even now.

He hears the sound of chair wheels rolling across the floor and moves toward the sound. His legs carry him to a room located behind the lobby, a room he hasn't ever seen. It is, he finds out when he rounds the corner, the squad room, and everyone in the station looks to be crammed into it. But they aren't milling around, making casual conversation or barking out orders or refilling their coffee cups. They are all frozen, speechless. Sheriff Hal York, who must've been speaking before, now stands silent at the front of the room, his head bowed.

When Kenny enters the room, their heads all swing around to look at him in unison, their faces a mixture of shock and confusion. For a moment, he wonders if the looks on their faces are for him. But then he hears a woman start to weep. She pushes past him as she exits the room, her hand on her mouth in a futile effort to stave back her sobs. One by one, they turn away from him, turn back to look at their desks, their coffee cups, their feet encased in utilitarian nondescript shoes, the kind worn by people who expect to be on their feet all day.

He is left blinking and scanning the room, wondering why no one has demanded to know why he's out walking around. He thinks maybe he should just turn and leave. But something keeps him rooted to this spot; something tells him to hold on to this moment, because it is a moment he will remember for the rest of his life. He feels a new fear, fresh and tight, in his throat.

The sheriff catches his eye, nods for him to come forward. Kenny nods back and goes to do so, but his feet are stuck to the floor. He cannot figure out how to unstick them. His brain commands his feet to rise, but they remain frozen in place. His mind knows what his feet do not: he must not go to the sheriff because the sheriff is going to tell him the worst bad thing. He sees Annie at the school dance in the eighth grade, refusing to smile because she doesn't want anyone to see her new braces. She thinks she looks ugly. He should've told her that nothing could make her ugly. That to him, she was—and is still—the most beautiful girl in the world. He should've been braver. And now it is too late. He knows this before the sheriff speaks a word.

Hal York calls out, "Whoa, whoa!" as he crosses the room toward Kenny with his long, loping stride. For a moment, Kenny cannot figure out why Sheriff York is telling him to "whoa," when he isn't moving at all. But then he realizes that, while his feet aren't moving, his body is. He sees the floor rising up to meet him. Only when it is too late does he try to put out his hands to catch his fall.

JUNE 2

One Day after the Wedding Day

Body of Missing Bride Found
By Laurel Haines, staff reporter

"This was absolutely not the outcome we wanted," said an emotional Sheriff Hal York upon relaying the news that the body of Annie Taft, a Ludlow bride reported missing on Wednesday, was found in a wooded area deep within Eden Hill State Park. Taft appears to have fallen to her death. Sheriff York has promised a full investigation into the circumstances surrounding her death.

Annie Taft was the only witness to the death of her mother, Lydia Taft, when she was just three years old. The three-year-old identified her mother's killer as Cordell Lewis, a family friend. Lewis served twenty-three years in prison for the murder but was recently released.

The town of Ludlow grieves with Taft's friends and loved ones, many of whom are still gathered in town for what was to have been her wedding ceremony. The *Ludlow Ledger* will provide funeral details as soon as they are released. We invite all citizens to pray for this family as they are again touched by unspeakable tragedy.

Faye

Now she must make "the arrangements." She and Clary are going to the funeral home in a bit. They are picking a casket, figuring out where to have the service, where to bury Annie. They must wait until her body is released and the investigation is over before they can bury her. She has begged Hal to be as expedient as possible, and he has promised he will move things along as fast as he can.

Faye simply cannot make it all work out in her mind: how they are planning a funeral when they are supposed to be recovering from a wedding. It is like a horrible, cruel joke that someone is playing on her. She keeps waiting for someone to say, *We were just kidding. Annie is fine. Of course she is.*

Annie, Annie, Annie, child of my heart. You cannot be gone. This is not right. Faye thinks this again and again, like a song stuck in her head.

Hal comes to tell her what happened to Annie. He brings the recording of Kenny giving his statement. They sit side by side on Faye's bed as they listen.

"Well, Mr. Spacey," Hal says. "You ready to give your statement?"

Faye hears Kenny's voice, still thick with tears after receiving the news that Annie is dead. "Yes, sir," he says. "I'm ready."

"You going to tell the truth now?" Hal asks; he has his cop voice on.

"And nothing but," says Kenny. She can hear the nerves in his voice. "So help me God."

"Well," Hal says, "let's hear your story."

"I met Annie Taft on the night of May twenty-eighth, because it was the last time we would be able to be alone before her wedding. We agreed that it would be the last time we would see each other, that we wouldn't see each other again after the wedding because it wouldn't be right, her being married and all." Kenny pauses, but no one says anything, so he continues.

"She wanted me to drive her new car, because she said that way she could always picture me sitting there, even when she was in Georgia and I was here. She said that way I could still be part of her new life. So I drove the car to Eden Hill State Park, because she wanted to go there."

Faye hears Hal's voice. "And she was in the car?"

"Yes, sir," Kenny responds.

"In the passenger seat?" Hal asks.

"That's right," Kenny says. "She was feeling sad about her mom not being there for her wedding, and she was also upset because she felt guilty about Cordell Lewis being in jail all those years. She said she knows now that he didn't do it. She said she wanted to go there—where her mother was killed—because she thought she would have a memory come to her if we did. She wanted to go at night because her mother was killed at night. She said that she had a suspicion, but she couldn't be sure yet."

"Did she say what the suspicion was?" Hal asks.

"No, she didn't. She said she wasn't ready to talk about it yet. Just that something had happened, and she'd had this feeling that it was tied to her mom. She wouldn't say any more. But she promised she'd tell me once she knew for sure."

"Okay," Hal says.

"I begged her not to go because it had started raining. But when she got like that, there was no stopping her. So, we get to Eden Hill, and we park in this out-of-the-way place she always parks in. She never wants anyone to see her car and figure out she's gone there. So she always hides her car."

"I didn't know that," Faye interjects.

Hal quickly stops the recording. "You didn't?"

"No. I mean, I knew that's where she went whenever she was upset, but I had no idea she took such precautions to keep it a secret."

Hal shrugs. "Maybe we all need our secrets," he mumbles before quickly pressing "Play."

"Once we parked, she was about to get out of the car, but I reached over and stopped her. I asked her to sit with me a minute and, well, I—" There is silence, but Faye can hear Kenny's ragged breathing. "I just went for broke, I guess you could say. I told her I was in love with her and I knew she loved me, too, and I wanted her to call off the wedding and let me take her to England, like we'd always talked about. I told her I'd do anything. I . . . begged."

There is another period of silence. Then Hal's voice says, quietly, "What'd she do?"

Faye hears Kenny take in a long, shuddering breath. "She told me she had no intention of calling off her wedding or of going with me to England. She told me that, yes, she loves me, but not like that. Not like a husband. And I said, well isn't that interesting, since we just did what husbands and wives do back at my apartment? And she said, 'Don't be gross,' and I said, 'I'm not being gross; I'm being factual.' And she said, 'Look, you were my first time'—I was, you know—'we were each other's first time, and because of that, you'll always be special. But, Kenny, surely you know I can't marry you. Back at your apartment? That was goodbye.'"

There is another pause. Faye hears Kenny sniff, hears his voice go funny. "I just lost it. I started screaming at her about how she was a selfish bitch and how she used me all these years and how I hated her and never wanted to see her again. Then she just jumped out of the car and ran off into the woods."

"And did you go after her?" Hal asks.

"Of course I did," Kenny says, "Though not right away, to be honest. I debated just leaving . . . but of course I couldn't do that." In his voice Faye can hear the raw devotion, the pure love. "By the time I got out of the car it was raining even harder. I ran after her, but it was dark, and I couldn't see a damn thing. I called her name again and again, but I'm not sure she could hear me calling on account of the pouring rain. I searched as best I could, but . . . I never found her. Finally, I just decided maybe she was hiding somewhere, waiting for me to leave. Then she'd come out, ya know?"

Hal's voice says, "Mm-hmm."

"So I left the keys in the front seat of her car, left it unlocked, and started walking home. I laid awake all night hoping she'd call, but she never did. Nothing the next day, either. And then my girlfriend came home, and I convinced myself that that was it, that it was over. She was done with me. We'd never see each other again. She'd get married, and we'd go on with our lives. And I'd keep my promise to never tell anyone. I didn't know she was missing until the cops showed up at my door."

Then there is a beat, and Kenny adds, "I swear on my mother's life."

"And that means a lot to you, does it?" Hal asks. "Your mother's life?"

Kenny's answer is barely audible. "Of course."

No one speaks, but Faye can hear papers rustling as the recorder plays on. Someone clears his throat. She opens her mouth to tell Hal to shut it off, that she's heard enough. But he holds up a hand and points at what is coming next. On cue, she hears a low, mournful keening noise, the kind of choked, strangled cry that can come only from the deepest part of someone's soul.

"It's my fault," Kenny says, the words one long, painful moan. He sobs for a few seconds more, then she can hear him working to compose himself.

Hal's voice says, "It was an accident, son."

"No," Kenny argues, drawing out the word in anguish. "She's dead because of me. If I'd gone and gotten help instead of giving up on her, maybe someone could've found her. Maybe she could've been saved. If I hadn't left her there. If I'd done something—anything—other than what I did."

"Turn it off," Faye says.

Hal does. "There was nothing else anyway. Just me trying to reassure him, then us taking care of the formalities."

"Is it his fault?" she asks, her voice raspy with grief. She can feel it again, that need to blame someone, to punish a guilty party. Anyone but the person who died. She'd wanted to punish someone for Lydia's death all those years ago, but what if Lydia had done something different? If she'd been wise and mature, not so impetuous and wild. She'd had no business camping alone with a three-year-old in the middle of the woods. And now, with Annie, who'd jumped out of a car and gone running off into the woods in the rainy darkness.

Accidents happen. Life goes sideways. And people get hurt. Her sister and her niece are both lost to her now, largely due to situations they put themselves in. Is Kenny to blame? Maybe in part. But Annie's insistence on their secret relationship put him in that impossible situation. And now he's going to have to live with the what-ifs for the rest of his life. The what-ifs and the loss. She and Kenny will have that in common, she supposes.

Hal stands to leave. He pulls her up, too, and holds her close before he goes. He kisses the top of her head, and her eyes dart toward her open bedroom door. He puts his finger under her chin, lifts her head until her eyes meet his. "Don't worry about that," he says.

"Someone could see," she says. And as she says it, she is so tired of those three words, words that have governed her life for far too long. She is tired of secrets, of hiding, of lying and denying. No more rules. She cannot do this with Hal anymore. She wants to live in the open, in the bright light of day. She wills him to say the right thing, to tell her he will stand up for her, that he will claim her.

But instead he just says, "No one will see." And she knows that he expects to go on being invisible with her. But Faye is tired of being invisible. She wants to be seen. She wants to belong somewhere, with someone. As it should be.

"You should go," she says.

He starts to argue, but something stops him. He nods once and leaves.

Clary sticks her head in the door as soon as he is gone. Her voice is quiet and weak when she says, "Mama?"

"Yes?" Faye responds.

"I saw Hal leave," Clary says, and swallows. She comes over to where Faye has flopped back onto the bed, sits in the spot Hal just occupied.

"Yeah, he had to get back to the station," Faye says. She knows how this must look to Clary, Hal back here in her bedroom, sitting on her bed. The intimacy of it must look strange no matter what the situation is. Policemen usually deliver news to victims in living rooms. "He played Kenny's statement for me," Faye says. "I don't think he was supposed to, but he . . . feels sorry for me, I guess."

Clary holds up her hand, a weary look on her face. "Mom," she says. "You can stop now."

"Stop . . . what?" she asks, her heart kicking hard against her rib cage.

Clary gives her a smirk, looking exactly like she did when she was a teenager and thought she knew better than Faye about just about everything. "I know." She thinks about it for a moment, looks upward, and smiles at someone who isn't there. "We knew."

"We?" Faye asks, though she knows what it means.

"You thought we had no idea. But we lived with you. We saw the way you looked at him, the way he found flimsy reasons to come by here. We used to laugh about it. We—" Clary's voice breaks, and Faye's hand goes out to her daughter, a reflex, like when she slams on the brakes and uses her hand as a human seat belt. It's funny, the things that come naturally.

She rubs Clary's back as Clary cries. She cries, too, both of them grieving Annie together. Annie, who is gone but not gone. Faye supposes she will have both Annie and Lydia on her shoulders now, one for each. She will carry them both with her.

Clary regains her composure and continues with what she was saying. "Annie and I figured it out." She swallows, looks Faye in the eye. "Together," she finishes, her voice steady this time.

Faye nods, doing her best to look properly chastised and penitent when what she really feels is an overwhelming sense of relief. She has not had time to let the implications flood in. That will come later, after the funeral, when there is time again for real life. Do the next thing. Isn't that what she's always done? It's gotten her this far. It will have to get her the rest of the way.

"I'm sorry if I wasn't a good role model," she says. "I let you down."

"You didn't let me down," Clary says. "You didn't let either of us down."

Faye gives her a skeptical look.

"You didn't!" she says. "We just felt sorry for you. That you love him so much and he's married. We just want you to be happy. Same as you always said for us."

Faye presses her lips together, gives Clary the thinnest of thin smiles. She looks at her daughter and sees life going on. She sees the circle of their lives—hers and Clary's with Annie—closing. They are skaters on a very large rink, making a figure eight, one circle complete, a new one taking shape.

"You ready?" Clary asks. "We should get going."

Faye attempts another smile and this time manages to get the corners of her mouth to turn up ever so slightly. She will be there for her daughter. She will do the next thing, the thing that is most needed at this present moment. She will make the arrangements to bury her niece next to her sister. She will help her child grieve, and she will grieve herself. She will close one circle and skate right into the next one. Because this is what she does. It is what she has always done, no matter how hard it is.

"I'm ready," she says.

JUNE 3

Two Days after the Wedding Day

Clary

On Monday afternoon, she goes to Miss Minnie's to drive her, just like she always does. Faye begs her not to, says no one expects her to do anything, that Glynnis can care for her own mother. But Clary needs to do this, needs to do something besides sit in their silent house now devoid of policemen and searchers, because there are no more searches to be done. Annie has been found, and everything has changed.

And so she goes to Miss Minnie's to hear the story she's heard a thousand times, to drive the same route she drives every day and distract her brain from thinking about what all this means. She goes to do something she can do because she doesn't know anything else to do.

Glynnis and Laurel are both there, clearly not expecting her when she knocks on the door, startling them as they sit at Minnie's kitchen table talking about who knows what. They both look at her like they've seen a ghost. Glynnis leaps to her feet and tut-tuts over Clary, asks after everyone but, mercifully, keeps it brief, shuttling Minnie off to the car and giving them a cheery wave as Clary shifts the car into reverse. Laurel hovers in the doorway of Minnie's house, watching. When she looks at Clary, there is a longing in her eyes, a hunger for a story. But the story has already been told.

Clary lowers the radio like Minnie likes, so that she can be heard. She expects Minnie to launch into the story about the time they hit the turnoff onto the main road, just like she always does. But Minnie remains silent. Clary looks over at her passenger, but the old lady is staring out her own window, watching the same roads she's traveled all her life, turned new every day by a mind that cannot hold a memory. And yet she holds just one.

Clary prompts her. "It was a perfect day," Clary says aloud, hoping that it will get Minnie going.

But Minnie is silent.

They round a curve, and she tries again. "Henry said, 'Let's go for a drive, Sugar.'" She thinks that if she feeds Miss Minnie a line, she will just pick up and go with it. For a frantic moment, she wonders if this, too, has been lost, if Minnie has lost her one remaining memory. Clary cannot take one more thing going wrong. She tries again with another standard from the story she knows by heart. "Family is the most important thing."

That does it. Miss Minnie turns from the window and gives her a smile. "It is, honey. It really is." Miss Minnie takes a good long breath, and Clary feels heartened, expectant. She knows that the old woman will tell her story, and they will drive their route. There is still one thing she can count on in this world. But what Miss Minnie says next is off script.

"It was because of my family that I told Henry he had to do it. He had to make that girl be quiet." Minnie continues looking out the window. Her voice is quiet but clear as she adds, "She was going to tell everyone about him and her."

Clary feels her blood run cold as she grips the steering wheel harder and tries to keep her foot steady on the gas, the car on the road. She glances over at Miss Minnie, expecting her to still be looking out her window, but instead she is looking directly at Clary with those cloudy eyes of hers.

"You favor her, you know. I've always thought that since the very first day you came here to drive me. And you kind of act like her, too. A little wild, a little different. She didn't have those tattoos like you do, but she was always doing crazy things with her hair and whatnot. She had a wild streak in her. The kind a man likes to think he can tame." Minnie cocks her head. "Has any man ever tried to tame you?"

Clary makes her face stay calm and emotionless as she stutters, "N-no."

Finding no good place to turn around, she executes a three-point turn in the middle of the road. She almost wishes a cop would come along and ask her what in the Sam Hill she's doing. Then she could get out of this car and away from this crazy old woman.

"He told me all about it that day," Minnie continues, seemingly oblivious that Clary has changed their route or that she is about to completely freak out. "He said, 'Let's go for a drive, Sugar.' And I had an idea why. I had suspected. He just up and confessed it all while we drove. Told me about that hussy we hired seducing him, causing him to stray. Said he had to get it out in the open because she was making threats about telling people. He said she had proof, that she could make real trouble for us. He said that he had to make it right, and he would do anything. He said *anything*, and he meant it.

"We drove right along this way, and it was a beautiful day. We talked about the kind of things that don't really matter in the end but you talk about anyway. Because at the time they seem like they need sayin'. Then we went to watch Neil's baseball game. And after the game, he dropped me at home and went to find her. She was camping that night, using equipment he gave to her out of our store. He said he knew right where she would be, and he would make sure it was over. Of course I didn't know what he meant by that. I found that out later."

Clary's heart is pounding so loudly and she is shaking so hard that she's afraid she will have some sort of attack and not make it back to the house where Glynnis is. She wills herself to just get there, to put Minnie out of the car so she can call Hal York, the man her mother loves, and tell him what she has just heard. She presses down on the accelerator, and the car picks up speed as Minnie shakes her head.

"Did you know she had her little girl with her that night? We were always so afraid that little girl would tell someone what she saw, that she would recognize him. But there was nothing we could do about it. It's not like we could harm that sweet child—not without further risk to us both. We had to just hope for the best. And then the best happened. That little girl told the police it was someone else who did it." There is silence. Then Minnie speaks again.

"She came to drive me the other day. Did you know that?"

Clary keeps her eyes on the road, forces her head to nod up and down.

"I told her that I knew who she was. But I don't think she knew what I meant." Minnie clucks her tongue. "Now that little girl is dead." She shakes her head. "Isn't that just a shame?" Minnie thinks about it for a few minutes, then turns back to look at Clary as they finally make it back to Minnie's driveway.

She throws the car into park and staggers out, away from Minnie's cataract stare, before falling on all fours into the strip of grass running along the drive. The smells of earth and grass waft up as the blades tickle her nose. She retches, then vomits as Glynnis comes running out of the house. "Oh, you poor dear," Glynnis hollers. "I shouldn't have let you take Mama today. I just knew it was too much."

Glynnis stands over Clary as she spits into the grass, talking as though nothing is happening. "Did Mama upset you? She said she had something to tell you. But I didn't pay it any mind. I just thought she'd tell you the same story she always does."

Glynnis wrings her hands and continues to babble on. "She's not been right ever since Annie came over here to drop off that handkerchief, if you want to know the truth. She just sits and worries that handkerchief to death. Then she saw on the news that Annie was dead and, well, she's just been more confused than ever. So don't pay her any mind—whatever she said. Okay?"

Glynnis glances over at Minnie, who is still sitting, unfazed, in Clary's front seat, then back at Clary, who is sitting up on her haunches, wishing for water. "You poor dear," she says to Clary. "Do you need anything?"

Clary nods, looks up at Glynnis, the afternoon sun a halo over her head. In the doorway of the house, Laurel watches, openmouthed. Clary wipes her mouth with the back of her hand. "I need you to call 911."

JUNE 8

ONE WEEK AFTER THE WEDDING DAY

Kenny

His girlfriend was actually Annie's idea. An idea he resisted for a long, long time. But once Annie accepted Scott's ring, he told her he was going to go for it. He'd worn the shirt he knew she liked when he told her this, the one she bought him for his birthday. She said it brought out the color of his eyes. He wanted Annie to see what she was losing when he told her about this girl he'd met, one he was interested in. And he was interested. That part wasn't a lie.

The girl who would become his girlfriend was pretty and kind and had a way of talking to him that reminded him ever so slightly of Annie. He was drawn to her—just not as much as he was drawn to Annie. But that ship had sailed, as the saying went. And he needed to move on. Just like Annie had told him to. He replayed those words in his head, in Annie's voice, so that she was always with him, even when she wasn't supposed to be.

When he told her about the girlfriend, he expected Annie to say all the things she usually said. Things about moving on and letting go and such. But instead, Annie started to cry. She cried until snot ran from her nose and tears poured from her eyes, and then she got up to go to the bathroom because she was embarrassed about the way she looked. But he thought she looked beautiful, and he told her so when she returned from the bathroom.

She started to cry again when he said that, and this time he got up to get her a tissue, but all he could find was a roll of paper towels, so he tore off a few and brought them back to her. She accepted them and blotted her face, looking mournful.

"I'm a coward," she said, her voice muffled by the paper towels. "I do everything everyone else expects of me and nothing I want to do."

"Well, what do you want to do?" he asked her.

"I don't know!" she screamed into her hands. And she began to cry all over again.

Sometimes he feels hurt down deep in his heart, but it's so deep he can just pretend it isn't there at all. He would have to be like a miner and go down where it is completely dark to find the hurt, to excavate it and bring it up to the light. Instead, he just lets the hurt stay where it is. And that is how he has learned not to let life kick his ass. That is how he has learned to live with his love for Annie. Annie who loves him but cannot be with him because she does not know what she wants. And because she does not know what she wants, she does what other people expect. She accepts Scott's ring, and she plans a big wedding, and she keeps trying to be The Girl Who Turned Out Good.

He has told her he would not pressure her to get married like Scott has. They can just live together. They can be best friends. And they can talk about things and share their wildest dreams when it's dark outside and it seems like it's just the two of them on the whole Earth and anything is possible. It can be like it's always been between them, but all the time. He tells her this, but she says no, that that's not the way life works, that there are some things he just doesn't understand.

"I wish I could outgrow you, like you outgrow eating Nerds or wearing overalls or going to the skating rink on Friday nights," Annie says.

But Annie does not outgrow him. She calls him when Scott is gone. She comes over when she gets lonely. She tells him that she is sorry, sorry, sorry for using him. But he just says, "Use me all you want," which makes her kiss him and ask how come he puts up with her.

266

"Because I love you," he tells her.

"I love you, too," she says back. But it is not enough. Sometimes love, Kenny has learned, is not enough. It was not enough for them to be together, and it was not enough to keep Annie here on Earth where he needs her.

There is a knock at the door, and for a moment, he feels that burst of euphoria that is her name resounding in his chest. It will be a long time before he doesn't think, *Maybe it's Annie!* when the phone rings or when there is an unexpected knock at his door. It might be for the rest of his life.

He shuffles over, hoping it's not more cops, wanting to ask more questions. He is tired of cops, and besides, there should be no more questions. Not for him anyway. They say it wasn't his fault. Everybody says that. For the first time ever in this town, he sees compassion and sympathy in people's eyes when they look at him. As much as he values their acceptance, it will be a long time before he can agree with any of them. He shouldn't have yelled at her, called her those names, driven her to run away from him.

But it isn't a cop. It's his girlfriend standing there, or the girl who used to be his girlfriend. She looks pretty and sad and a little afraid. He wonders if she is afraid of him or of what he will say. But he does not ask. He just gives her a little smile and says, "Good to see you." Because that is not a lie. She is a sight for sore eyes, as Annie used to say.

"Are you okay?" she asks. She points at his black eye, his busted lip.

"I fell," he says, and as he says it, he sees it again, the sheriff running across the room to try and stop his fall. He didn't get there in time, but he tried.

"But I'm fine," he adds quickly.

Of course he is not fine. He is miserable. But how can he tell her that he is miserable because the girl he loved most is dead? He has lost the great love of his life. And all the while, he'd let the girl standing in front of him believe she was that girl. It was wrong of him to do it; he sees that now. A thought occurs to him for the first time: it was wrong of Annie to ask him to.

"I heard about the girl the police were asking you about. Your . . . friend from high school?"

"Annie," he says, and her name hurts to say out loud.

"It's terrible what happened," she says.

"Yes," he agrees. She looks as awkward and nervous as he feels.

"I wish you'd told me about her," she says, and her words are not angry anymore, just sad.

"She asked me not to," he says. He feels the sharp sting of tears prick his eyes. He does not like to cry. It gives him a headache. He has not cried for Annie yet. He is afraid to start. But looking at the girl-friend's sad face, he wants to cry. He wants to cry over losing both of them. "Would you like to come in?" he asks, remembering his manners.

Sarah smiles, nods. He steps back and holds out his arm, the universal sign of *come in, you are welcome here.* But she does not see it as such. Instead, she sees it as the overture of a hug. And so she hugs him. She hugs him right there in the doorway, where anyone could see. She is not ashamed of him, she does not question him, and she never has. He hugs her back, tightening his arms around her. She is not Annie. She is Sarah, and she is here.

"I'm sorry," he says.

"It's okay," she says. And it is not okay, but he doesn't point that out. There in the doorway, with Sarah in his arms, it occurs to him that it might be okay again. And in that moment, just that feels like enough.

Faye

They leave her alone to do Annie's hair and, once the door closes behind the funeral director, she sets about arranging the things she will need in the order she likes to have them: round brush, comb, flat iron, hair spray. She does not let herself think too much about what she is there to do. She tries not to think about the circumstances or the setting. She just ignores the cold and gets started, willing her fingers to cooperate instead of freezing, willing her heart and mind to leave the building while her body does what needs to be done.

The other girls from the shop offered to do it, of course, but she wouldn't let them. She was to have been the one to do Annie's hair for the wedding. It is only right that she will do it for the funeral. There is a symmetry to it that fits somehow. She was not there when Annie was born. She had wanted to be, but her husband wouldn't let her go. She'd talked to Lydia on the phone moments after, promised to come as soon as she could to see her new niece. But Annie was more than a year old before she laid eyes on her.

She might not have been there when she entered the world, but she is there to see her out. She will do what her sister could not. She blinks back tears and uses the comb to work out the tangles. Per her request, the funeral home has already washed and dried her hair, but they've done a terrible job of combing it out.

"I keep thinking I'm going to hurt you," she says to the still and silent girl on the table, her voice loud as it bounces off the tiled walls.

They have already dressed Annie in what she will be buried in: the outfit she was going to wear to leave her reception, a little white lace shift dress. They'd bought that dress together in Greenville. She tries to think of that day, of Annie happy and alive, Annie singing, Annie trying on outfit after outfit until Faye was plumb exhausted and begging to go home.

"I keep expecting you to fuss at me," she tells Annie. "You were always so tender-headed." She chuckles to herself, remembering the hell of combing out both girls' hair after baths when they were little. There was not enough No More Tangles in the world.

"You should tell your mama what a good job I did," she says to Annie now. "I mean, you're welcome to lie a little." She thinks about this, then adds, "'Course I guess where you are, that's not allowed." She chuckles again, half expecting Annie to laugh along. Her eyes stray to Annie's face, wishing she would find the trace of a smile. But whoever dressed her also arranged her face into a nonexpression expression. She is Annie, but devoid of any emotion or humanity.

"Remember when I did your hair up for prom, and you hated it? You went to your room, and I hollered that you'd better not take down those hours of work."

She can see the scene perfectly in her memory. Annie stalking off to her room, calling out, "I won't, Aunt Faye," even though they both knew that was exactly what she intended to do behind the closed door of her room.

Sure enough, when she came out, her updo was undone, and Clary, the traitor, had snuck in and used a big fat iron to add long curls to Annie's otherwise stick-straight hair. It had looked better than the updo, but Faye had never once admitted it. Instead, they hadn't spoken for days.

Faye blinks back tears again, clears her field of vision as she untangles the last of Annie's hair, and begins to use the straight iron, smoothing her long locks into a loose, glossy sheet of hair. The child always did have the loveliest thick hair. Poor Clary was always messing with hers, coloring it just about every color in the rainbow at some point in her life. Faye always suspected it was because she knew her hair was simply not as beautiful as her cousin's. Clary hadn't gone to prom, opting to stay home with Travis and boycott.

Faye continues talking as if they are just chatting like usual. "I guess you know this already—because I'm sure you're watching all of this—but Clary got quite a confession out of Minnie Porter. The mystery of what happened to your mother is finally solved, thanks to your cousin."

Her daughter has solved a mystery that has plagued the whole town for decades. "You would've been so proud of her," she tells Annie. "And that bird of hers. The one she was missing? Do you remember that, how upset she was?" She sighs. It was only a few weeks ago, but already it feels like years.

"Well, that bird somehow ended up sitting where you were! It's what led them to you, or I'm not sure they would've ever found you. I never paid any mind to those birds—never cared to, as I'm sure you know—but Clary always said her doves are special. Now I go outside every day to see them. I'm learning all their names, and Clary even let one sit on my finger. It started flapping its wings and stirred up quite a wind. Messed my hair all up!" She finds herself chuckling, even as tears run down her cheeks.

And speaking of hair, she is nearly done with Annie's. She will add some hair spray, which is silly, but it feels necessary. She stops, takes a moment to let herself really be there, to appreciate the gift this is, this moment alone with Annie to say what she has never been able to say. She hopes Annie can hear it and senses that, from where she is now, she does. This is, she realizes, why it had to be her doing Annie's hair and no one else. Because there is something she still needs to say, and this is her last chance to say it.

"You saved my life," she says to her niece. Her voice sounds thick, strangled, and she swallows. "I don't know what would've happened to me if I'd stayed in Virginia, if I hadn't come here for you. I think T. J. might've killed me. Or if I didn't actually die, I would've died inside. I already felt like I was dying when the phone rang that night."

She rolls her eyes at herself, laughs a nervous laugh. "I know, I know. 'Oh, Aunt Faye, you're being dramatic again.' And I guess I am. But when I think of my life—of all that it became—you and Clary and Hal, my salon, it feels . . . meant to be. It feels like I turned out exactly like I was supposed to. But I couldn't have—wouldn't have—any of that without you. And I'm sorry—" Tears form in her eyes, and this time she doesn't blink them away. "I was always telling you what you should do. But there were things I should've done that I didn't."

She lets the tears run down her cheeks, taking her mascara with them. She places her hands on her niece's still, silent body. "I'm so sorry I ever let you believe it was my sacrifice to stay here and raise you. When it was my privilege." She scans the room, the ceiling, wishing for a sign, a confirmation that Annie can hear her. She has to believe she can. She rests her hand on Annie's cheek for a moment, gets one final look at the job she has done, and, satisfied, she exits, leaving the room in a cloud of hair spray. Which, Annie would say, is just as it should be.

Laurel

Tyson Barnes comes to Annie's funeral. He finds Laurel sitting alone in a pew near the back, uncertain why she's there except that she feels like she should be. Her mother refused to come, fretting about the way it would look, leaving her to brave the crowd alone. But Annie's story was her story—*is* her story—and she feels obligated to see it through to the end, though this is not the end she had hoped for.

She is so grateful to Tyson Barnes for acknowledging her existence that she almost hugs him. "May I sit?" he asks. There is an empty spot on both sides of her. He can have his pick.

She doesn't know whether it is appropriate for her to be there. The revelation of what her grandmother confessed is still reverberating through the town. Tyson takes a seat in the pew, making her feel less conspicuous. She finds herself scanning the crowd for Damon's face. She wonders if he will keep his distance now that the truth has come out. She will not blame him if he does. Her family's good name now has a big black *X* beside it. If her grandmother is to be believed, her grandfather killed Annie's mother. She can still scarcely believe it.

"How're you holding up?" Tyson Barnes asks, keeping his voice low. Around them, other mourners file quietly into the church, heads down. She sees some of them look at her, then look away. The news has traveled fast. Bad news always does.

She shrugs. "I'm still sort of in shock, I guess," she whispers.

He shakes his head. "I knew Cordell Lewis didn't do it. But I had no idea who did," he says. "I want you to know that."

She nods, looks down at her feet.

"Hey," Tyson says. She looks up. "You've got nothing to feel bad about, you know. You didn't do it."

She presses her lips into what passes for a smile of acknowledgment. "I know," she says.

"Then hold your head high," Tyson says. "Don't apologize to any of these folks for who you are. Your grandfather did something awful. But you didn't."

"Then why do I feel like I did?" she asks.

"Because they're your family. It's guilt by association, I guess. Because this whole town has spent years despising an innocent man, and we were all, unwittingly, a part of perpetuating that."

"I had even thought about writing a book about it," she says, and her voice is too loud when she says it. She covers her mouth with a stricken look and lowers her voice to a whisper again. "I wanted to make my mark by writing about someone else's tragedy."

Tyson Barnes looks at her. "So you're saying you shouldn't write about it now that it's your tragedy, too?"

His words catch her up short. She cocks her head. "What do you mean?"

He grins at her like she's a child he just needs to have patience with. "Before, you were willing to report it. That's the easy part. It's different when you have to live it. But maybe that's where the heart of a truly good story comes from. Maybe when you're in it—fully in it instead of watching from a distance—you'll find out what kind of writing you're really capable of." He shrugs. "But what do I know? I'm a defense attorney. I take up for scumbags."

She is about to tell him that Cordell Lewis isn't a scumbag. That her grandfather, a man who used to carry butterscotch disks for her in his pocket and taught her all the words to "Get Rhythm" by Johnny Cash, was the scumbag. But then she hears someone say, "Is this seat taken?" She looks up to see Damon standing there, his hands in his pockets and a hopeful look on his face.

She scooches over, and as he takes the seat on the other side of her, she feels relief wash over her. She was afraid he would turn his back on her now that she's the granddaughter of a murderer. She was afraid that he would fire her, even. That his father would make him do it to avoid the negative association. Her grandmother's confession has upended her world. But sitting there in that church, she realizes that sometimes worlds need upending. Sometimes the story has to go a completely different direction in order to conclude the right way. The sheriff walks up to Tyson, and he turns to speak to him, his back to Laurel and Damon.

Damon uses the opportunity to lean over and whisper in her ear. "Is he my competition now?" he asks, pointing at Tyson's back.

She pulls back, shocked, and looks at him. "Competition?" she whispers.

He rolls his eyes and sighs. "I've already confessed my crush. This should not be news to you."

"From when we were kids, yes," she says. "But . . . now?" She knows the confusion is registering on her face.

He grins and nods. "Now."

"Well, that is news to me."

Damon sits back against the pew, looking relaxed. "Good thing we're in the news business, you and I."

"Yes," Laurel agrees, feeling lighter than when she walked into the church, lighter than she's felt in a very long time. She thinks about what Tyson said about writing the story better now that it's her story, too. Maybe that's what she's been missing—the part that involves her heart, her soul, the part of herself she's always held in reserve. "It *is* a good thing," she agrees. The organist begins to play a hymn, and note by note, the music swells, filling the room with its sound.

Clary

As Travis is wrapping up his sermon, she slips out of her seat and goes out the side door of the church. She walks to the display cage where the doves are waiting for the release, the four of them clustered together inside the smaller space of the cage, making their little roosting noises. Gently, she scoops them, one by one, into the basket she will use for the release. She closes the lid until it is time to open it and let them fly away.

Mica is still too weak, so she has left him in the loft at home. He needs time to heal. There is a time to heal, and a time to soar, a time to hold on, and a time to let go. There is time for all of it. She tips her chin toward the sky, takes in the fluffy white clouds, the bright, blinding sun. She breathes in the hot June air, feels the sticky humidity fill her lungs, smells the hydrangeas blooming nearby, feels her feet firmly planted on her hometown soil. She has something Annie doesn't have; she still has time.

She has done dozens of funeral releases, but she has never done one when her dove represented the soul of a person she loved. A few of the congregants begin trickling out, but Clary keeps looking up at the sky, thinking, as she does, of Aunt Lydia waiting up in heaven for Annie to arrive, the joyous reunion they must be having. It was only ever her mother who Annie wanted, after all. Clary takes comfort in this thought. That little girl and her mother are back together again, not wishing on the stars but living among them. She tries to take comfort in anything she can as she grapples with all that has happened.

The service lets out, and she stands, silent and still, holding the basket, waiting for the mourners to gather in the grassy area where she will do the release. She nods at people who nod at her, but no one smiles; no one calls out. Everyone is somber and serious, as they should be. A reverence is called for, expected, needed, at a time like this. Clary is not a religious person and yet, she is a believer.

She believes in souls taking flight and a God who takes them home. She is a believer in love and destiny and hope. She is a believer in everything, somehow, working out. She thinks of Travis, of the daughter she gave up, of her mom and cousin, of all that has come before and after. There is, she believes, purpose in every goodbye and every hello, in every win and every loss, in every rough patch and every smooth place. As she opens the basket and the doves fly past her, she feels all those things at once.

The birds furiously flap their wings in their effort to take to the skies. The wind they stir up takes her breath away in a powerful rush that she will carry with her for the rest of her life. She feels emptied and filled at the same time. She feels very brave and very afraid. She feels simultaneously larger than life and smaller than a speck of dust. Most of all, she feels an unexplainable, indescribable peace. She thinks of something she heard once: "All shall be well and all shall be well and all manner of thing shall be well." Yes, she thinks: that.

She holds her breath as the doves climb higher and higher into the sky. "Goodbye, Annie," she whispers as her eyes fill with tears and the lump in her throat seems to grow larger. "I will miss you every day." With the rest of the congregation, she watches as, together, the doves circle and circle overhead, getting their bearings, finding their way home.

BOOK CLUB QUESTIONS

1. There are several main characters in this book. Did you see yourself in any certain one? If so, which one and why?

2. The first time we see Annie, she compares her car to her fiancé, calling them both "new, reliable, and suitable." How is this description significant to who Annie is?

3. Two major themes in this book are regret and release. Discuss how each character—Annie, Kenny, Laurel, Faye, and Clary—deals with both regret and release.

4. When Faye recalls the time she lost Annie as a little girl, she remembers that Annie and Clary each wanted to ride a different ride. What ride did each girl choose? Are their choices as children indicative of their personalities as adults or contrary to them?

5. Which character did you find yourself rooting for? What did you want for her or him?

7UP CHICKEN MARINADE RECIPE

2 cups 7UP
1 cup soy sauce
1 Tbsp. horseradish (optional, but you know Faye included it!)
1 cup vegetable or olive oil
Boneless, skinless chicken breasts

Mix all ingredients except chicken in bowl. Pour over chicken breasts and marinate for at least eight hours in refrigerator. Grill chicken. Serve with roasted or baked potatoes and a green veggie. (Or slice and serve over salad, just like Faye did.)

ACKNOWLEDGMENTS

This is the part where I try to remember to thank everyone who provided help as I wrote this book. This was a tough one, as I battled several health issues while writing and required much more of my friends and family than normal. So, sit back, relax, maybe get a refreshment. Here we go . . .

Huge thanks goes to my husband, Curt Whalen, and our children (Jack, Ashleigh, Matt, Rebekah, Brad, and Annaliese) for both taking care of me and managing to live in peace with me throughout this time. I know it was not easy, and I am grateful for you guys. (Curt also, he would want me to mention, helped me immensely—he would want me to say immensely—with the story arc between Faye and Hal York, who he now refers to as Hopper.)

Ariel Lawhon, you know what a terrible human I can be and yet you love me anyway. That's the true definition of a best friend. Thank you for the gift of your friendship. Ashley was right—it really is like no other.

To my mom, Sandy Brown, you've always believed in me, and that belief gave me the confidence to go forward with some crazy dreams. Without your voice in my head spurring me on, there's no way I would or could have. I am grateful for your continued love and support no matter what.

To my agent, Liza Dawson, and her team: The other day one of my friends remarked that you are the perfect agent for me. And I said with a big smile, "She really is." You really are. And Jodi Warshaw is the perfect editor for me. Jodi, every time I'm around you, I like you all the more, and I appreciate both your patience and your positivity. I'm so grateful to have found a home at Lake Union and marvel at all you guys do for your authors. I was fortunate to have two very talented developmental editors help me with this book: Caitlin Alexander and Faith Black Ross both made this book better in their own individually unique, editorially gifted ways. And Nicole Pomeroy and her crackerjack copyeditors, especially Stacy Abrams and Sarah Engel, made me look ever so much smarter than I really am.

As for the friends who hung in there, prayed for me, and never failed to ask "How's the book going?" I have to specifically thank Tracy and Douglas Graham (you guys got a character named after you in this one—sorry if she's a bit annoying; no parallels were intended), Jill and Billy Dean, Lisa and Mike Shea (DSW!!), Misty and Carl Howard, Amy and Clay Gilliam, Beth and Steve Burton, Maria and Micah Swett, Jen and Terry Tolbert, Rachel and Rick Olsen, and Christy and Alex Kennedy. (If I forgot anyone, I am so sorry!)

Lisa Patton, thank you for the time to work in your gorgeous home and for being your delightful self. Likewise to Shannon King: You offered your beautiful home as a gorgeous and inspiring writing space. You also provided lunch with wine—which is the best kind of lunch.

Chelsea Humphrey, words can't express how much your help spurred me on. I hope I can return the favor someday. Ahem.

Christopher Rice, your kindness about *Worthy* was a huge boost, and your continued kindness and funny comments have been an unexpected and welcomed addition to my life.

To the members of the never defunct Authors Out of Carolina: Kim Wright Wiley, Joy Callaway, and Erika Marks. You are my writing cohorts, and I am grateful for your wisdom and encouragement. Kim, your help was especially invaluable for this one. Turns out Carrabba's in Myrtle Beach at four o'clock on a Monday is a place where magic happens.

Donna Ruth Powell of Charlotte White Dove Release was an amazing resource who opened her heart and home to me. She made that part of this story come alive and gave me insight I couldn't have gained by simply reading about doves.

Nancy Malcor, cousin extraordinaire, once again provided valuable legal advice. Whatever I got wrong is not your fault. Whatever I got right is to your credit. It's good to have a prosecutor in the family, especially one as stylish, smart, and hysterical as you are.

Thank you also to Mia Brown Geiger, friend of Nancy, who clued me in on what really goes on in hair salons.

Thanks also to my daughter's former roommate, Taylor Newcomb, who came to dinner at our house and told us the story of an elderly relative who repeated the same story every day, day after day. Taylor said that, my brain went to, "But what if one day the story changed?" and a key part of this book was born.

Rohn Brown, you get a thank-you this time, as you introduced me to Monty Python. I've now mentioned *MPATHG* in two different novels, so clearly your spot-on impressions made a lasting impact, especially on a nine-hour drive to Kentucky.

To the artists who sang the songs that became the soundtrack (in my head) to this novel: "When We Were Young" by Adele, "This Town" by Niall Horan, "Castle on a Hill" by Ed Sheeran, "Learning to Fly" by Tom Petty, "Roll Me Away" by Bob Seger, "Say I'm the One" by Griffin House, "Here with Me" by The Killers, "Vice" by Miranda Lambert, "Hazard" by Richard Marx, "Marry Me" by Thomas Rhett, "Misunderstood" by Slow City Hotel, "Take It to Heart" by Michael McDonald, and anything by P!nk, as she's the inspiration for Clary. I'm sure there were other songs, but these are the standouts, the ones I could always play to help me get inside the minds and hearts of these particular characters.

HUGE thanks to all the readers (and booksellers!) who buy/sell my books, come to/organize my events, ask me to sign books, tell their friends/customers about them, send me encouraging emails, and so on. I always try to picture my intended reader as I write, and your faces are what I picture. Thank you for being on the other end of this process.

And finally, to the Holy Trinity, who show up a few times in this book and show up for me every single day, in more ways than I can count. Apart from You, I can do nothing (Psalm 109: 26–27).

ABOUT THE AUTHOR

Marybeth Mayhew Whalen is the author of *When We Were Worthy*, *The Things We Wish Were True*, and five previous novels. She speaks to women's groups around the United States and is the cofounder of the popular women's fiction site She Reads (www.shereads.org). Marybeth and her husband, Curt, have been married for twenty-seven years and are the parents of six children. Marybeth divides her time between the suburbs of Charlotte, North Carolina, and the coastline of Sunset Beach, North Carolina. You can find her at www.marybethwhalen.com.